I0762288

UNDER THE WILLOW

MADGE HURLEY JONES

UNDER THE WILLOW

madgerjones1@gmail.com

Hardcover ISBN: 978-1-7365630-0-7
Paperback ISBN: 978-1-7365630-1-4
Ebook ISBN: 978-1-7365630-2-1

Book and cover design by The Brand Huntress
TheBrandHuntress.com

First printing 2021

To my beloved grandchildren
Aaron, Danielle, Samuel, Nathanael, Briella, and Elliot
Because I want to leave something of me to you

1

ONE LITTLE KISS

Bethany struggled to breathe while she stopped long enough to gather her gown. Fortunately it was dusk, so she could not be seen by the guests assembled on the Jacksons' lawn.

As she started down the slope toward the willow, a strong hand grabbed her wrist and jerked her to a halt. Bethany was whirled around and forced to look into his eyes. "It didn't mean anything!" he foolishly blurted.

"Why Stew? Why would you? Here? Now?" She glared at him in disbelief. "This is our engagement party! Our wedding is in two weeks."

"I'm sorry! I...I don't know how it happened. It...it just did," he stammered as he pulled her to his chest attempting to comfort her.

In confusion, she relented, but while pressed against his chest, she saw Rica Adams leaving the garden shed with a lantern.

"Rica Adams?" A painful look swept over her face as she forced Stew away.

"You know what Rica is capable of. She would stop at nothing to tear us apart! Yet, you were with *her*?"

"Calm down! It was only one little kiss! I guess it was a...a moment of stupidity on my part. I humbly apologize." He rolled his eyes, trying to make light of the circumstances and hoping to convince Bethany she was overreacting. He had no other defense since he was unable to think clearly at the moment.

"You were embracing her, Stew! I saw you!"

"Wait! There's no reason to be this upset. Listen...it was out of view of the guests, and there's no reason for anyone else to know about this. We can discuss it after the party." Stew hoped to sway her in order to come to an agreement quickly.

In the fading light, Bethany could see no convincing remorse on his face. *Does he actually think he can talk me into letting this incident pass? Is he only concerned for his reputation?* Hurt and confusion took control of Bethany's heart.

"I didn't realize you and Rica had become close." Bethany's voice was filled with sarcasm as she turned from him and tried to collect her thoughts. She had never suspected Stew was attracted to Rica. Bethany had known Stewart all her life and was desperately in love with him.

The two of them had grown up serving the Lord in the same church. He was responsible for helping shape many of her Christian values, and they had planned to instill those same values in their children.

How could Stew have wanted that moment with Rica so much he would risk our love? What else don't I know?

Stew gently cupped her shoulders with his hands in another consoling gesture, but Bethany pulled away.

"Come on, Beth. Please, forget this. You know I'm in love with you. Let's put this situation behind us and enjoy the rest of our evening together. This party is a once-in-a-lifetime event, and we've had to put it off far too long." The statement was tenderly spoken and his eyes seemed filled with love, but she no longer believed his words or what she read in his countenance.

"You honestly think a few soothing words can make everything fine between us? Stewart, you've been unfaithful to me. This is something I could never have imagined. I...I can't just let this go. You were with *Rica*! But, even if it had been another woman, it would still be the same." Her lips were quivering as she stared into his eyes.

"I wouldn't call it being unfaithful. I never intended for this to happen. I confess it was a bad situation, but let's not overdramatize." Stew took the liberty of scolding Bethany, hoping to gain control of the misunderstanding.

"Oh, Stewart!" Even though Bethany managed to hold back the tears, her voice revealed her anguish. "You're not truly in love with me!.

"Don't be ridiculous, Bethany! We've been hopelessly in love with each other for years! Surely you're not going to go into all of this right now. This isn't the time or the place. We can discuss it *after* the party." Even though he was trying to rationalize the situation, Stewart Jefferson knew he had no reasonable explanation.

Stunned by his words, Bethany turned and looked up into his face with sadness and acceptance in her eyes. "You're right Stew. There's no reason to discuss it now. It's over and done with. We can't change it."

Evidently Stewart was taken by surprise, for it was several seconds before he released the breath he was unaware of holding.

Stew's shoulders relaxed as he reached out and lovingly lifted Bethany's chin. "There now...I'm glad you see how foolish this has been on both our parts."

"No, Stew–" Bethany started to correct his statement, but the first notes of the string quartet drifted toward them.

"Oh, no! It's time for the greeting line! I...I don't think I can face our friends right now..

Bethany noticed Stew's face took on the confident look which often comes with having won an argument. He began to instruct her. "Of course you can. Just take a couple deep breaths and relax. You'll do fine. But we need to hurry, or our guests will wonder where we are.

"Let me see your face. Well...it might look like you've been crying a little, but people expect a few tearful moments at this type of celebration. Now give me your hand."

As Bethany looked up into the face of the tall, handsome man beside her, she offered a defeated reply. "You're right Stew...we must go through with this." Bethany again lifted the skirt of her gown, and the couple ran back to the party hand in hand.

2

FALLING IN LOVE

Once Stew and Bethany were near the house, they had to spend valuable time finding a suitable place to slip back into the party. Stew caught his foot on a chair and stumbled a little. It caught the attention of a few, but, after Stew flashed them his most charming smile, they went back to their conversations. He then escorted Bethany to the gazebo for the formal greeting of the guests.

As a beautiful love song played in the background, Bethany forced herself to face the line of guests. Her jumbled mind began reviewing her relationship with Stew over the past several years.

Bethany had known Stew for as long as she could remember. During the spring when she was fifteen and he was nineteen, their close relationship had begun to develop. Their pastor had mentioned it was unfortunate the local churches did not associate because of denominational differences. The congregation of Faith Chapel was touched by the truth of the statement and decided to sponsor a bible quiz contest for the youth of all the churches in the Remington area.

Stew had been elected captain of the team and was asked to be an assistant coach because of his biblical knowledge. Practice had begun immediately after the first invitation was accepted from one of the churches.

Even though the entire youth group was very bright, it was only a short time until it was apparent Bethany was much more advanced than the others and her ability to memorize was outstanding. To top it off, Bethany's eagerness to learn was spurred by competition.

The coaches quickly became concerned because the rest of the group seemed discouraged by Bethany's abilities. It was even rumored that some of the youth were thinking of dropping out.

After some consideration, it was decided Bethany should be coached individually. Since she could put most of the adult coaches to shame, Stewart was given the job.

The two were allowed to meet at church with the rest of the youth so they could be supervised and still visit with their friends during breaks. The adult coaches felt there was no reason to take a chance of intimidating the rest of the team before the quiz, so the two would not join the others until the actual competition.

The day of the competition turned out to be a huge affair which included games, boat rides, and a picnic lunch. Children and adults had a great time socializing with other Christians in the community, and Faith Chapel had the honor of winning the first Bible quiz banner. Everyone went home exhausted, and the friendly competition became an annual event with the banner being passed to the winning church each year.

It had been a great, fun-filled summer for everyone, and Bethany and Stew had become very close, despite their age difference. He had worked hard tutoring Bethany, and she had responded enthusiastically. It was no secret Stew was revered by his many friends due to his extraordinary good looks and personality; therefore, it was only natural Bethany had grown to admire him during that time.

Over the years he had been seen with Mandy, Adel, and other girls from their church and high school, yet Bethany did not remember that he had spent a long period of time with any *one* girl. There were always girls nearby when Stew was around. He could have had his pick of any of the young ladies. Before *now*, Bethany had never given this much thought.

Stew had left for college shortly after the church picnic, and when he returned to the area there was seldom time for more than a polite exchange between them. Yet, two summers later when the young people of the church took a trip to the state fair, Bethany became totally smitten by him. Being seventeen and the youngest, Bethany was assigned to Stew's group as a protective measure. Their mission was to spend the main part of the day passing out gospel tracts and witnessing. The evenings were set aside for seeing attractions at the fair.

Bethany had been amazed at Stew's ease in engaging people in conversations about the Lord and his sincerity when talking to them. The chaperones and others were impressed as well. It was a glorious week, and Bethany was spiritually motivated by the deep relationship Stew possessed with the Lord.

On the last evening, everyone in the group wanted something different from the food booths. Stew and Bethany were going in the same direction, so they agreed to meet the others near one of the entrances to the grandstand. Since their booth was the farthest away, the two made every effort to hurry so they would not cause anyone to be late for the riding competition. However, when they arrived back at the meeting point, no one in the group was there. Bethany waited while Stew checked the other entrances, but he could not find their friends. Finally, they went inside to watch the event. Afterward, Stew and Bethany had no choice but to return to their host homes on foot.

The couple had walked several blocks when Stew had to stop to remove gravel from his shoe. However, as soon as he sat down on the curb, a hand reached out and grabbed Bethany. She was quickly pulled to the chest of a drunken man whose slurred words produced a strong odor of alcohol.

"Well! What d-do we h-h-have here? You're a perty lil' one, ain't ya? Can ya d-dance with an ol' fella? Just furrr a lil' spell?" the drunk asked, not waiting for a reply.

"Please sir, let go! You're hurting me!" Bethany was terrified.

"Hey, pal! That's a respectable young lady you're addressing in such a familiar manner. I'll thank you to release her and be on your way!" Stew towered over the man when he stood to his feet. He grabbed the drunk by the collar and easily placed him in a heap on the bench by the tavern. Ripe for a drunken slumber, the man was too intoxicated to get up or even respond.

"He didn't hurt you, did he?" Stew put a protective arm around her and led her away from the area as quickly as possible.

"No...I'm fine. It just took me by surprise. I wasn't expecting anything like that to happen. I...I guess I live a pretty sheltered life. I just didn't expect it...that's all." Bethany began to tremble and was embarrassed by her reaction toward the harmless drunk. "Will he be alright there? Maybe we should do something...

"He'll be fine. I'm sure it's not the first time he's slept one off on the street. Besides, my only concern is to get you safely away from here." As they walked away, Stew scanned the area for any other apparent danger.

It was at least four blocks before Stew slowed their pace and relaxed his tense grip on her hand. Yet, he did not let go of her hand and she did not pull her hand from his. Their steps became slower and slower.

"I'm starting to recognize some of the homes, so we should be safe in this area. I'm sorry the evening turned out like this...at least for your sake...but to be truthful...I'm glad it has. I mean...I always enjoy spending time with you. You're quite a girl," Stew confessed.

"Thank you...I also appreciate the person you are," she timidly admitted. "I've enjoyed every minute." She secretly hoped the walk would never end. Then their steps slowed to a stop. He looked into her eyes and then gently brushed her lips with a kiss.

Immediately, he was remorseful since he had not meant to treat her disrespectfully. "I'm sorry! I don't know what I was thinking. That was out of line. Please, forgive me."

"Please...don't apologize. I don't mind that I received my first kiss from you."

"You're every inch a lady, but you're still young. I've acted foolishly. Please...I beg your forgiveness."

"And I accept," she answered with a soft, forgiving smile. "Now let's put it behind us."

Once the two arrived at the home where she was staying, they learned the rest of the group had become ill from something they had eaten earlier in the day. Fortunately, Bethany and Stew had been detained while witnessing to a young couple and had not eaten with the rest of the group.

That was how their romance had begun. It had always been such a sweet memory for Bethany.

"Bethany. Bethany! My, you're a nervous bride-to-be! I was just telling Stewart what a lovely time Lawrence and I are having tonight. If your family was concerned about such matters, this event would certainly have made the social column for party of the year. The decorations are lovely. No! They're beyond lovely. They are extraordinary! Thank you so much for remembering us on your guest list," Mrs. Rosenthal gushed with her usual bright smile, as her husband offered a cheerful agreeing grin and a handshake.

"Mr. and Mrs. Rosenthal, you have always thought too highly of me and everything I do. But, I accept your compliment with the love and thoughtfulness in which it's been offered. And, may I add, you have been an encouragement to me throughout my life. You lift people's spirits wherever you go. Thank you very much." Then Bethany gave them both a hug.

In a moment's time, Bethany went back into her daze and was barely aware of their other friends and relatives passing through the line. Bethany caught a few words of advice and was capable of returning hugs and an occasional kiss. She remembered thinking she must have been responding appropriately to their comments since no one, except Mrs. Rosenthal, had requested much of her social input.

Still, it would not have mattered if each person had noted she was being inattentive, she could not stop her mind from returning to the memories tucked in her heart, nor escape the grief reviewing those memories created.

As Bethany recalled, it was their summer commitments which extinguished the first sparks of their relationship. Stewart left on an overseas mission trip, and she had spent the rest of the summer visiting with her sister, Tanna. They had exchanged letters a few times, but his traveling from place to place had put an abrupt end to it. Their paths had only crossed briefly at a couple gatherings during the holidays that year. Although it hurt, Bethany had tried to convince herself that Stew's lack of attention was for the best.

It was not until late spring the following year during an ice cream social that Bethany and Stewart came face-to-face. He had breezed around a corner with Adel on his arm when he bumped right into Bethany, accompanied by Jerald Wilkerson. Bethany, to her shame, recalled being pleased she was at the social with a friend—and a very good looking one at that.

The encounter had taken Stew completely by surprise, and his facial expressions clearly indicated his jealousy over her being escorted by one of his friends. His feelings became even more apparent when his lighthearted mood quickly dissipated.

Embarrassed by the situation, Stew nodded politely and passed Bethany and Jerald without conversation. Bethany was glad Adel never took Stew's attention seriously, and she was certain her date was pleased to know Stew had seemed a tad envious of him.

A few days later, Bethany had received a dozen red roses from Stew with a card asking for her to accompany him to dinner. Unknown to her, Stewart already had met with her father to ask for permission to see her.

Now looking back, Bethany could see she had been very young and naïve during that time. She had always prayed for God's guidance in their relationship but wondered if she had truly listened.

Her mind strayed to the time she had been brought to tears by a conversation she had overheard between Adel and Mandy. They were both newly-weds, and Mandy was expecting her first child. It was their turn to clean the chapel, and Bethany had walked to the church to pick up some literature left for her mother on the pastor's desk. Bethany entered quietly, so they had not been aware of her presence.

"I'm a bit concerned about the romantic interest Stew is showing toward Bethany," Mandy said.

"Oh, I know! It's all I can do to keep from approaching him. He's much more experienced in the world. There are so many girls after him, and he could have his pick of any of them. Why Bethany? She's so young. Granted she is beautiful and would look great on his arm. But, to be serious about her? Surely not!" Adel added in agreement.

"God knows what he has in store for the two of them, but right now I'm concerned about it," Mandy replied, ending the conversation.

Bethany remembered crying and being hurt for days. She admired Mandy and Adel and had always considered them to be close friends. Had Stew chosen one of them instead of her, she would have been happy for them. She could not believe they did not feel the same for her. But, now, she was wondering if she had misunderstood their conversation.

Suddenly, a whole flood of questionable incidents came to mind. Bethany had always wondered why Stew had helped Marjorie Willard with her college paper last fall. Marjorie was quite bright and had several close friends who were very intelligent. Now, Bethany was doubting that Stew had been needed.

Then there was the time when she was looking for Stew after church and found him comforting a crying Nellie Kessler. Supposedly, Nellie just needed someone to listen for a moment.

As her mind recalled various incidents, image after image of Stew with girls—and more recently young women—flashed through her head. Bethany felt foolish and wondered if Stewart was a ladies' man.

She was young and flattered when he turned his attention to her; she had never once considered his behavior toward other young ladies.

"Beth! Bethany, it's time! Let me have your hand," Stew instructed.

Bethany obediently held out her hand to him. He was right...it was time.

3

THE END

As the quartet continued to play, Bethany took a moment to view the party in candlelight. At each round table sat eight loved ones; many had turned their chairs around to get a better view. The dishes had been cleared, the table cloths changed, and the centerpieces of white candles wreathed with purple roses all looked even more impressive than when the party had first begun. The gazebo was aglow and seemed to sparkle in the darkness. Everything was exactly as she had planned.

Bethany had to pull her attention from the loveliness and what it meant, or she would not be able to get through the trial she was about to undertake. She prayed for strength.

The air was no longer filled with music but had come alive with the applause of their beloved guests.

Stew cleared his throat, put on a smile, and began his speech. "Thank you, everyone," he said with conviction. This was followed by more applause from the audience.

Stew continued, "First of all, I apologize for my late arrival which made it impossible for us to offer a proper greeting earlier. Nonetheless, Bethany and I want to thank you all for spending your evening with us. We want to express our appreciation to each of you for the part you've played in our lives. I don't believe one invitation was issued for this event, or the wedding, that wasn't from our hearts. We wanted to share this time with you because everyone present is special to us." The anxious listeners responded once more with applause.

It was now Bethany's turn to speak. "Yes. We are touched by your well wishes, love, and presence. Words cannot express how we feel toward all of you. However..." Bethany paused to gather courage. She refused to break down.

"However, I am afraid your generosity and loving kindness have unknowingly been misused. Stewart and I have just realized that the love we share...is a love in Christ and not the kind of love on which to base a marriage." With this statement, Bethany was forced to pause as an audible shock filled the air. She could hear speculation being voiced, but many sat quietly and shook their heads in disbelief.

Bethany noted her parents were sitting directly in front of her, and they had managed to continue smiling while keeping their composure.

"Helen, were you aware?" Her father tried not to move his lips while asking the question.

"Not at all," she answered in the same manner.

While Bethany gave their guests time to settle down, she received a quick chastising glance from Stew. Then with the original smile still plastered on his face, he quietly spat out, "so...you've decided to be spiteful?"

Once a hush was established, Bethany proceeded. "This evening's event has caused us to realize we have mistaken our friendship for true love. I'm sure you understand this is a very painful discovery...yet an unavoidable one. We humbly beg your forgiveness and ask for your understanding, prayers, and support. God bless you all. Now, if you will please excuse us, we will take our leave."

Stewart then took Bethany's hand and led her to the stable's tack room. He was very cautious not to draw attention, but he certainly meant to have it out with her.

Meanwhile...slinking behind trees and bushes and trying to catch every move the couple made was a tall, black-haired beauty with a hateful grin.

Immediately after the couple left, Bethany's father stood before the crowd. "Please, do not feel you must leave at this time. While this news may have left you all a bit shaken, we'd prefer you enjoy the rest of the evening at your leisure. Feel free to leave in your own good time. God bless each and every one of you for your support and thank you for coming."

Even with Mr. Jackson's kind invitation to stay, those present did not feel it was proper to intrude on the family any further. There was hurt and disappointment in every heart. Out of their deepest respect for both families and for the couple which was so dear to them, the guests quietly dispersed.

Once inside the tack room, Bethany again was brought to an abrupt halt, whirled around, and forced to look into Stewart's eyes.

"I can't believe you could be so vengeful! I've always known you as a forgiving person, but you just *ruined* the engagement party and the wedding for us...our families...our friends! How could you do such a horrible thing?" Stew spewed in hurt and disbelief.

"Stew! If you recall, *you* were embracing and kissing Rica Adams. *I* haven't ruined anything. *You* did! That's why I called off the engagement and wedding." Bethany was trying to remain calm, but it was more than she could do.

"We have a wedding in two weeks, and you've just made fools out of both of us! How are you going to fix this mess before our wedding?" He ran his fingers through his hair and began to pace from the anxiety. His head and heart were pounding.

"I'm not! Haven't you heard anything I've said? I'm *not* marrying you now or ever! The engagement is over, and the wedding will *not* take place!" Bethany was no longer calm and was speaking distinctly to make it perfectly clear to him.

Stew was shocked. He could not believe such words had come out of her mouth so heartlessly. "Why are you persisting with this? The guests are still here. Go correct this *now*!" he ordered.

"Stew, it's over." Bethany tried again to calmly emphasize her stand.

"You are taking this too far! I know you love me, but for some reason you're refusing to disregard that stupid incident!" He had suddenly taken on a condescending air.

"Quit, Stew!" This time Bethany was adamant.

"This is ridiculous! Listen! I have no feelings for Rica! I'm in love with you!" Stew was beginning to see Bethany was more serious than he ever thought possible. "We're in love. Let the kiss go! This is our future you're toying with." He pulled her close and looked into her eyes.

"Stew! That kiss was wrong in every way." This time she had a catch in her voice and tears in her eyes.

He opened his mouth to continue the argument, but the truth in her statement was more than he wanted to admit to himself. He froze in silence as he stared into her eyes.

"Stewart! I don't even know you! I was in love with the man you *portrayed* yourself to be. I was in love with the man I *thought* you were. But...I'm not in love with *you.*"

Bethany made the next statement with all of the honesty she felt in her heart and with sincere sadness and determination in her eyes. "I don't love you, Stew."

It was the sincerity in Bethany's eyes that made Stew realize their relationship was over. She wanted him out of her life—now and forever. Her heart was hardened, and there was nothing he could say to change her mind. He could not argue his case because he had no reasonable explanation for what had taken place with Rica.

Though he continued to look into her eyes, Stew could not speak because he was too emotionally stricken to form words.

Bethany watched as Stew's expressions changed from a look of realization to devastation, to blank lifelessness, and then to indignation.

It was the look of indignation which caused Bethany to believe he refused to examine the seriousness of the situation which had led to their broken engagement. Stew obviously felt no remorse for what he had done, and that was all Bethany needed to know about the man she thought she had loved. Nothing could change her mind.

Stew removed his hands from Bethany's shoulders, turned from her, and left.

The light from the full moon exposed the hurt in Bethany's eyes as the feeling of emptiness filled her heart. Bethany was alone.

4

WICKED CONFESSIONS

After a word with their closest friends, Mel and Helen Jackson walked past their guests as if unscathed by the night's events and disappeared behind the wide doors of their stately home. Neither spoke, but both instinctively went to the study. Mel lit the lamp while Helen closed the door.

They turned and looked at one another. Mel sighed, and Helen looked away as tears came into her eyes.

After a few minutes of contemplation, Mel was the first to speak. "Where do you suppose she is?"

"I don't know, but I can hardly..." Helen, having to take a seat, replied in a tearful voice.

Mel crossed the room and put a comforting hand on his wife's shoulder. "There now. Bethany is a strong girl. She'll get through this just fine. She's young and very wise." He paused for a moment and then added, "I should go find her. Will you be alright, dear?"

"Wait, Mel. Just a bit. She'll need some time to herself," Helen cautioned. "I believe Stew has left. I'm sure I saw his carriage going down the lane as we were crossing the lawn.

"Of course. It's just so hard to stay here while knowing our little girl is alone out there," Mel had never felt so much pain for one of his girls.

"Mel, was I mistaken? Wasn't Bethany bubbling with happiness throughout dinner? Helen was trying to recall anything which might have indicated there was a problem between Bethany and Stew.

"I believed so. I even saw her giggling with Sarah and a few of her friends not long after. She seemed as joyful as she had been before the party began." Mel shook his head in bewilderment.

"What do you suppose—" Trying to keep her composure, Helen pretended to straighten a doily on the table next to her.

"I don't know, dear."

"I didn't notice anything unusual, but I was busy visiting with guests." Helen's voice indicated she was feeling guilty for not noticing their daughter's distress.

"You were doing exactly what you should have been doing, Helen. It's probably best neither of us knew anything was going on. If we'd interfered, she might not have had the courage to carry off the announcement so coolly. Still a parent's first thought is always to protect their children. But she isn't a child anymore."

"No dear, she isn't. But I still feel she is." Helen looked up at Mel and gave a faint smile.

"I feel the same." Mel smiled back in understanding, wishing he had the words to comfort them both.

"I'm sorry, Helen. I believe the guests are gone. I must go and find her. I just can't wait here any longer."

Mel grabbed his hat from the rack, smoothed back his hair, and placed the hat above a furrowed brow.

Stewart had allowed his horse to walk down the Jacksons' lane before ripping carelessly down a side road. He was furious, hurt, and bewildered. God was not in his thoughts, and a feeling of revenge was rising within him.

The buggy was tossed as it leaped rut after rut. Several times Stew came close to being dashed onto the road, but he did not notice or care. He just wanted to get away. He wanted to escape his thoughts and the pain in his heart.

I don't love you, Stew. I don't love you, Stew. The words resounded in his head until he thought he would lose his mind.

At the same time, he was concerned that he might come across someone returning home from the engagement party. Stew's pride was still intact. He would rather die on the road than have anyone know why Bethany had broken their engagement or know that he, Stewart Jefferson, had no say in the matter.

He had chosen wisely, as far as the road was concerned, for the route was vacant. Stew began whipping Storm furiously—something he had never done before—frightening the horse and making him gallop down the dangerous path for an unfair distance. Fortunately, the horse stopped the madness on his own before any damage was done. The gelding had never been conditioned to gallop for long periods under such conditions, but Stew had no compassion for his faithful friend. He continued to whip the animal until long after the horse drew to a halt. He would probably never be able to regain Storm's trust, but in the heat of the moment, Stew did not care.

Exasperated that the buggy had come to a complete stop, Stew became more infuriated. He hurled himself to the ground and turned the whip around to beat the horse with the handle. One... two...three...four...but on the fifth attempt to brutalize the animal, Storm reared so defiantly that it frightened Stew. Then using all of his muscular strength, the horse lunged forward to break away. The action flung the buggy toward Stew allowing only enough time for him to dive into the ditch to avoid being hit.

Stew lay beside the road in a disheveled pile too enraged to notice the muddy conditions around him. He stayed there several minutes—his chest heaving. As his breathing slowed, he began to assess his conduct. He could not believe he had stooped so low as to abuse the horse he loved so dearly. Stew was ashamed of his actions, for never in his life had he allowed himself to lose control in such a display of anger.

Stew knew he needed to trust God to deal with the breakup but was not in the mind to do so. He was just grateful no one was around to witness the madness.

"Hello! Stewart...Stewart, is that you?" a lovely, young voice trilled as a feminine figure stepped delicately from a small buggy.

"Are you alright?" Rica Adams asked, acting as though she had just happened to be passing. She shined a light to add to the already near daylight effect of the moon. "Stewart! What on earth happened? Were you thrown out by your horse?"

Stew, who had heard nothing to warn him someone was approaching, moaned at the greeting and laid in the ditch a short time longer, not wanting to deal with her. When he turned over, the first words out of his mouth were not stated with the politeness

Rica was hoping to hear.

"Why are you here, Rica?" Stew questioned with anger. He got to his feet and turned to face her. "Haven't you destroyed enough lives for one night?"

"You seem a bit out of sorts, dear," she said mockingly, while hanging the light on her carriage to free her hands. "After all, I am prepared to offer assistance."

"Well, how convenient for me to have picked the rutted path you would be taking. What is it? About four...five miles out of your way to the main road?" He was beyond being sarcastic. "So where were you camped out to follow me?"

"Now, Stewy...be nice. After all, it was your attraction for me that just saved you from marriage," Rica replied in baby talk, using pouting lips.

"Stop it, Rica. I've had enough of your cleverness for a lifetime. If you were a man I would have swung at you by now. Just get out of here and leave me alone," Stew demanded in disgust.

"Oh...I see you're blaming me for the little indiscretion. Aren't you forgetting *you* were involved?" Rica was more than happy to bring up the subject.

Stew grabbed her arm and held it in a tight grip to question her. "How did you manage to get the locket, anyway? I couldn't get back from my business trip in time to pick it up before the party, so Mr. Kelts assured me he'd deliver it to the Jacksons' home."

"Let go of my arm. You're hurting me!" Rica jerked her arm from Stew and went proudly into her story. "Mr. Kelts didn't lie. Mother and I were looking at pearls when you stopped at the jewelry store last week to order the locket. We were there watching while you chose the chain. If I recall, you were in a terrible hurry. Well...after you left, I simply offered to stop by and pick up the locket on my way to your engagement party. Uncle Rodger—or Mr. Kelts, as you refer to him—was most grateful."

"Wait! I know you weren't on the guest list. How did you manage to get an invitation?.

"Silly, I didn't need or want an invitation. I just wanted to be there. As it turned out, I was there on business." Rica openly continued, "I parked down the lane by the garden shed and waited until the party was in full swing. Then I walked right up to the front door. The staff at the Jacksons' was very obliging once I informed them I was on an errand from the jewelers. Of course, you had instructed them to inform you as soon as the representative arrived, so I just told them you could meet me down at the shed to inspect the locket before accepting it. You remember the message, don't you? Oh, yes. I almost forgot. I *also* left a note for Bethany. She was instructed to go to the shed shortly after. You certainly did have a surprise for her, didn't you?"

"You planned this?" Stew wanted to shake her but instead hit his fist in his hand. Fortunately for Rica, he was still mortified by his bout of violence toward Storm.

Rica was leery but hoped to call his bluff. "Oh, stop the dramatics! I'm sure this isn't the first time you've strayed along the path to matrimony. To refresh your memory, *you* were the weak one in this little travesty. It's not likely the marriage would have lasted. Eventually, you would have grown tired of her. You and I are alike in that way. We love attention. The only difference between us is...I don't mind if the attention is *bad*." Rica meant for the comparison to be a slur.

"How dare you compare my life with yours? I'm in love with Bethany and want to spend the rest of my life with her!" Stewart would not have admitted it, but Rica's insults had hurt him.

"No doubt, you're in love with Bethany. However, it took only a few seconds for you to take me in your arms. I'd only meant to give you a little congratulatory kiss, but Beth saw everything. Her timing was perfect." Rica was enjoying the taunting much more than she had imagined.

"It wasn't like that!" Stew understood her tactics but could not help reacting to them. "You did this to break our engagement!"

"Excuse me! I was just an innocent girl making a delivery for my overworked uncle. And *I'm* free of any commitments. *You*, on the other hand, were engaged. Two weeks until the wedding, wasn't it? You couldn't even be faithful through your own engagement party. As I see it...*I'm* the heroine here."

"Don't flatter yourself. You're far from innocent. Not only have you hurt Bethany and me, but you've injured our families. You've ruined our engagement party and our wedding plans. I don't understand a mind like yours."

"Stew, aren't you forgetting something here? You took the test and failed. Badly, I might add." He was making this too easy for her.

Stew stared at her with contempt in his eyes. "Why did you do this? Was it to hurt Bethany?"

"I must admit that I love tormenting her. I also like seeing the look that only she can give. You know the one—the sad, painful look of bewilderment, like a puppy that doesn't understand why it just got a good spanking from its master. I wonder if a horse feels like that after its owner gives it a good thrashing.

"Besides, Bethany has all of those loyal friends to baby her afterward. But I get the satisfaction of knowing she's miserable." Rica turned and looked at him with a devious smile.

"So Rica, you're jealous of Bethany and get pleasure from hurting her? I sometimes thought Bethany was imagining your attacks, but you're pleased to admit your maliciousness. Still, there's no reason for you to harass her. You're wealthy and attractive enough. You don't run in the same circles. What interest do you have in her life?" Stew couldn't believe anyone would admit to such a horrible existence.

"You've always found me attractive...and you never seemed upset when I played one of my little pranks on Bethany. You weren't exactly her great defender, were you?" She took a moment to laugh at him.

"If Bethany hadn't been around, you might have chosen me. You may be a so-called Christian, but you love it when a pretty face admires you. Actually, I believe every pretty face is a challenge to you." Rica's accusations were intentionally provoking.

"That day in the jewelry store, I decided I was going to take you away from her because I knew I could. We belong together. Humiliating Bethany Jackson only added to the pleasure. In fact, our little encounter couldn't have gone more perfectly."

Rica took hold of his arm, but he yanked his arm away. "Stop! You're ruthless! I feel sorry for you. You've stood here and admitted to being despicable, and you're proud of it. We have nothing in common. I love Bethany and you hate her! You stay away from me! Furthermore, keep away from Bethany!" Stew was seething.

By this time Stew's head was killing him, but he had managed to deliver his message. Then he got in his carriage and faded into the night.

Shaken by the realization that a relationship with Stew would never develop, Rica reacted completely differently than she or anyone else would have expected. Instead of chasing after him and issuing threats, she just stood and watched him drive away. He had sized her up and had the gall to tell her what kind of a person she really was. No one else had ever dared to do so...and Rica didn't like it one bit.

Stew had managed to get the better of her. Rica was not *quite* sure what she was going to do about that.

5

SLITHERING AROUND

The husbands of Adel Lewis and Mandy Yonker took the front seat of the double buggy to allow their wives to sit together in the back. It was obvious the ladies were shaken by the unexpected announcement and needed time to console one another.

"I just can't believe it. It's so completely unexpected. Everything seemed perfect between them... until that moment. I did notice she seemed distracted in the receiving line, but I never dreamed—" Mandy was overcome with disbelief.

"I'm afraid I may have a theory on what happened tonight." Adel did not want to believe what she knew in her heart was true.

"Then it *was* her?" Mandy asked guardedly, realizing she truly had caught a glimpse of the uninvited guest.

"Why should we have expected anything less from Rica Adams? Even as a grown woman she's staging her nasty tricks as if she were still a child. What is the woman's motive in finding ways to hurt Bethany? Bethany would do anything for anyone—even Rica. I guess I'm speaking out of turn. I don't have any hard evidence to prove Rica was behind the breakup," Adel backtracked, feeling somewhat bad for the accusation.

"*I'm* certain she had something to do with it...if not everything." Mandy had no problem adding to Adel's thoughts. "After all, we both know the Jacksons didn't invite her."

"Rica wasn't trying to mingle among the guests. She was dressed in black, slithering around and pretending to conceal herself in the shrubbery. I'm sure she planned and executed her scheme well...whatever it was. I'm also positive Rica *wanted* to be seen by the guests," Adel accused.

"If so, I don't think her strategy worked well," Mandy broke in. "By then, the candlelight had brightened against the darkness, so I don't think anyone could have picked her out, even if they'd been looking for her. All of the guests were in front of the gazebo with the candelabras around the perimeter. It was too bright to see outside the circle."

"That's good to hear." Adel relaxed a little. "Luther and I never moved into the circle with everyone else. I can assure you, it was Rica."

"It seems as if the little sneak *might not* have carried off her sabotage as smoothly as she'd estimated." Mandy gave Adel a faint smile. The thought lightened their mood somewhat.

"Bethany seemed so happy this evening. She was excited about moving to Bay City. There's no doubt in my mind Bethany was hopelessly in love with Stew before the receiving line. Remember, she told us they were planning to officially announce the wedding date would be moved up from September to June since Stew was to start his new job earlier than expected," Adel recalled.

"Yes, I remember now...and a note arrived a few seconds afterward. That's when Bethany excused herself. Whatever was in the note might have had something to do with what happened between Bethany and Stew. I'm almost sure of it."

"Of course, I'd forgotten about the note!" Adel agreed.

"I guess it really isn't any of our business. We may never know what took place. Still, we need to pray that whatever happened won't become public knowledge. They don't deserve to suffer further shame. Tonight was bad enough."

To put an end to the conversation, they joined hands and prayed that Stew and Bethany would seek God's comfort and wisdom during such a trial.

6

UNTHINKABLE

Mel had checked several places on the property, including the willow and the garden shed. He was just about to leave the stable when the moonlight revealed Bethany's silhouette between the tack room windows.

"Bethy?"

"Yes, Papa," Bethany answered weakly, using the name she seldom called him anymore.

"I've been looking for you." Her father put out his hands to receive her.

"Desperately, Bethany threw her arms around her father's neck. "Oh, Papa. It hurts so badly," she told him. Then the tears rose, and she allowed them to have their way.

He wrapped his arms around her in the protective and loving way only a father can. He intended to hold his daughter for as long as she needed him. "Go ahead, sweetheart. Let it all out."

Eventually, Bethany and her father made their way back to the study where Bethany was met with the comforting arms of her mother and older sister, Tanna. No one asked any questions, but Bethany felt she owed them an explanation. Finally, she collected herself well enough to attempt telling the story.

"Dear, there is no need for you to speak of this matter tonight. It will be too difficult. It can wait until tomorrow when you've had enough time to rest. Please, let's get you into bed," her mother begged.

"Thank you, Mother. But I'm much too shaken to think about sleep. At least, not yet. I—I really would like to talk. I need to try to make sense of what has happened. Do you mind terribly?" Bethany still could not believe what she was about to convey was reality, but she wanted them to know what happened since they were hurting too.

"Then will you at least sit in the wingback chair? It will be much more comfortable."Her mother's request was filled with insistence.

To please her, Bethany graciously moved.

"You might have noticed Stewart and I were missing from the party for a while this evening."

Tanna spoke up, "I believe I caught a glimpse of you talking with some friends after dinner, but then you seemed to have disappeared."

"Yes, that was when Margaret brought out a card requesting me to go to the garden shed by the lake. Of course, I believed it to be from Stew. I thought he just wanted to see me for a few minutes. We hadn't been alone since he'd returned from his trip. We sat briefly together at dinner, but we were separated during the party while we talked to our guests."

Mel interrupted, "Wait! You never mentioned you and Stew

were having second thoughts. We're confused by all of this. It seemed to have come out of nowhere. Are we correct in thinking the two of you hadn't thought of breaking up before tonight?"

Bethany had to stop for a moment to regain control of her emotions before she could go on.

"You aren't up to this. Really, dear, let's drop it for tonight," her mother encouraged.

"No, Mother. We're all upset and confused. I want to get this over with," Bethany understood her mother was trying to be protective, but it wasn't helping.

"Now...to answer your question, Father—no, we had no thoughts of calling off the engagement before tonight."

"As I was saying–I excused myself from the conversation with the girls and took the path to the garden shed. I had to hurry to make it on time, but when I arrived outside the door, I could hear a girl giggling. I wasn't intentionally sneaking up on them, but I slipped inside the door and saw Stew..." Bethany had to stop. Telling the story hurt almost as much as when she witnessed it.

"Please, don't worry. I'm fine. It's just a little difficult.

"As I was saying, I slipped inside the door just as I saw Stewart...embracing and kissing...another girl." Once again, she felt the stab of betrayal in her heart.

Bethany watched as looks of unbelief and shock overtook her family.

"No, dear, you must be mistaken. Stew loves you so very much. He would never intentionally hurt you. You're just exhausted from the preparations for the party and the stress caused by changing the wedding date—not to mention all the packing to move."

"Thank you, Mother. I appreciate you trying to reassure me–but there is no mistake. I caught Stewart being unfaithful to me." Bethany took a shaky, deep breath.

"Bethany? This is an unthinkable charge against Stewart. Maybe you mistook the meaning of the embrace. Could it have been a relative?" Her father was convinced there was another explanation for Stew's actions.

"Father, the shed was brightly lit. I startled them and he broke away from her. I was able to see her face clearly in the light."

Like her parents, Tanna still believed Bethany was mistaken. "Then who was it, hon?"

"It was Rica—Rica Adams."

The anticipated gasps were followed by a sickening silence. If true, the family knew there was no chance of reconciliation. The relationship was over.

7

SKELETAL REMAINS

The next morning, Bethany awoke to the sun streaming through the French doors of her room. She forced herself to reach for the bell cord to let the maid know she was awake. The thought of facing a bright and beautiful day seemed impossible, so she stayed in bed longer than she had intended.

Bethany was aware that, not far from her balcony, the tables, chairs, and candelabras waited to be taken down. They were the skeletal remains of what might have been. If only sleep had allowed her to escape the pain she felt, but it had not been a comfort. Yet she had to get up. She could not burden her parents further by being despondent. They had enough to deal with after the disgrace of last night's engagement party and the cancellation of an extravagant wedding. She wondered how she could ever make it up to them.

Out of consideration for her family, Bethany forced herself to throw back the covers and place her feet on the soft rug beside the bed; it seemed to take all her strength to do so. Sickness filled her stomach, but she was determined to go through a regular morning routine, no matter how she felt.

After straightening the bed to make it easier for the housekeeper, she went to the bathroom, disrobed, and sank deep into the tub of warm water that had been prepared. She strummed the water with her fingers and stared blankly at the wall in front of her. Once again, the hurtful words Stew had spoken came to mind—*It didn't mean anything.* She wondered how he could have had the nerve to make such a statement.

When it was time to dress, she did not call the maid. The closet was full of clothes, and it did not take much intelligence to find something to wear. It felt good to be alone and not have someone hovering over her. After fighting the urge to crawl back into the security of her bed, Bethany sat down in front of the mirror to examine her eyes. There was little evidence she had been crying. Relieved, she started to put her hair up but decided it brought attention to how tired she looked. Being one to rebel against hair styles dictated by fashion, she was glad to leave it down.

Bethany dreaded facing anyone but left the room determined to be strong. However, when she started down the stairs, it finally occurred to her that the future she had planned to live was no longer there. It was an agonizing realization. She wasn't ready to adjust to a new life. Still, Bethany forced herself to keep moving.

On her way to the kitchen, she passed the dining room and heard the tinkling of the silver and crystal. The sounds meant the tableware brought out for the engagement party was being put back into storage for the next special occasion. All other reminders of the wedding had been removed from within the house and placed out of sight.

Bethany pushed open the swinging door and entered the dining area of the kitchen. She often ate there when she missed breakfast in the dining room.

"Well, good morning," Mary greeted with a soothing tone and a smile. "I knew my girl would be up and about early. I've never known anything that could keep you down. What would you like for breakfast?"

Bethany was grateful to Mary for handling the situation in such a discreet manner. She was not in the mood to discuss the details of the broken engagement.

Bethany sighed. "Now that I'm here, I don't think I can eat a thing. I just don't have an appetite."

"Nonsense. I'll be right back with some dry toast and tea. You know your Mother will fret if you don't eat something. You might as well eat and get it over with." Mary started toward the kitchen. Bethany knew she was right and would eat for her mother's peace of mind. Mary soon returned with toast, tea, and a loving smile, and Bethany ate as instructed.

Mary Zimmer and her husband, John, lived in a small house about two miles down the road from the Jacksons' estate. Mary was just a newlywed when she started working as the Jacksons' head housekeeper. John had been injured in a farming accident, so she had needed to find a way to supplement their income. After John's recovery, she decided to keep the position since she enjoyed the job and the money. The Jacksons, who refused to acknowledge social standings, considered the Zimmers part of the family. Bethany loved and trusted the housekeeper, and the two often shared their most personal thoughts and secrets...but not today.

After the meal, Bethany left through the front door and took the path to the willow. She did not want to be at the house while the yard was being cleared. Besides, the sooner she visited the scene where the breakup began, the sooner she would be able to put it behind her.

The warm sunshine and gentle breeze were welcome and calming. So Bethany moved near the water's edge to listen to the swishing of the willow and the sound of the gentle waves that enticed and teased from the bank. For a few moments, she was able to enjoy the peacefulness, but it soon melted away as unwanted thoughts came to mind.

Evidently, she had been wrong in accepting Stew's proposal and in believing God wanted them to marry. She wondered if she had ignored God's will because of wanting the relationship so badly.

Father, I know you're there to support and love me, but I feel so alone. I'm hurt and confused. Help me to move on. Bethany took a few deep breathes to relax, then walked over to the willow and allowed its branches to hide her from the world.

Bethany's time alone by the lakeside was short lived. His approach seemed deafening. She was not prepared for a confrontation nor had she anticipated one.

"Why are you here, Stewart?" She didn't turn to face him. "I thought we'd settled everything last night. I have nothing further to discuss with you."

"I was hoping you might see things more clearly after a night's rest. I've certainly had a change of heart. We need to talk this through." Stew's heart was racing.

"Surely you don't expect me to repeat myself," Bethany replied.

"I haven't changed my mind. I meant what I said last night."

"Bethany—I'm sorry for the way I talked to you and for the way I left things. I was distraught and angry. I've never treated you or anyone else in that manner, and I'm ashamed of myself. I will never demonstrate such behavior again. Please, forgive me," Stew apologized sincerely.

"I see no reason to hold it against you, and I appreciate your apology. It was a difficult circumstance." She noted he had made no reference to the incident with Rica.

"Is that all you have to say?" Bethany asked.

"No—but—will you please turn around and face me?" He tried not to sound agitated.

Bethany did turn to him, but her unwavering expression spoke volumes. His words were having little impact.

Stew then ventured his final plea, "I have come to ask you to continue with the arrangements for our wedding, so we can go on with our lives as planned. I'm desperately in love with you, Beth, and I believe it *is* God's will for us to be together."

"Stop it, Stewart! I told you I'm serious about breaking the engagement. I'm not trying to be cruel, but I must be truthful. The man I loved didn't exist. I don't love you, Stew. You proved last night you don't love me." Bethany made the statement distinctly and firmly.

Stew was totally crushed and not prepared to defend himself against the hurtful words. He had never seen Bethany demonstrate such mature strength and would have admired her for it if it had been under different circumstances.

He was devastated but covered his reaction with a farewell

statement, "Well—I believe you've made a very foolish choice and have no desire to learn the truth. I don't know what has come over you, but obviously you aren't the person *I* perceived *you* to be either. Despite that, I wish you well. I hope we will always be friends.

"As it is, I have to catch the train for Hastings. You'll be in my prayers, Bethany."

Bethany would not allow herself to watch him walk away. She was afraid she might run after him and plead for him to stay. Yet she believed this was the way it was supposed to be. God evidently had other plans for their lives.

After she was certain Stew was well on his way, Bethany walked back toward the house. The chairs and tables were gone, and the gazebo stood alone as a last reminder.

Her father had built the gazebo with his own hands as a wedding gift to surprise her. He had chosen the place where she would have the best possible view of their estate and her precious willow by the lake. Bethany loved her father dearly, and she would not allow last night's occurrences to destroy the memory of love in which the gift was given.

8

THE FLIRT

Stew's knees were shaking by the time he reached the carriage. He was so stricken with grief from Bethany's final rejection that he was not sure he could climb into the buggy. The guilt of whipping Storm, along with the angry quarrel with Rica, added to his distress. His heart was pounding, his head was throbbing, and his forehead was beading with sweat. He desperately needed to take time to recover but refused to do it. Gripping the seat of the rig, he pulled himself up with what little power he could rally. He grasped the reins and gave a lash just to get the horse moving. Storm instinctively turned the rig and headed down the lane. Stew was relieved the horse had taken it upon himself to do so without any further prompting. Ironically, he was at the horse's mercy.

Storm was acting extremely skittish toward him, and Stew felt the full effect of remorse for having betrayed the trust between them. It no longer seemed right to take Storm from a luxurious country life to a cramped city stable, so he decided to give the horse to his father as a parting gift. His dad was an avid horseman and had always admired Storm. The animal was superior to all the finer horses in the area, and Stew felt his father deserved the best.

Stew knew his parents would be hurt when they realized he had left without saying goodbye, but he could not face them after last night. He had left a letter on his father's desk giving a brief explanation of why the wedding was cancelled and of his plans to attend the seminar in Hastings before going on to Bay City. Of course, the letter did not include anything about Rica. He wished he had spent more time composing the letter but was too burdened to think it through.

Upon arrival at the station, Stew pulled Storm to a stop under a shade tree and took a minute to regain his strength. *Bethany, why have you done this?* He could never have envisioned Bethany being so stubborn and vindictive.

Taking out his handkerchief, Stew mopped his forehead and wondered if he looked as unraveled as he felt. After securing the reins, he made his way to the depot.

The station was busy and Stew found it aggravating. Of course, he was not in his normal good humor, but he managed to put up a front. He checked his bags and hired a man to deliver Storm back to his parents' home.

Then Stew purchased a newspaper and took a bench. He attempted to find an article that would hold his attention but was unable to concentrate no matter how hard he tried. Eventually, he gave up the pretense of reading and laid the paper aside.

As he watched the people passing by, he caught sight of two attractive young women. Being deep in thought, Stew unintentionally continued to stare at them, and it was not long until they noticed his gaze. The more flirtatious one with the dark hair piled high on her head looked directly into his eyes and smiled. She then lowered her head and raised her eyebrows to let him know she appreciated his interest. The blonde, a little younger and attired much like her companion, continuously giggled as they walked toward him. He reacted by giving the ladies his usual friendly smile and a slight nod. The girls bobbed their heads in return, assuming they knew how his stare and smile were intended. Once Stew realized he had been staring, his conscience was pricked for not averting his eyes. Still, it might have been discourteous, so he dismissed the incident.

Soon after, he boarded the train and found a seat across the aisle from an attractive redhead. He gave her polite recognition, not thinking anything of it since finding a seat near pretty girls was a common occurrence.

More than ready to leave town, Stew reached for his pocket watch. To add to his frustration, the watch was last year's Christmas gift from Bethany. He wished he had thought to exchange it before leaving home. The last thing he needed was to be reminded of her whenever he checked the time. He would replace it.

To his relief, the train gave a jolt, indicating it was leaving the station. He watched as people on the platform tried to squeeze in final goodbyes to loved ones. A little girl ran several feet alongside the train waving and crying. The scene tugged at Stew's heart, and he gave her a sympathizing smile as he passed by.

Several minutes later, he leaned his head against the window to nap, hoping it would relieve his aching head which was now sore to the touch. Unfortunately, it was not long before he heard someone trying to get his attention. "Sir...sir!"

Stew opened his eyes and turned to see the lady with the red hair standing over him. "Yes?" Stew's head was pulsating, but he tried to appear more alert than he felt.

"I'm sorry to disturb you, but your hat has fallen on the floor and some water or something is running toward it. It looks like a new hat. I couldn't reach it, so I had to wake you."

Stew leaned over and snatched the hat up just in time. "Thank you very kindly! I had no idea it had fallen. You may have saved me the price of a new hat."

"If I may, my name is Stewart Jefferson," he said courteously to introduce himself.

"And I'm Pearl Sawyer." Having just removed her glove, she held out a hand for Stew to take.

"Nice to meet you, Miss Sawyer," Stew replied. "I'm sorry you caught me napping, but I've had a very trying week which has robbed me of my normal rest."

"Nothing serious, I hope?" Miss Sawyer asked.

"Nothing life threatening," he answered, hoping the conversation would end there.

"I wish there was something to make train rides more interesting. I get restless sitting for hours with nothing to do. One can only read so long." She was being overly friendly, but he continued the conversation because he did not want to be rude.

"Well, it doesn't look like you'll be a "Miss" for long." Stew was still holding her hand since she made no effort to let go of his. He did not know what to do about it, so he thought commenting on the ring might cause her to release his hand.

"Oh, you're referring to my ring. The wedding is set for September," she shared.

"That's quite a ring," Stew mentioned only out of politeness.

"Thank you! Clarence is most generous. When I saw the design, I refused to consider any other. After all, it's my engagement ring, and I'm the one who'll be wearing it. Don't you agree?" Miss Sawyer questioned.

"Certainly," Stew answered, wondering why he should care if Clarence didn't. Stew actually thought it looked gaudy but gave it a close inspection to please her. "*It is* eye-catching."

"It's three karats and a perfect stone," the redhead stated loudly so others could hear.

"Excuse me! I'll thank you to turn loose of my fiancée's hand," a base voice requested and none too pleasantly. Stew looked up into the stern face of a large man.

"I beg your pardon, sir. I can see how this looks, but I was just admiring the engagement ring you gave—uh—Pearl. Otherwise, I wouldn't be holding her hand." Stew tried to explain.

"Clarence! This is Stewart—" Miss Sawyer began.

"On the first name basis, are we?" Clarence said accusingly.

"I don't appreciate the friendly way you've addressed my fiancée. You're out of line, mister!" Clarence gave him a cold stare.

"I can assure you I only used her first name because I couldn't readily recall her last." Stew stood to his feet. He did not feel a gentleman should stay seated in such a situation, nor did he want the other passengers to get the impression he could be bullied. "I hope you'll accept my apology. We've only been talking a couple of minutes, if that long. Now if you'll excuse me, I feel it would be best for me to find another seat." He was insulted and hoped the explanation shamed Clarence. Stew was not the brawling type and had no intention of getting in a fist fight over...Pearl.

"I'd prefer it." Clarence made a point of using his deepest voice.

Stewart picked up his belongings and walked toward the back of the car. He passed a few seats and finally asked an older woman if he could take the seat beside her.

"Please, by all means!" The lady was thrilled he had asked and slid closer to the window.

"Thank you, Madam. My name is—"

"Stewart Jefferson—Yes, I heard. My name is Marjorie Haines." The woman was obviously amused by his predicament.

"I'm so sorry if that couple caused you embarrassment. You were unmistakably in the right and a gentlemen about the whole thing. She knocked your hat off when she stood to remove her wrap. I'm sure she did it on purpose. It's clear to see, she feels herself quite the attraction. Now, you just sit there and forget the whole thing." Marjorie patted his hand.

Stew felt self-conscious because of the incident but tried to hide it. Since there was a lot of whispering going on, he discreetly glanced around to determine if the other passengers agreed with Marjorie. To his relief, all eyes rested on Clarence and Pearl, who were obviously not speaking to one another. Nonetheless, they soon got off the train, and the occurrence quickly became a fading memory.

Consequently, Stew spent the first part of the ride to Hastings in pleasant conversation with Marjorie Haines, which was a welcome distraction from his troubles.

9

SOMETIMES WE DON'T WANT TO KNOW

Bethany entered the house through the front door. She never tired of seeing the huge, cherry staircase that swirled down into the center of the foyer.

Many times she had walked down those stairs to meet Stewart. He always seemed mesmerized when she appeared. Stew was extremely handsome and wore a constant smile. He was tall and a little on the thin side, had dark hair, blue eyes...and Bethany had been totally in love with him.

Every moment they had spent together seemed precious. His last year of college had felt like an eternity. Running down the stairs to him on his final return from his senior year was her fondest memory.

Stop, Bethany, she thought, pulling herself out of the daydream. *It was fantasy!* The sickening sadness within her heart grew larger. She wondered how long it would take for the torture to end.

"Bethany! I was wondering what time we would see you today. It's good to see you're up and looking so pretty. How are you doing this morning?" her mother asked hesitantly.

"It comes and it goes," Bethany said, trying to sound perky.

"Thank you for asking, Mother.

"Stewart was here, you know." Bethany had not planned to mention it because she was not sure how her parents would react to the news.

Her mother was surprised to hear he had returned so quickly. "I'm sorry to meddle, but what did he want?"

"He wanted me to reconsider...he did apologize...somewhat... but, he didn't speak about the incident with Rica. He believes I'm being unreasonable."

"Please forgive me, but I still find it all so hard to believe on Stewart's part—not that I doubt what you've told us. He's so loving and accommodating toward you—toward everyone, for that matter. We've never had reason to question his character." Helen, like the rest of the family, was fighting a battle of questions.

"Mother! Until last night, I had never considered his actions toward other women. I just felt privileged he chose me."

There was a long pause, but finally her mother broke the silence. "Bethany, I don't mean to speak out of turn, but, sweetheart, are you positive a complete and final break between you and Stewart is the right thing? What happened last night was a terrible shock. You haven't had time to pray this through.

"Don't misunderstand, Stewart seems to have committed a terrible offence, and you didn't deserve it. But when we've been hurt, we tend to react with our emotions instead of with God's guidance. It's hard to tell the difference—sometimes we don't want to know the difference."

"Mother, I cannot love a man who treats love or marriage so carelessly. Last night Stew was like a complete stranger. I was stunned by the way he acted. As for knowing if I've done the right thing—I couldn't have made it through the announcement if I hadn't believed God was on my side."

"On your side, Bethany?" Helen questioned.

Both were aware she had not answered the questions satisfactorily, but her mother yielded, "All right, dear, I won't press the issue any further.

"Would you like to take a walk or maybe we should spend time with Tanna since she'll be leaving soon?"

"No, not at present. I really don't know what I want. I just need time alone."

As Helen was leaving the room, Bethany called to her. Helen turned to face her daughter. "Mama, thank you for your honesty."

Her mother gave an understanding smile and left the foyer. She waited until Bethany had gone upstairs and then knocked softly on the study door before entering.

"My beautiful wife...to what do I owe this pleasure?" Mel said lovingly as he looked up from his desk.

Helen was not aware of the look of admiration her husband's smile reflected. He did not see the graying of her hair or the slight weight gain which the passing of years brings; she was beautiful in his eyes and a lady above all others.

It was uncomfortable for Helen to admit why she had come. She felt as if she was betraying her daughter's trust, but Mel was Bethany's father. He was just as concerned for Bethany as she.

"How are you, darling?" she asked as she crossed the room and gave him a kiss on the cheek. "I'm sorry to interrupt you this time of day, but I just spoke with Bethany. Have you talked with her this morning?"

"No, dear, I haven't. I'm not exactly the bravest man in dealing with matters of the heart, and since this involves my little girl, I'm afraid I can't trust my judgment just now."

"Unlike you...I usually speak first and think things through afterward...but I felt it necessary to question our daughter before someone else did. I wanted her to consider her actions. Was God leading her or did she react from a broken heart? I thought I was in God's timing, but I may have been overly zealous." Helen looked uncertain.

"The questions needed to be asked," Mel reminded in his usual diplomatic way.

"Thank you," Helen replied, as she bent and gave him another kiss. "You always have the right advice when I need to be consoled."

She sat down in the chair in front of Mel's desk to continue the conversation.

"Stew was here to talk to her this morning. I assume he caught her under her willow tree. He knows her so well."

"I thought I heard his rig but believed it was my imagination." Mel leaned back in his chair.

"He came to apologize, but Bethany still believes Stewart is blaming her for the breakup since he didn't address the situation with Rica Adams. No doubt, there was more to be told, but she seemed to have shared all the information she cared to reveal. I didn't pursue it.

"Mel, I feel guilty. I have misgivings about Bethany's perception just now. I love Stewart as a son, and I'm devastated he won't be in our family."

"Don't chastise yourself, sweetheart. While Bethany comes first, we have feelings to deal with in this breakup too.

"He was like a son to us long before he and Bethany noticed one another. I started fishing with him when he wasn't much bigger than the fish he caught. I stayed out in the woods hunting on many a cold day—chilled to the bone because the little rascal refused to give up. We have a lot of time and love invested in the boy. I remember being very pleased when I learned he was interested in our daughter." Mel's eyes glistened, and his voice started to crack.

"To be honest, one moment I'm mourning the loss of a son, and the next minute I want to give him a good, sound thrashing. Not exactly the Christian attitude, is it?" Mel admitted to Helen.

"I must admit it does disturb me that Stewart didn't mention the Adams girl. Stew does have a way with young ladies, but he has a way with all people. I considered those traits before I allowed Bethany to see him," Mel pointed out.

Helen was glad to hear her husband's opinion of Stewart mirrored hers.

"I do need to speak to Bethany today. What kind of father would I be if I ignored my daughter during such a trying time?"

With everything having been said, Helen lovingly patted his hand and left the room feeling comforted by her husband's Godly wisdom.

10

THE GOWN

When Bethany arrived at the top of the stairs, she went straight to her mother's sewing room. The unexpected visit from Stewart had drained her emotionally, but it had not overpowered the curiosity of seeing her wedding dress for the first time.

The Jacksons easily could have afforded the most expensive wedding gowns for their daughters, but it was never considered since Helen's passion was sewing and design.

As a bride-to-be, Bethany had dreamed of the white, silk dress she had sketched in her imagination over the years and trusted her mother to make the dream come true.

When she opened the door, Bethany realized she had never fully appreciated her mother's talent. Not only was the gown exquisite—it was captivating.

She took several minutes to study the design and to note all the intricate details. The number of hours of labor involved in making it was inconceivable.

The front of the bodice was a tapestry made of glass beads which extended onto a high, standup collar. The bodice also came to a delicate point at the waist, where the beaded skirt gathered to give it a sophisticated bell shape. Down the back of the dress was a tight row of covered buttons which ended well below the waistline. A lengthy train flowing from the back of the dress rounded at the end and had its own elaborate beadwork to leave a lasting impression.

The sleeves were also arrayed with beading, puffed at the top and slightly puckered along the seams to give a draping effect. Then just above the elbows, the sleeves tapered to a tight fit which came to a point over the hands.

The floor length bridal veil was sprinkled with pearls and trimmed in silk. It cascaded from a headpiece covered to match the beaded bodice.

"Bethy?" an apprehensive voice questioned.

Bethany turned to see her mother standing in the doorway with an anxious look.

"It's magnificent. Beyond any of my dreams." Bethany rushed toward her mother, and Helen reached out to receive her daughter into her arms.

"You don't deserve what happened after all of your hard work. I'm sorry I won't be wearing it. Our friends and family should have seen it. The gown should be worn by a princess." Bethany did not have enough words to compliment her mother and secretly wished the lovely gown was not part of the terrible memory.

"Sweetheart, I'm overjoyed you like it, but—" her mother tried to warn.

"Mother–it's remarkable!"

"Honey, don't concern yourself about this dress because—" Helen tried again.

"Don't concern myself? The hours–a shameful waste." The

regret on Bethany's face brought pain to Helen's heart.

"Sweetheart, I must explain," Helen insisted.

"Explain?"

"I'm sorry but...this isn't *your* gown," Helen admitted sorrowfully.

"Not mine? But the wedding was to be in two weeks. You've had time to work on someone else's gown?"

"No, of course not. But, this isn't the one you designed in that pretty, little head of yours. Your dress is hanging over there by the cutting table. It still needs several hours of work. I was planning to put it in storage today."

"Then whose is it?

"It's a long story, and this isn't the time."

"Mother, I want to know about this dress...please," Bethany begged pitifully.

"If you insist—" Helen did not want to cause her daughter any further stress but felt trapped.

"Do you remember much about your sister's wedding gown?"

"Yes, I thought it was the most beautiful dress I'd ever seen...until today."

"If you recall, Tanna was never one to care about details, so the design of the dress and most of the wedding plans were left to me."

"I remember. The wedding was perfect for them. Tanna loved the dress—as everyone did." Bethany's mind was taken back to the day.

"I almost didn't meet the deadline. It was difficult with Tanna being abroad and not being here to make decisions. Nonetheless, I'd always known what I wanted to design for her. I just made it the way I saw your sister as a person.

"After Tanna's wedding, the dress I'd pictured for *you* kept burning in my mind. First, I made a few sketches, so I wouldn't forget the way I had envisioned it. Not long after, I started experimenting with the bead work and material. To be honest, I just got carried away, and I couldn't stop myself from working on it. I'd planned to surprise you. It was completed just before Stewart asked for your hand.

"When I realized you had your own ideas for a gown, I was too ashamed to tell you what I'd done. You know how I can be. It was ridiculous." Out of embarrassment, Helen looked away from her daughter.

"I wish you'd told me." Bethany felt sorry for not realizing how difficult it must have been for her mother not to be included in designing her gown.

"Sweetheart, it was *your* wedding—not mine. You imagined your dress differently, and a bride should wear the gown of her dreams."

Bethany took her mother's hands and kissed them, "I would have preferred *your* gown."

Helen's face lit up. "Really? Do you mean it?"

"Yes, I do. And should I ever marry, I would—" Bethany didn't want to finish the sentence.

"I didn't intend for you to see it. And, I wouldn't want you to feel obligated."

Bethany smiled tenderly at her mother. "I've never been more sincere."

"Wonderful! I'll put it in storage." Helen was comforted by the thought of Bethany wearing the gown someday.

"What would you like me to do with the *other* dress when it's completed?" Helen thought the decision should be made while the subject was open; it would be less painful if not revisited.

"Could you make a few changes and give it to someone who can't afford a wedding gown?"

Helen smiled approvingly. "Certainly."

11

FRIEND AND FOE

It was midafternoon when the train pulled into Hastings. The gentle movement along the tracks had allowed Stew to relax, and he had been able to rest for the remainder of the ride. On the other hand, the trip did leave him looking a bit scruffy, and it bothered him since he was sure to be recognized on campus.

After paying a hefty tip to have his bags delivered to the hotel, Stew left the station and headed toward the downtown area. It was a gorgeous day, and it put him in a better frame of mind.

He had missed breakfast and lunch so decided to stop at the café where he had shared many meals with friends during his college days. Since Stew wanted to enjoy the atmosphere and watch people passing, he asked for a table outside. After looking over the menu, he ordered his usual soup and sandwich.

While waiting for the meal, Stew decided to look over the information on the seminar. It was a disappointment to discover the author he had wanted to hear had been replaced with an unfamiliar name. The list of other speakers assured the next couple of days would prove to be boring.

"Stewart!" a lady's voice paged. Stew was caught off guard

when he looked up.

"I can't believe it's you!" the young lady squealed with delight. She took him by the hand and pulled him to a slightly more secluded area. "What are you doing here? I heard you'd accepted a position in Bay City and had moved the wedding to a much earlier date. I can't imagine you had the time to come to Hastings."

He recognized the face, but nothing else came to mind—especially not a name. He did his best to smile and act as if he were glad to see her.

"Millie—Millie Kendal!" another young lady called out. "I can't stop, but can we meet in an hour for tea."

The young woman holding onto Stew's arm acknowledged the invitation with a slight wave of her hand.

Millie Kendal. Oh, yes. The pesty one. I tutored her a few times for a professor, Stew recalled.

"Miss Kendal...I wasn't expecting you to be the first person I would meet in Hastings." Stew pretended to be cordial.

"I knew it!" Mille insinuated knowingly. "The wedding has been called off!"

"What makes you think that?"

"I can just tell. And you've come to see me!" she said with a self-convinced look.

"Actually–" he started to reply, bewildered by her reaction.

"Don't say anything! I have a pressing engagement which can't be put off another second. I must run, but can we meet at the Bradford for dinner about five?"

"But–" he tried to protest, but she placed a quieting finger on his lips.

Oh, no! he thought. Yet what else did he have to do this evening. Even if he did not relish the idea of spending time with this girl, he needed to get things cleared up. Stew gave in and nodded to accept.

Excitement filled her face. "We must be discreet though. My father's a judge, and my parents are constantly warning me to monitor my behavior in public." Millie leaned over and gave him a peck on the cheek. "Until this evening!"

"Strange girl," he said under his breath, as he returned to his table.

After lunch Stew went to the hotel and was pleased to find his bags were unpacked.

He had no idea The Regency had such fine accommodations. Had he known it, his family would have enjoyed staying there when they had visited him at college. Stew could only imagine how nice the suites might be. The place suited him.

After looking around, he finally sat down and took the newspaper from the night stand. Searching for an article to hold his attention was still a waste of time. As soon as he laid the paper aside, his mind went to thoughts of Bethany. His love for her was unshaken, although he was still furious with her for humiliating him in front of friends and family. He then recalled the times she had mentioned how blessed she felt to be the one he had chosen to be his bride; he had felt equally blessed. He knew he had been a fool not to attempt an explanation of what had happened when she found him with Rica, but he could not. Stew then pressed a hand to each side of his head trying to stifle the racing thoughts.

The hope of catching a short nap was gone. Stew realized he needed to stay busy since being alone allowed him to dwell on the past.

What better way to stay busy than to have dinner with an old friend like Millie...or whatever her name is. Stew decided to bathe, put on a fresh suit, and go for a walk around campus to pass the time before the five o'clock appointment.

It had only been a short time since he had been on campus, so not much had changed. The construction on the new library was near completion. Some building material had been delivered to change the old library into much needed dorms. Hopefully, the job would be completed by the fall semester.

"Stewart!" a muscular, young man called out as he grabbed Stew's hand and gave it a good shake. "What on earth are you doing back here? If I remember correctly, you're to be married in a couple of weeks."

"Matthew! Good to see you!" Stew increased the hardy handshake. "How are things going for you? Did you get that job in Albany?"

"Sure did! Start first of the month. So I decided to burn some time here at the seminar. Have to keep busy. You know me.

"Say, did you happen to notice Joyner was replaced?" Matt questioned. "I can't say I'm happy to have come all this way to listen to someone I'm unfamiliar with." Matt's brow furrowed in aggravation as he waited for Stew's reaction.

"My thoughts exactly. I expect several people are of the same opinion. I've come to the conclusion I'm going to ask for a refund if the speaker isn't as good as Joyner. It was my understanding Joyner was the original reason for the seminar."

"Hey! Where's that pretty bride-to-be I've been hoping to

meet? I almost considered catching a train and surprising you at the wedding."

Well—there it was. Stew had hoped not to have to answer that question for some time, especially since he had not made up his mind how to reply. *Now—should I just say the wedding was supposed to be Saturday after next? No—that Millie girl is already certain the wedding is cancelled. She doesn't appear to be the type to keep quiet.* Since several of his buddies would be attending the seminar, there was the possibility of running into a friend at dinner. He knew it would be best to be straightforward about the wedding.

"We've called the wedding off." Stew tried to act nonchalant.

"What? I'm sorry! If I'd known I wouldn't have mentioned it." Matt's face reddened.

"Oh, it's fine. We just realized we loved each other, but we weren't *in* love. And that's not what a marriage should be based on. We parted as friends."

There—I've said it. He was now committed to an explanation for the breakup. Stew had taken his answer from Bethany's announcement at the engagement party. He hoped it sounded optimistic. But telling the story was painful, and he had to fight to keep it from showing.

"I sure am sorry to hear it. She sounded like a fine girl. Still, a bride means a man is limited to one woman. That might've been rough on a guy like you." Matt laughed and gave Stew's hand another shake. "Say, I...uh...I have to hurry off. I'm running late, but maybe we can get together for dinner tomorrow evening...about seven...at the usual place?"

"That sounds great, but I'm not positive I can make it. Not

sure about my schedule." Stew was still shaken and unable to give a straight answer.

"Well, come if you can," Matt yelled as he walked away.

Stew did not respond; he was weighing the statement Matt had made about a guy like him being limited to one woman. He did not understand the meaning of it and was slightly offended. Making things worse, it was obvious that Matt had ended the conversation because he was uncomfortable after learning about the broken engagement.

Admitting to the breakup hit Stew hard, so he walked to a small courtyard where he could collect himself.

In less than twenty four hours, he had lost Bethany and endured more hurt and conflict than he had known in his entire life. His ability to fake a good mood was nearly depleted.

When he walked into the restaurant, it was immediately assumed he was the gentleman the young lady was expecting. The waiter led him to the table by the window where Stew cautiously greeted Millie before taking a seat.

"You're late," she whispered once the drink order was taken. "I don't mean to scold, but I was afraid you might not come. I should have known better.

"I'm in love with you. I couldn't say it before because you were promised to someone else," Millie gushed.

"Millie!" Stew broke in. "I have no idea what—"

"It sounds silly, I know. But there's nothing to stand between us now," Millie rattled on.

"Tell me—did *you* stop the wedding? It's clear to see you're happy about it," she continued.

"I wasn't intending to discuss it with you," he informed her.

"You can tell me. Let's get it out of the way so we can go on with our relationship," she persisted.

"Actually, there's not much to tell. We decided to stay friends," he said dismissively, refusing to give her any further information. He was quite perturbed with the young woman and her assertions. Unfortunately, the information encouraged her to take more liberties.

By this time the waiter had returned with their drinks and asked if they were ready to order.

"Yes," Millie answered, "I'll just have the salad."

"I'll have the same." Even though he was hungry, Stew just wanted to set things straight with this young woman and leave. He knew he should have been blunt with her when they had met earlier and should not have accepted the invitation.

The waiter collected the menus and started to leave, but Stew motioned him back. "Millie, would you care for dessert later?" Stew questioned.

"Do I look like a lady who eats dessert?" she questioned in return, with more pride than she should have.

"Since neither of us care for dessert, would you please bring the check right after you've placed the order?" Stew requested. "I'd like to take care of the bill so we're free to leave when we're ready."

"By all means, sir. I'll be right back with the check," the waiter answered.

"You're in a hurry for us to be alone just as I am! We'll discuss our plans then." She smiled assumingly.

"I haven't asked. How was your trip? Was it pleasant? Did you doze?"Millie made the statements loudly so those seated nearby would assume they were a couple.

"Like most people, I can usually sleep on a train. I guess it's the motion. Do you travel by train much?" he asked dryly, trying to keep the conversation to the blandest topics.

"We seldom travel. My father doesn't care to, and mother doesn't like to venture far without him. We haven't been out of the country for ages," she stressed.

Mother and I do have a trip planned for late summer, but it can be cancelled," Millie hinted.

Stew was determined to ignore the insinuations until he could get the girl alone. Wanting to avoid further conversation, he picked up his cup and sipped slowly.

"Excuse me, sir. I have your bill." The waiter politely placed the bill on the table. "I'll return for it in a few minutes."

"No! No! That won't be necessary. I—I'd like to pay now," Stew insisted, nearly knocking over his chair as he rose. He pulled out his wallet and handed the man a bill.

"I'll be right back with the change."

"That won't be necessary! Keep the change!" Stew didn't want anything to interfere with a quick departure and hoped the waiter would bring the salads immediately.

"Thank you very much, sir." The waiter was impressed; he had never received such a large tip from someone who was not having a complete meal. "Your salads should be ready. I'll bring them immediately."

As promised, the young man promptly returned with the two salads. Stew thanked him and asked for a second glass of water to create another diversion while he and Millie dined.

Stew dug right into his salad, hoping to give the impression he was in a hurry to be alone.Seeing this, Millie ate a small portion and then acted as if she could not eat another bite.

"I'd like to leave. Are you ready?" Millie asked candidly.

"Certainly!" He assisted Millie with her chair, as he would have for any lady in his care. Millie took hold of Stew's arm as they left the restaurant.

"Let's walk to the park. We won't be disturbed there. It's always full of young couples who are only interested in each other," Millie suggested.

Stew let out a long breath. He had not wanted to leave the area, but even though he was weary with Millie and her childish ideas, he did not want to be rude.

"We're alone—and we have every right to be!" Millie hugged his arm.

"I'd like you to meet my parents as soon as possible. When can you come for dinner?"

"I'm afraid I can't, Millie. The seminar begins tomorrow, and I have plans to meet with a friend tomorrow night. I'll be leaving for Bay City on Tuesday afternoon right after the final speaker... if not sooner."

"Tuesday? Why would you leave so soon? You won't be starting your new job for quite some time!"

"I have business obligations to take care of, and I'd like to use the time to familiarize myself with the city." He had hoped to let the girl down easily, but her persistence made it impossible.

"Then if you must go—take me with you. I'm sure one of my cousins would be more than happy to accompany me. Then you and I could—" Millie began enthusiastically.

"Land sakes, girl! What on earth are you talking about?" Stew finally asked in utter amazement. "Why do you keep talking as if we're in love or something?"

"Aren't we?" Millie looked at him with an admiring smile.

"You must have me mixed up with someone else." Stew was trying not to sound angry, but he had reached his limit.

"What do you mean?" Millie seemed astonished at the suggestion.

"I tutored you a few times. That doesn't mean we're in love. We hardly know each other." Stew recapped their relationship to point out they were only acquaintances.

"You said you'd come for me if you didn't marry the other girl!" she enlightened him.

"I never said any such thing!" Stew denied.

"But you did!" This time, Millie was emphatic.

"I'm certain I didn't use those exact words," he protested.

"It was the last time we met. You told me—if you didn't marry her, you might be back to get me." Millie went over the scenes to refresh his memory.

"You thought I wanted to marry you?" As far as Stew was concerned, Millie was an overly imaginative, young woman who had intentionally misconstrued a simple statement. He could not believe his actions were being misunderstood by someone *again*.

"I'm sorry if you've mistaken something I said. But I'm in

love with *Bethany*."

"But I thought you decided to be friends!" Millie reminded him.

"That's not your concern," Stew said coolly.

"If I recall, when I arrived at our last study session, you were crying over a young man who was no longer interested in seeing you. I was trying to cheer you up—like a big brother or a friend—I only meant to make you smile.

"Millie, the only reason I'm in town is for the seminar." Stew made his defense as calmly as possible.

"Why didn't you tell me earlier?" she snapped.

"I didn't want to correct you in such a public place. Now—I think it's about time for me to take you home before this conversation gets any further out-of-hand."

Millie was humiliated. "I will most certainly not allow you to escort me home!"

"I'm uncomfortable with you walking alone. I must insist." Stew was sorry he had been so blunt and had upset her to such a degree, but the damage was done.

"You will not! I prefer to take my chances by walking alone!" Millie glared at him.

"Also...it might comfort you to know there will be one less woman swooning over you tonight! Now...if you'll excuse me, Mr. Jefferson!" Millie's dismissal was an attempt to save what little dignity she had left.

"Then if I can't persuade you," Stew relented, "I do apologize for the misunderstanding, and I'm saddened by it. Good evening, Miss Kendal." Stew respectfully tipped his hat.

12

JUMPING A TRAIN

Stew walked into the bistro and saw Matt sitting at a table near the back. He chose not to wait to be seated and went directly to join him.

Once the waiter noticed, he took Stew a menu and coffee.

Matthew's face brightened with pleasure when he saw Stew. "I wasn't expecting you to make it!"

"Well, I'm glad I did!" Matthew's enthusiastic greeting had lifted Stew's mood. "I didn't notice you at any of the sessions, but I'm not surprised since there were so many people."

"I hate to say it, but I'm disappointed in the speakers. My first session tomorrow is the replacement for Joyner. I've a good mind to grab my bags and take the next train for Albany. I think I'd rather read the newspaper at the station than sit through another assembly. I expect it to be as worthless as the ones I've just attended," Matt complained.

"I was thinking of doing the same thing myself. As far as I'm concerned, this has been a waste of time. They should have sent out notices when Joyner cancelled.

"Honestly, I *do* think I'm going to gather my belongings and head for the station," Stew said decidedly.

"Then I'll be right behind you," Matt announced, "Eventually, there'll be a train that will connect to Albany."

"Say! How would you like to come to Bay City for a few days? It won't be a problem to catch a train for Albany from there. It'll be like old times. Just like our first years of college... before we actually had to buckle down and study!" Stew reminded Matt.

"I don't know! Are you sure you want me tagging along while you're trying to get set up? But—I might be interested...if you're serious." Matt found the offer too tempting to refuse.

"Of course, I'm serious! I've had my fill of being on my own the last couple of days. I'm ready for some good company. I'd enjoy it more if I had someone there to share a few laughs with before starting a full time job," Stew reassured Matt.

"Well, then, I'm your man! There's no real need for me to get to Albany right away. My living arrangements are made, and I know the town well enough." Matt was thrilled with the invitation.

"Then we'll have dinner and meet back at the station. I should've packed and sent my bags ahead," Stew said.

The waiter returned, ready to take their order. Since both men were in such good humor, they decided on the hardiest meal on the menu—steak, baked potatoes, salad, and the restaurant's famous yeast rolls—which made their mouths water just thinking of them.

The place was packed, and they had to wait for an inexcusable length of time to be served, but they were so involved in conversation that neither of them noticed.

Even though they were stuffed after the meal, both decided to indulge in a dessert of hot, blackberry cobbler with ice cream. It had been a long time since either of them had allowed their appetites to rule.

After paying the bills, they went their separate ways to pack. It was much later than they realized, so they had to hustle to make the train.

Matt was the first to arrive at the station and was still standing in the ticket line when Stew finally showed up. The two barely made it onto the steps of the train as it pulled away from the station. Fortunately, Matt had thought to purchase both tickets.

"I've heard of people jumping trains, but I've never wanted to do it. Not exactly my style," Stew joked.

"By the way, we won't be sleeping in luxury tonight. The guy before me got the last berth."

"I'm not complaining—just glad to get out of Hastings!"

After pulling themselves together, they made their way inside the car and found a seat about midway down the aisle. Stew stepped aside to give Matt the window, but noticed Matt looking at the pretty young lady in the seat next to them. Matt took the seat offered to him and thought nothing of it since Stew was always considerate. Stew was sorry he had been polite this time but went ahead and took the seat across from her.

Stew watched the young woman until she finally lifted her eyes in response to his gaze. She smiled at him curtly and returned to reading.

"What an impressive way to get a lady's attention! I know what you're up to. You're still trying to find me a wife. Listen...I don't have the time or the patience to socialize with every girl you find for me. So if you don't mind, I'll skip this one and try to get a little sleep," Matt murmured, then put his hat over his eyes and started whistling as if already asleep.

Stew overlooked the comment. He waited a few minutes, and then spoke, "That must be an interesting book. May I ask the title?"

"If you were speaking to me, I'm afraid I didn't catch what you said. Would you mind repeating it?"

"Then I was right. It *is* an interesting book, and I've spoiled your concentration. As for my question, I was merely inquiring about the book's title."

"The title?" The lady turned the book over. "*A Suit of Armor*. Why do you ask?"

"No reason. I was just trying to start a conversation since my friend decided to nap his way to Bay City. I'm sorry. I didn't catch your name." Stew was trying to be subtle.

"I believe you didn't catch my name because I haven't given it. Would you suppose that to be true?" she quizzed staunchly, letting him know she did not appreciate the intrusion. "I do sympathize with your desire for conversation. However, I was absorbed in my reading. So if you'll excuse me, I would like to continue." She emphasized the statement with a little shake of her head.

"I beg your pardon, miss. I can assure you I was only trying to make polite conversation and nothing more. By all means, continue," Stew relinquished, embarrassed and a bit shocked by her response.

"No offense taken," she said as she lowered her eyes again to read.

It was apparent to Stew that she was not in the habit of entering into a conversation for mere pleasure. He could hear a faint snickering coming from Matt, who was pretending to be asleep.

"That must be embarrassing," Matt whispered, trying not to laugh and still maintain his fake sleeping pose at the same time. He was hoping to aggravate Stew, and it *was* funny.

"Yes, but at least *I* was brave enough to find out why she'll end up an old maid," Stewart responded out of the corner of his mouth.

"Whoa! You hurt my feelings!" Matt's lips twitched as he tried his best not to crack a smile. But it was no use, so he picked up his hat and placed it further down on his face to hide the overly satisfied smile. Then he lifted it slightly to speak. "Don't worry. I'll find a girl...someday. In the meantime, feel free to start working on your own love life and stay out of mine. But I do want to point out that this is the first time I've ever known a woman to get agitated with you."

"Lately—I seem to be on a roll," Stew admitted truthfully.

"Wish *I* had a book to read," Stew jested, causing them both to break out into a roll of laughter. They were both overly tired and were enjoying falling back into some of their younger, college days' behavior.

With that, the young woman snapped her book shut, stood, and walked down the aisle in disgust. They then broke into hysterical laughter as lighthearted and free as a couple of ten-year-olds.

"Old prude. I can understand why she picked *that* book," Stew joked.

"I wouldn't say that!" Matt teasingly defended her. "I think you might have hit on something. She might be just the girl for me. Yep! Her nose stuck in a book and out of my affairs." The young men tried to gain control, but the half-baked humor started another roar of laughter that ended up bringing tears to their eyes.

It took them a few more minutes to get everything back into perspective, but once they settled down, they could see things weren't nearly as funny as they had thought them to be. The two were ashamed for using the girl's frustration for their entertainment. It was uncommon for them not to behave as gentlemen.

"I suppose we should attempt to look the lady up and apologize," Matt suggested.

"I believe I'll seek my forgiveness from God and pray she'll find it in her heart to forgive our rude behavior. In other words, I don't believe I care to tangle with her anytime soon," Stew speculated with a faint smile.

"You may have a point, at that." Matt gave a little laugh as he studied his friend's view.

When they finally sat back to relax for the remainder of the trip, Stew was able to do so with a lighter heart. But before trying to rest, Stew began to deliberate on why he had never talked to Matt about where he stood with the Lord—especially after all the time they had spent together in their earlier years of college. Outside of being a great guy, there was no indication Matt might be a Christian.

13

BILLY JOE PETERSON

Late in the night when Stew had finally fallen into a light sleep, a tug on his sleeve brought him back to life.

"'Scuse me, sir," a small voice paged. "Is this seat anybody's? Thought I saw a lady here before."

"No, I don't believe so. I'm sure she isn't coming back. So, if you're looking for a place to sit, then it looks like you've found one," Stew politely answered.

"Thank ya, sir!" The little, freckled-faced boy flashed a smile of relief and hurried to the back of the car.

"Here, Mama! I toad you I'd fine ya a comforbull seat. There's not nobody smokin' in here. You'll breeve just fine. And I can try to open the window 'cause wer in the country."

The little boy grabbed the hand of a desperately, tired-looking woman to lead her down the aisle. Knowing the space between the seats was too narrow to walk beside her, he stepped out in front, turned sideways, and gently coaxed her along.

It was easy to tell the mother was very ill. She looked little more than a skeleton adorned in skin. Stew feared she would not be able to maneuver the distance to the seat even with the use of an old cane. He stood to his feet ready to offer assistance if needed. It was obvious she was terribly exhausted but was determined to reach the seat for the benefit of her son. Once she was seated, Stew and those watching breathed a sigh of relief.

Stewart's heart wrenched as the little caretaker lovingly sat down by his mother and took her frail hand for security. Unfortunately, it looked as though the security the mother's hand gave the child would not be there in the very near future.

Stew could not help but study the mother and son. The boy did not look more than five or six years old, yet he bravely tried to care for his mother's needs as if he were an adult.

"Isn't this a nice place, Mama? You'll feel real good purdy soon, won't ya? Don't ya think this is the best place we've had to ride so far?" He looked up into her eyes for assurance, but the woman could only offer him a faint smile in return.

The youngster sat quietly so he would not disturb his beloved mother any further. A little while later, he propped his elbow up and tucked his little hand under his chin to support his head. His straight, light blonde hair was nicely cut and formed neatly around his small face. His clothes, though worn, were clean and pressed.

The mother's clothing was wearing thin but had been laundered and pressed as well. Even though they did not seem to have much in worldly goods—one another was all they needed at present. Such qualities commanded respect for the mother and child.

Suddenly the mother began to struggle while trying to take a breath. A look of fright passed over the boy. He jumped up, remembering his promise to open the window. Since they were both so slight, he easily slid in front of her. Even though he stood on the corner of the seat, he was unsuccessful on his first attempt. Refusing to be discouraged, he was reaching to try a second time just as Stew's hands gripped the latches and easily opened the window. The mother, though she barely seemed conscious, took in the fresh air and soon seemed to be restored to a more normal breathing pattern.

"Thank ya very much, sir. I forgot to open the window," the lad said gratefully.

"You're welcome. Let me introduce myself. My name is Stewart Jefferson. My friends call me Stew." He reached out his hand in introduction. "And may I ask your name, my fine gentleman?"

"My name is Billy!" The little boy flashed a full set of very white baby teeth.

"Well, Billy, do you have a last name?" Stew asked with a smile.

"Yep, I do! My name is Billy Joe Peterson, and my mama's name is Lilly Mae Peterson.She's not feeling so good. Wer goin' out west. They have good air there, Mama says. Uncle Jake lives out there and wer goin' to go live with him so my mama can breeve. My daddy's dead. He got killed by a tree. I miss 'em, but it's alright 'cause he's with Jesus, Mama said. Is your daddy dead?"

"No. My father is very much alive, but I'm very sorry to hear about your father," Stew said sincerely. "Do you know your Uncle Jake?"

"Nope, I never knowed him yet. But my mama knows him. He dranks, and we kin take care of him maybe. Wer a surprise. He don't even know wer comin'. I bet he'll sure be happy to see us. Don't ya think? You know what? We don't got anymore money. We use to live in a big house, but the people at the bank liked our house and horses and furniture so much they decided to keep 'em so we could move west. And now wer surprisin' Uncle Jake. Don't ya think it'll be fun?"

"Yes, that could be quiet fun, I imagine," Stew replied, trying to sound impressed, "How long has your mother been ill?"

"I don't know, but she won't be sick when we get to Uncle Jake's. Don't ya know? The air! The doctor said." Stew could tell Billy wanted to believe the promises he had been given and tried to demonstrate confidence in what he spoke; however, he was an intelligent child, and his eyes seemed to state otherwise.

Stew could tell it was a very touchy time for the lad's mother. He was certain she could not travel the long distance to her brother's home without medical attention. Unfortunately, if she continued to deteriorate at the present rate, she might not even make it to the Bay City station.

"Billy, would you please excuse me for a minute. I'll be back in a little while, and maybe we can continue our conversation." He tried not to sound nervous.

Stew found himself nearly running to locate the conductor but had to turn around because he had gone the wrong way. As he passed Billy on his return, he was relieved to see the little guy was already fast asleep holding onto his mother's hand. It was a sad, forlorn picture. He believed he would never be able to erase it from his memory.

When Stew arrived at the caboose, he banged on the door. "Yes! Coming! I need time to get to the door!" the conductor yelled from inside the car, but the noise outside was too loud for Stewart to understand the man's reply.

It seemed like an eternity since he had left Billy's side, so Stew was posed to knock again when the door opened. "Is there a doctor on the train? I need a doctor! Quickly!" Stew's questions came off as an attack of criticism to the conductor.

"Calm down, young man! What's this all about? Don't you think I have the right to a few minutes to myself?" The conductor looked Stew over suspiciously. He was accustomed to being confronted with any number of outlandish requests.

Stew did not argue with the man but spilled the story in hopes of getting things moving. "There's a young boy and his mother on the train, and she's very ill. I'm afraid she may be in danger of dying if she doesn't get help immediately!"

"I have no way of knowing if there's a doctor on the train. If what you're telling me is true, then the only way to find out is to go from car to car and ask," the conductor explained.

"Well, let's get busy! I fear there's little time!" At this point Stew was ready to beg.

"Wait just a minute, young man! We're not doing that until I see if this supposed illness is legitimate. Take me to this woman so I can see for myself. I can't allow you to go through the cars disturbing people. They're sleeping!" The grouchy, older man motioned for Stew to get moving, and Stew was more than willing to lead the way.

"Good grief, man! Can't you tell I am serious? Follow me!" Stew could not believe he had to wait while the man took time to lock the door behind him. "Can't you forgo a rule or two to reach out to another human being in distress?"

Seemingly unshaken, the conductor followed Stew, making a

point not to go out of his way to hurry. In another rebellious response to Stew's question, the old man lagged farther and farther behind costing them valuable time.

When they finally reached the women, the conductor could instantly see she was in trouble, and he immediately told Stew to check the rear cars while he checked those in the front. It was not long until they both returned, but neither was successful in finding a doctor.

"When is the next stop? Can we get help there?" Stew asked.

"There are no stops where she could get medical help!" the old man snapped. "Best we can do is just keep an eye on 'er."

By this time, Matt had awakened and pitched in to help. "Can you get some towels and cool water to bathe her face? That might be somewhat reviving for her. I wonder how long it has been since she had anything to eat or drink. Maybe the dining car would have some broth. Let me move our stuff and put the boy over here out of the way. I think he's so tired that he's beyond waking. I doubt he'll even stir when we move him."

Stew scooped the boy up, laid him on their seat, took off his jacket, folded it neatly, and placed it under Billy's head. He could not help but gently stroke the boy's hair. He was so young and innocent; no child should have to face what was before him.

"Bathing her face is a great idea, Matt. They'll have water and towels in the kitchen and maybe some ice and broth, won't they, sir?" Stew grilled the conductor again.

"Well, I guess it's up to me to go and get it. They might not give it to you," the conductor said sarcastically.

Stew was irritated with the crotchety, old guy and was just

about to reprimand him when Storm flashed into his mind. The thought instantly changed his attitude, and he approached the man as a Christian should. “Look, sir, I’m sorry if it seems I’m treating you disrespectfully. I’m not meaning to boss you around. It’s only that I’ve never seen anyone this close to death. I’m a bit worked up. It has nothing to do with you.” The explanation was the best Stew could do at the time, but the older man responded gratefully.

“I appreciate it, son.” The conductor’s answer made Stew feel ashamed of his actions.

“Excuse me. Maybe I can be of some assistance. I’m a nurse,” a calm voice interrupted. Stew, Matt, and the conductor tuned to face a women dressed in a traditional nursing uniform. “Is this the person who needs a physician or have you found one?”

“Yes, Madam, this is the lady. We didn’t find a doctor, but you most certainly can be of help. This is Lilly Peterson, and she’s having breathing problems. Beyond that I know nothing else about her health. That’s her son, Billy, sleeping there in the seat. We were about to get some broth along with some towels and cold water to bathe her face. I’m sure she hasn’t eaten for some time. She and Billy took this seat only minutes ago. It was all she could do to get there. A few minutes later she started gasping for breath, and we opened a window to ease her breathing. I think she looks much worse than when she sat down.” Stew told the nurse everything he knew, hoping the information might be of some use.

“Please–get the ice water and towels. Bring the broth, just in case, but I’m afraid she won’t be able to take anything in if she continues to struggle for breath. It could easily be aspirated into her lungs, and we’d lose her for certain. She looks very weak. I’ll need my bag so I can listen to her heart and lungs."

Seeing she was ready to take charge, the conductor hurried off to get the needed supplies while Matt got the bag.

The nurse then dropped to her knees and began to open Mrs. Peterson's blouse. Matt and Stew found seats which had been vacated because of the commotion.

The nurse had been with the patient for several minutes when the conductor returned with a pail of ice water, towels, a couple of blankets, and a pillow. "Oh, bless you for being so thoughtful. Please, hand me the thin blanket to cover her. I need to leave her clothing unbuttoned so I can check her breathing when needed. I'll take one of the pillows to prop her head in a more comfortable position. "What about the soup?"

"The porter will be bringing it right away," the conductor answered.

"There–The pillow placed in that position should ease her breathing somewhat." The nurse spoke loudly enough so all concerned could hear. "We must get her to a hospital soon. There appears to be little time. How far are we from the nearest one? Can we make an emergency stop?"

"Sorry, but to my knowledge there are no hospitals close by. Most of these towns out this way are very small, and the people have to travel for miles to see a doctor. Our best hope is to make it to Bay City. We're going to have to wait this one out," the conductor regretfully informed the nurse. "There's nothing to be done in that respect unless someone on the train knows the area better than I do. I don't suppose it would hurt to check though."

Matt and Stew immediately responded to the possibility but returned with the same conclusion; Bay City was the closest and best chance for medical help and any other attempt would be too risky.

"Is there anything else, nurse?" the conductor asked respectfully.

"No, not just now, but thank you for your trouble," the nurse replied.

"Well, then it's time for me to get back to work. Please, keep me informed." By this time the conductor acted as if he would like to stay and help.

"We will, and thank you. I appreciate all you've done." Stew shook the conductor's hand. An appreciative smile flickered on the man's face in response.

The nurse asked for the pail so she could wring out the towels when she needed them. Nevertheless, Stew thought it would be best if he took the seat beside Billy so he could keep the towels ready for her.

It was at least fifteen minutes before the cold towels made a noticeable difference for Lilly.Unfortunately, it was not enough to make a difference in her actual condition.

The nurse tried the soup, but Lilly choked on the tiniest spoonful. It was too risky. Nourishment would have to wait until they could get her to a hospital.

"We must pray," the nurse encouraged, "I hope she's a child of God. When I know a patient has given their life to the Lord, it makes my job much easier. I don't relish seeing anyone leave this world without knowing where they will spend eternity."

The same thought had crossed Stew's mind earlier. "Ma'am, the little boy mentioned his mother assured him his father was with Jesus. Although I can't be certain what he meant, I hope it will ease your mind some."

"Thank you. It *is* a comfort. Keeping her comfortable is all we can do for her physically, but praying is the best thing we can do for them both. That little boy needs his Mother...and *she* needs a miracle."

Stew nodded his head in agreement.

"Ma'am, there wasn't time for introductions earlier, but my name is Stewart Jefferson and this is a close friend of mine, Matthew Wilson. May I ask your name?" Stew spoke up to help take the nurse's mind off of the sadness for a moment.

"Grace Harper." She smiled sweetly, but said nothing more.

Further conversation seemed out of place, so each resolved to keep watch from a nearby seat and pray for the sweet, little mother. The tension of impending death made waiting feel as if their heartbeats were ticking away the minutes of Lilly Mae Peterson's life.

Matt was at a loss in knowing how to pray. He had never earnestly prayed in his life beyond a memorized child's prayer, but he managed a few words.

Although his prayer was short, he felt better for it. He was glad to do anything which might help spare the life of the little boy's mother.

14

QUESTIONING GOD

Stew was having a difficult time responding to the tapping on his shoulder. He was awake enough to know someone was softly calling his name, but he was resting comfortably and didn't want to be interrupted. *I don't love you, Stewart!* Bethany's hurtful words shot through his mind and forced him to consciousness.

"Mr. Jefferson, please! I didn't mean to frighten you, but I need your assistance immediately. I'm sorry, but you and your friend must help me. There is little time before the other passengers awake," the nurse prodded in desperation.

"What? Yes...what is it?" Stew responded making a serious effort to get a grip on where he was and what was taking place. As he rose from his seat, he gave Matt a shove on the shoulder to hurry him awake.

"Mr. Jefferson and Mr. Wilson, it's our little mother. It pains me to say that...we've lost her."

"No!" Stew whispered in shock; he had not really expected her to die. "Surely this can't be! She has a child!"

"I'm sorry...but it is absolutely so. It has only just happened. Thank goodness the child is still asleep.

"I didn't wake you, but sometime earlier Lilly indicated she wanted the boy with her. She had him lean against her and mouthed that she loved him. She ran her fingers through his hair...as best she could...and looked at him lovingly. It was only for a short time. Then they both fell back to sleep. I thought she might be getting better, but she was saying goodbye. She seemed to be resting comfortably but suddenly just took her last breath.

"Mr. Wilson, would you mind getting the conductor? We need to take her to a secluded area quickly. The child must be told, but I don't want the little one to see her until after I've made her ready. It would also be disrespectful to allow others to see her in this state. She must have been beautiful before she fell ill. This is such a tragedy."

"I'll find the conductor. Poor little tyke..." Matt whispered as he was leaving.

"What should we do about Billy when we move her to another area?" Stew was concerned the boy would awaken and ask for his mother.

"I thought you or your friend might stay with him just in case he wakes up. Hopefully, he'll continue to sleep until I have her ready for viewing. We'll allow him to see her then."

"Are you sure he should be told of her death here on the train?" Stew questioned.

"Mr. Jefferson, even though he's small, the child deserves to be told the truth of his mother's passing as soon as possible. Most children are very perceptive." Nurse Grace checked the blanket to make certain it was secure enough for Lilly to be moved discreetly.

Just then Matt returned with the conductor, and the nurse

whispered her requests to him. He responded with a nod and headed to the back of the train. "One of you will need to carry Lilly to the back. The conductor doesn't look in good health, so I didn't have the heart to ask him to carry her."

"I'll do it," Stew volunteered. "Matt, will you stay with Billy? Bring him to the back if he wakes up, but hopefully he'll sleep a while longer."

"Certainly." Matt looked sorrowfully across the aisle at the little orphan.

"She's covered properly, so we should take her to the back of the train to the conductor. He'll direct us from there," Grace instructed. "Hopefully he's had enough time to find a place to lay her."

Stew felt honored to be the one to carry her. He was certain Lilly had been a wonderful Christian wife and mother. Holding her and knowing she was precious to God made death much easier to accept, and seeing death did not trouble him as he had always supposed it would.

"As they entered the caboose, the conductor indicated where Lilly's makeshift resting place had been prepared. It was the conductor's own little cot, and he had spread a clean white sheet over it.

Stewart gently laid Lilly down and stepped back while the nurse gave more instructions.

"Do you know if there is any luggage? I must have everything ready for the undertaker when he arrives. They will take her immediately, so there won't be much time since this will most likely be a pauper's burial. I would like for her to look nice since her son will be seeing his mother for the last time. I'll need soap, water, a hairbrush, and anything else of the sort. She needs a decent dress. It would be unkind for the boy to view her in the shabby dress she's wearing. His last memory of her should be as the angel I'm sure she was."

"I don't believe there's any baggage to speak of. Maybe a few articles in a sack. Billy seemed to indicate they only had the clothes on their backs," Stew answered.

"Then, conductor, can you help me out here?" The nurse looked at him with pleading eyes.

"I reckon I can come up with the basic stuff, but I can't help with the dress and ribbons and the like. They'd have my job if I started askin' the passengers for those sorts of things. I'm sorry...I can't help you there."

"Surely, there must be a way to find a dress for her. What if Mr. Jefferson asked the passengers?"

"I'm sorry, but I can't condone that either. It's part of my job to stop anything such as that...you understand...botherin' people for handouts and the like." The conductor hung his head.

"I'll be more than happy to purchase a dress when we arrive in Bay City," Stew suggested.

"There won't be time, I'm afraid." The nurse was becoming a little anxious since their time was growing short.

"Wait! There may be another option, but I'll need you to back me in prayer if I'm to undertake it," Stew said reluctantly.

"The young lady who was upset with you and your friend?" the nurse questioned with raised eyebrows. "Indeed, you will need prayer, young man, but the Lord's work isn't always easy. Please be quick. There's little time. And tell Mr. Wilson he'll be informed when to bring the child. Now, go!" Nurse Grace ordered.

He hurried off, only taking a moment to inform Matt of what was taking place with Lilly and the mission he had just been sent on. Matt would have had a hardy laugh if the situation had not been a serious one. Stew was glad to see Billy curled up and still sleeping soundly.

Stew asked God to give him favor with the young woman whom he and Matt had upset. He methodically searched the train and hoped to find her awake. It was not until the third car that he noticed her seated by the window. Fortunately, the seats around her were vacant.

The young woman did not notice him as he leaned forward to get her attention. "Miss, I'm sorry to bother you, but please hear me out," he spoke quietly.

"What on earth are you doing here? Please! Leave me alone, or I'll call the conductor." The young woman's voice was a step above a whisper.

"I understand your feelings. You have every reason to be upset. My friend and I were overtired and in rare form. We were shameful, and I do sincerely beg your forgiveness. But right now, I need to speak with you over a serious matter which has taken place on the train." Stew knew his plea was on shaky ground by the expression she wore.

"I'm not interested in any problems you might have!"

"Wait—" Stew was ready to plead the case anyway.

"Mr. Jefferson, do you need some assistance in speaking to this young woman?" the conductor intervened, concerned the conflict might disturb the other passengers.

"Thank you, sir."

"Miss...there has been a tragic circumstance take place on the train. This young man thought you might be able to help in the matter. Please, hear him out." With that said, the conductor hurried up the aisle to the next car.

"I'm truly sorry for the confusion," Stew apologized.

"Then what do you want from me?" she spat.

"Late last night, a small boy and his mother took the seat you had been sitting in. The young mother was extremely ill. She passed away not even fifteen minutes ago. We believe her only clothing is the worn out dress she's wearing.

"The nurse who cared for her is asking for a proper dress for the little boy to view his mother in for the last time. We will be arriving in Bay City very soon. The boy is still sleeping and doesn't know about his mother.

"The body will have to be taken soon after we arrive in Bay City. Her son will need to see her before then. She's very small like you. By chance, would you have a dress you could donate?" Stew tried to be as diplomatic as possible.

"I see. Well...the child should see his mother looking presentable, and I do happen to have just the thing. It's a simple, lace dress my aunt gave me as a parting gift when I left Hastings. She'll never know. It's right here in my bag." She opened the bag and handed Stew the box from inside.

The young lady's tone was still cold, but Stew surmised it was due to what had transpired between the two of them and not for lack of caring.

"Thank you for doing this. I guess this might explain why our paths crossed. Even though, it was unpleasant for you." Stew was hoping to end their meeting on friendly terms.

"Yes...it was unpleasant." She was not about to give him the impression he was forgiven, even if he had apologized.

"All things work together for good—" he quoted.

"Romans 8:28..." She was caught off guard by the Bible quote and had to rethink her position, "I must agree," she said with a faint smile.

Stew smiled back, gave a polite bow, and went on his way. God had taken a bad situation and used it for good.

As he passed Matt, Stew noticed Billy was still sleeping.

Stew hurried to the caboose and tapped on the door. The nurse peeked out to see who it was. She smiled when Stew held up the box. Without a word, she grabbed it and shut the door leaving Stew standing alone with the conductor; both were at a loss as to what to do.

Finally the conductor broke the silence, "I have other duties I should attend to. We'll be pulling into Bay City in less than thirty minutes. Send for me if you need anything. I'll make certain the proper authorities are notified for Mrs. Peterson." He turned and hurried off. There was nothing for Stew to do other than wait for the nurse to give him further instructions.

It wasn't long before Nurse Grace opened the door, "Mr. Jefferson, Billy's mother will be ready soon, and I don't feel she should be left alone. Since the boy has no idea who I am, I believe you should be the one to tell him about his mother's passing.

"It would be best to bring him to the back of the train before speaking with him. His feelings must be considered, and there's no reason to alert the other passengers," the nurse said compassionately.

"I know nothing about children and even less on how to tell a child he's lost his mother—especially after just losing his father. Surely you're more qualified for this task. I beg you to reconsider. I've never lost anyone close to me. I've no idea how to console a child." Stew's plea to the nurse was a desperate and sincere one. He reached for his handkerchief to wipe the perspiration from his forehead.

"Mr. Jefferson, you're very intelligent and well spoken. God will give you the words. If you wish, you may ask your friend to do it." She stepped back inside and closed the door behind her.

Stew was astonished the nurse had asked such a thing of him, but she was not the type with whom to argue. He had been assigned the job.

Stew wondered how he could tell the little boy that he had just lost the most important person in his life. He took a few minutes to pray, which gave him more confidence to cope with the matter. He looked at his watch and there was no time to waste.

Stew found Matt cradling Billy like a baby. Matt looked up. "He woke up a few minutes ago and asked for his mom. I told him she was with you in another part of the train, and he needed to get some more rest. The answer satisfied him, so he went back to sleep. He's starting to stir though. I couldn't stop myself from picking him up. He's too small to be alone in the world. I don't understand when things like this happen. I thought God was supposed to answer prayers."

Stewart would like to have discussed his disillusioned friend's questions at length but only had enough time to reply, "Unfortunately, death is part of life.

“Matt, it’s time to take him to the back. We probably shouldn’t wake him too abruptly. Carrying him back might be a more gentle way. The nurse asked me to tell him about his mother—unless you’d like to do it?”

“I don’t think so. None of this is within my expertise, and I don’t envy you, my friend.” Matt stood with the child in his arms and followed Stew.

Just as predicted, Billy was wide awake by the time they reached the car.

15

WHO IS RESPONSIBLE

As they entered the caboose, Stew noticed the nurse had arranged seating for three. He was glad a makeshift curtain had been draped to hide Lilly while he talked with the boy. The sun streamed brightly through the tiny windows taking away the gloomy look the car had possessed earlier.

"Billy...I need to talk with you. Do you think you're awake enough to sit here beside me," Stew asked.

"Uh-huh. Are we the only people in here?" Billy asked wide eyed. "I always wanted to go in one of these cabooses. I sure am proud to be in here."

"That doesn't surprise me. You look like the curious type," Stew kidded before allowing his face to take on a more serious look. "Billy...there's something I must tell you...you're going to have to be a very brave boy. Do you think you can be brave?"

"Sure! I'm brave a lot. I'm getting' to be a perty big boy. That's what Mama tells me all the time. Where is my mama? I didn't see her yet," he inquired suspiciously.

"That's what I need to talk to you about. You see..." Stew had to stop and regain his nerve. He did not want to show his emotions after asking the boy to be brave. "You see, Billy...sometimes when we make plans they don't turn out the way we hoped they would. You and your mother planned to go live with your uncle, but while you were asleep your mother became very ill. We tried to find a doctor, but there wasn't one on the train. We did find a very kind nurse. Her name is Grace Harper. She took very good care of your mother.

"Do you remember waking up and your mother holding your hand and loving on you until you fell back to sleep?" Stew was trying to break the news gently but could barely get the words out.

"It was Nurse Grace who woke you up and carried you to your mother. She tried very hard to make your mother feel better...but your mother kept getting worse until there was nothing more the nurse could do to help your mama.

"Do you remember telling me your mother said your father had gone to live with Jesus in heaven?" Stew asked.

"Did my mamma die too?" Billy courageously questioned—his eyes asking for honesty.

"Yes, Billy...she did. She went to be with your daddy, and they are both safe with Jesus." Stew felt physically drained by the time the words were finally out.

"I was 'fraid of that...I wish she didn't." Billy admitted, then tucked his head, and the tears began to run down his little cheeks.

Stew stood and placed his hands under Billy's arms and lifted him to his chest. Billy was crying in expression but was unable to make a sound. Stew was swept away by the boy's struggle, and sorrow pained Stew's heart. He did not understand or even realize such feelings existed, and he was glad he had never known them.

Death was a miserable thing for those left behind. How could a small child bare such a burden? Stew was able to forget his own grief to mourn with the little boy.

Stew encased Billy in his arms and sat down to comfort him while he wept for his mother. Matt could not deal with Billy's suffering and had to leave the car for fresh air.

It was several minutes until Billy, still breathing erratically, settled down into Stew's lap. By that time Matt and the conductor had stepped back in, and Stew motioned for Matt to bring Grace.

Nurse Grace came to stand beside them, and Stew turned Billy around to face her. "Hello, Billy. I'm Nurse Grace. I'm the lady who cared for your mother. Do you remember me waking you up to sit with your mama?" she questioned sweetly. Billy nodded, but his expression remained solemn.

"I'm very sorry you lost your mama. She was a very good patient." A sweet smile was on the nurse's face, and Billy's eyes responded.

"Was she a very good mother?" the nurse asked, trying to draw Billy out, but he only bobbed his head to answer. "Yes, I thought that was what your answer would be. I understand you lost your daddy not so long ago." Again, his head moved up and down with little, if any, facial changes.

"Mama toad me that someday she would go to be with daddy and Jesus. I'm sure she's there, but...I wished she'd stayed here wiff me," Billy was overcome with grief again and pushed his head into Stew's chest. The little boy in raggedy clothes continued to tug at the men's hearts. Neither could take their eyes off him. Tears welled in Matt's eyes, but instead of stepping outside, he reached for his handkerchief; he couldn't leave the child.

Grace handed Billy a handkerchief. He took it and wiped his eyes, then looked up at her and smiled. She was touched that a child so small and so full of sorrow could take time to offer a smile of gratitude for politeness sake.

Stewart put Billy down and then spoke softly, "Billy, we are almost to the city, and we don't have much time. I know this will be hard, but would you like to see your mother one last time. We'll go with you...if you'd like."

Again, Billy answered with a nod. Stew and Matt took him by the hand and led him behind the curtain where Lilly Mae Peterson lay.

Upon seeing his mother, Billy gasped, "Mama, you look just like an angel!"

Matt and Stew were struck with the same impression. Grace had combed Lilly's light blonde hair and laid it on each side of her shoulders. The dress was white silk overlaid with lace and was perfect for her small, delicate frame. A ray of sun streamed from the window onto her lifeless form causing her to look even more beautiful. Lilly lay with an expression of peace upon her face.

Soon Nurse Grace broke into their thoughts, "Billy, would you like some time alone with your mother? We can just step on the other side of the curtain, if you wish. I'm sorry, sweetheart, but this will be the last time you'll be able to see your mama. I know it will be sad, but I urge you to spend a few moments with her. Do you understand?"

"I understand. I want...I want to be here wiff her by myself." Billy was able to get the words out between sniffs.

"Alright then. We'll be on the other side of the curtain." Nurse

Grace and the others left the area to honor the boy's request.

Once they were on the other side of the drape, the nurse handed Stew a piece of paper with some writing on it, two tickets, and three dollars. "Mr. Jefferson, I thought you and your friend should see this. I found it on her person when I was changing her dress."

Stew held the note out so he, Matt, and the conductor could read it at the same time.

The script showed signs of having been done in a hurry, but the writing was still beautiful to the eyes.

Dearest Friend,

If you are reading this letter, then I have gone on to be with my Lord and Savior, Jesus Christ.

My name is Lilly Mae Peterson, and I am traveling with my young son, Billy Joe. We are on our way west to live with my brother, Jake Black.

I have prayed for my son to fall into caring hands. Therefore, I beg of you to look after him by seeing that he arrives at my brother's home safely. Jake is Billy's only living relative. However, I haven't been in contact with him for several years, so he will need to be notified of Billy's arrival.

My husband and I want Billy brought up in the teachings of Christ, and I believe God will honor our prayers.

Enclosed are two tickets, Jake's address, and the last of the money.

God bless you, and thank you for caring for my lit-

tle boy. Please, tell Billy I love him dearly and eternally.
In Jesus' name,
Lilly Mae Peterson

Stew and Matt could not look at one another; each had a lump in his throat and could not speak. It had most likely taken a lot of strength from the failing mother to scratch out this message on the torn paper.

The heartbreak the woman must have suffered at the thought of leaving her son stranded and alone was beyond either man's imagination. Neither Stew nor Matt had been brought up to know need or want.

"Nurse Grace, what will you do with Billy?" Stew whispered when he regained his voice.

"I'm sorry, Mr. Jefferson, I was meant to be an assistant of the Lord's for this journey, but once we arrive in Bay City, I must be on my way. I'm a nurse, and I have many obligations upon my arrival. I can't take on Billy or the problems he faces. He needs to be fed and looked after. I don't have the means or connections. I only hope his mother's plans for him are trustworthy," Grace Harper informed Stew honestly with a sweet but firm smile.

"You must realize we're nearing a large city where homeless orphans draw little attention from city officials. Our city orphanages are full with long waiting lists. Since he's been taken from his home state and was being moved to another area, I have no idea what jurisdiction would even take the responsibility. In my estimation, God has placed Billy in your hands. I can only stay long enough to inform the authorities of what I know. After that, I can be of no further assistance. As I said, I must leave immediately to care for those I'm assigned."

Stew looked at her in disbelief having suddenly understood the magnitude of the situation. "But Nurse Grace! Like you, I've only just met Billy! I don't have a clue how to get the boy to his uncle safely. I can't just stick him on a train and hope he makes it. What do I do with him?" Stew was horrified by the woman's insensitivity.

"Can't the railroad do something?" Stew turned and asked the conductor. The conductor shook his head no.

Stew couldn't believe a simple act of kindness had led to such complications.

"Mr. Jefferson, you and your friend apparently are well educated men. Surely the two of you are wise enough to figure this out," the nurse whispered out of exasperation.

Even though Stew was distraught, he had to agree Billy was no more the nurse's responsibility than his or Matt's. He didn't want the obligation, but he just could not leave the little guy stranded. He would have to come up with a plan.

"I'm not happy with this role being forced on me, but I'll see what I can do. Nonetheless, I would like you to give this money to the undertaker. I hope the man's dependable," Stew said, handing her a couple of large bills. "I'd like to see that Lilly has a somewhat decent burial and some type of headstone where Billy might someday be able to visit the grave."

Matt also handed the nurse money. "I'd like to help, too. Maybe some flowers could be added as well."

Stew looked in on Billy just in time to hear him say, "Mamma, I sure am sorry I didn't take better care of ya. I sure am awful sorry...I miss you...already." Then he started to cry again.

Stew leaped to his side. "Wait just a minute, little guy, your mama's illness had nothing to do with you. She just slipped into heaven. She's well now, and you know she didn't want to leave you."

"But I want to be wiff her!" Billy cried out.

"I know you do, son, but God has special plans for you here on earth. I know you loved your mama. You'll miss her for a very long time, but each day it will get a little easier. You must remember God will care for you, and He'll help you be brave through it all."

"It's awful hard to be brave. I want my mama!" Billy cried.

"I know...I know you do." Stew hugged the boy tightly to his chest.

At that moment, the train started slowing steadily as it neared the station. "Grace, if you don't mind, could you stay with Billy while he finishes saying goodbye to his Mother. Matt and I need to collect our things. We'll be right back for him."

By this time Stew's head was pounding again, but he had no choice but to ignore it. This had been a horrible week. He had left for Bay City to escape the trouble in his life, but instead the problems just kept mounting. Now, he and Matt were responsible for getting a small boy safely to an uncle out west, and he had no idea how to go about it. Still it kept him from dwelling on his own circumstances.

Billy and his mom had taken one train to get to Bay City, but to get to a small town in the west would involve changing trains and layovers. How could such a small boy handle traveling by rail all alone? Surely the conductor was wrong, the train systems must have some sort of plan for children traveling by themselves. He would stop by the ticket office to check.

Stew held the door open for Matt to enter the car. They grabbed their belongings, gave a tired sigh, and headed back to get Billy. Both would have liked a bath and a shave, but they could expect neither for some time.

When they reached the caboose, they learned the conductor had already summoned station employees to transfer Lilly's body to a remote area.

As tired as she was, Nurse Grace held Billy on her hip, and it looked as if it took all of her strength to do it. Stew knew he or Matt would have been doing the same if they had been left alone with him.

"There, now! There are your friends, Mr. Jefferson and Mr. Wilson. See, they came back for you just as Mr. Jefferson said." She handed Billy over to Stew.

It was time to leave, and there was no easy way for a child to handle being forever separated from his mother. It was a distressing sight for them to watch.

As they stepped out onto the platform, Billy nuzzled his face into Stew's shoulder and softly sobbed. Stew didn't talk but held Billy in a comforting grip and let him pour the hurt out in tears. Stew was not sure how long they stood there, but, while the little boy cried, the staff discretely moved his mother to a room in the station. People were so busy with their own affairs that the transfer went virtually unnoticed.

The small group of mourners stayed in their places in hopes that Billy would remain unaware of what had just transpired.

It was not long until Nurse Grace motioned to Stew and Matt that the undertaker had arrived and wanted to speak with them.

Stew tenderly put Billy down and walked him to a bench to sit while they talked.

"My name is Lester Tidwell of Tidwell Mortuary. I understand you happened upon this boy and his now deceased mother on the train. You are the individuals who have donated the money for a proper burial. Am I correct?" the undertaker asked seriously but compassionately.

"Yes. It's not a lot of money, but we want Billy to have a place to visit his mother. We'd like to have done more," Matt answered.

"I commend you both. I rarely witness such acts of kindness under similar circumstances. I did want to tell you that Mrs. Peterson's burial should be completed by three o'clock at Cedar Hill Cemetery. After that time, it will be fine if you would like to take the child to visit the site. Unfortunately, even without my commission, I can only provide the bare minimum and the smallest headstone with her name and year. Yet, it will be sufficient and decent. Is that agreeable?" the man asked respectfully.

"Yes. We thank you for your consideration and sacrifice as well," Stew said.

"I appreciate it," the undertaker said humbly. He touched the brim of his hat and walked toward the station.

As Stew and Matt moved back toward Nurse Grace and Billy, she rose from the bench and reached out one hand to Stew and the other to Matt. "This is where we must part. I've said goodbye to Billy. Although I'm sorry to abandon the three of you, I believe, with all my heart, God has brought you together. I will be praying." Her modest goodbye was appropriate.

"Thank you for all of your help and guidance. We'll need your prayers." Stew squeezed her hand.

As she departed, the men tipped their hats while giving a comrade's smile.

16

THE DECISION

As Stew, Matt, and Billy walked into the restaurant, Stew became aware of Billy's clothing. He looked around and saw people staring from every direction. It was bad enough he and Matt had been careless in not considering what Billy was wearing, but to see Billy hanging his head from embarrassment made it inexcusable. Stew had forgotten Billy was very bright and might remember a more comfortable lifestyle. Evidently, even a small boy could tell when he was out of place.

The headwaiter arrogantly glanced at them and then motioned the three to step aside while he proceeded to seat several customers before returning to them. The waiter's attitude was so haughty that Billy was aware of what was taking place. When the waiter finally started to direct them to a table behind a large plant, Stew spoke out. "No, thank you...we won't be staying." He then asked Matt to take Billy outside.

When the door closed, Stew spoke to the waiter, "I want you to understand you humiliated that little boy. The child recently lost his father in an accident which created many hardships, and this morning his mother unexpectedly passed away. Now, he's alone with a broken heart.

"I won't speak to the manager about your behavior. However, I suggest the next time a patron doesn't meet with your expectations you remember your position doesn't suggest wealth or social rank. Your family could easily be found in such circumstances if something happened to you." Stew's reprimand was just loud enough to make it perfectly clear his words applied to the diners as well as the snooty waiter. "You were cruel."

The waiter stiffened when Stew threw in the last statement, and his face turned bright red. Stew's words were not spoken harshly nor was he trying to be mean; still he felt, on occasion, thoughtless people needed a lesson in kindness.

When Stew stepped outside to join Matt and Billy, he ruffled the little guy's hair as he talked with Matt in a low voice. Then he walked ahead of them and turned left at the next corner. Matt took Billy to a park where he played until Stew reappeared with a small case.

Matt found a secluded area to help the little guy freshen up, and then Stew helped Billy into a set of new clothes. He opened the travel case to show Billy what was inside; Stew wanted to send the child off with a few changes of clothing and other necessities.

Although Billy showed appreciation for the clothing, he especially was pleased to see the brown bear. The little guy grabbed the bear and hugged it tightly, which was all the thanks Stew needed.

Then the trio walked a couple blocks to a restaurant where they were well-received. Consequently, it was only when the food arrived that Stew and Matt realized the boy was near starvation. Having been so involved with everything that had transpired on the train, they had not given any thought to when Billy's last meal might have been.

Matt quickly motioned to a nearby waiter and asked him to bring a glass of milk. They watched as Billy gulped it down. The sight made both men feel better.

The rest of the day was devoted to making sure Billy was treated like a prince. The men tried everything, including piggyback rides. They hoped indulging him would lessen the grief of visiting his mother's grave before leaving on the train.

When the time came, Billy stood reverently beside his mother's grave. There was no need to say a word; it was clear he knew what was taking place and what this meant to his life. Matt and Stew could not keep from admiring the little boy's strength of character.

Just before leaving, Stew, hoping the boy someday would visit again, showed Billy a way to find his mother's grave.

Few words were spoken on their return trip to the station, and even less once they arrived. Stew and Matt would not put Billy on the train alone, so Stew went to find what it would require to get Billy safely to his uncle.

As God would have it, Stew ran into a close friend from college. Andrea Landis was returning home from the seminar in Hastings. After hearing Billy's shocking story, she volunteered to be his guardian on the trip west. Miss Landis was pleased to accommodate them since she had a layover in the town near his uncle's home.

By the time they had finished discussing the details of the trip, Miss Landis was dedicated to the boy's welfare. Stew gave her the tickets, Lillie's letter, extra money, and then asked her to notify them as soon as the boy was in his uncle's care. Miss Landis waited while Stew telegrammed Jake Black to inform him of Billy's arrival and the death of his sister.

Stew felt even worse than before when he spotted the heart-broken boy sitting dejectedly beside Matt. Unfortunately, making the trip west was too risky for him or Matt to attempt with new jobs at stake. About that time, the conductor gave the call to board, and Billy looked up at Stew and said, "I'm scared, I don't wanna go!"

"I know, but we have to obey your mother's wishes," Stew said softly. Matt leaned over and picked Billy up. He was concerned for the lad and hated the thought of sending the child off before hearing from the uncle. Stew led them to meet Billy's new guardian. He gave him a sympathetic kiss on the cheek and then put him down in front of her for the introduction.

"Billy, I have a surprise for you. This is Miss Andrea Landis. She's going to be your traveling partner on the train. I'm sure you will be great friends in no time. Miss Landis will help you find your uncle. I've already sent word for him to expect you, so he should meet you at the train station." Unlike Matt, Stew seemed to be confident the trip would have a positive outcome.

About then, the final call to board was given. Matt assisted the attractive, young lady up the steps while Stew placed Billy beside her. Matt gave him a long hug and a wink. Then Billy took two steps, turned and looked at them, gave a slight wave, but showed no emotion. "Thank ya for yer kindness." His words were sincerely meant. He then turned and walked through the door and did not look back.

As the train pulled away from the station, they could see Billy and Andrea Landis through the window, but she was the only one to wave goodbye.

"I hope we've done the right thing," Matt sighed. "If I were certain his uncle was a fit guardian, I wouldn't worry."

"His mother had already made plans for him. we don't have the right to keep him from his only relative even if he drinks. Besides, he's most likely a good and caring person and will be overjoyed to have Billy in his life."

"Billy mentioned he and his mother were going to take care of the uncle. I don't know...it sounds like a bad situation to me, and why would a mother tell a young child his uncle drinks? Lilly hadn't been in contact with her brother for years. She might've only been going to live with him because they were desperate," Matt speculated.

"But in the letter, Mrs. Peterson asked for someone to help Billy reach her brother. Besides, we're strangers to the lad. We've known him less than twenty-four hours. What would either of us do with a child? You're going on to Albany in a few days, and I don't even know where I'll be living. Putting him on the train was the only choice we had to fulfill our duty to his mother. He has a traveling companion. He'll be fine. God will look after him." Stew was trying to put things into perspective for Matt—as well as himself.

"Well, it all makes sense, I guess. I've become overly involved in the little guy's affairs. Maybe he didn't even want to stay with us. He didn't put up much of a fight when it came time to leave." Matt was now trying to convince himself that Billy would be fine.

17

A BLUNDER

"Well, it's getting late, and I need to catch the landlord to cancel my lease. I won't need such a large apartment now."

They were dropped off in front of the building where Stew and Bethany were to have begun their life together. Matt was impressed that Stew had chosen a stylishly-decorated, furnished apartment which would have suited any woman's taste. Having no idea one could lease such extravagance, Matt surveyed the lavish quarters while Stew went to speak to the manager.

It was not long until Stew returned *without* the deposit and with the news they had to vacate the apartment promptly. Stew was agitated because he had foolishly told Miss Landis to have the telegram delivered to the apartment building. Now, Miss Landis had no *immediate* way to contact them if things did not work out for Billy, and Stew had no way to contact Miss Landis since he had forgotten to get her address. The whole arrangement made Matt ill at ease.

Stew had the driver take them to a hotel downtown near his new office building. They were both exhausted by the time they reached the room and retired early. Stew prayed for Billy's safety.

Even though Matt bowed his head, he still questioned what kind of God would take a little boy's mom when he needed her the most.

The next morning the two men had breakfast sent up instead of going down to the hotel restaurant; it gave them time to determine what their plans would be for the day.

Since it was a weekend, they opted to take a look around the building where Stew would be employed. The doorman was obliging, and Stew was grateful to get a better feel for the place before starting his new job.

Again, Matt was impressed. His own place of employment would pale in comparison to the huge, stately building where his friend would be employed. Of course, only Stewart Jefferson could land a job in such a place. Matt knew he was not as good-looking or as outgoing as Stew, but he felt his own intelligence and personality type had its advantages as well.

"I don't get it," Matt ventured. "Why are you starting out here in luxury while I'll be working in a small establishment decked out in last century's furnishings?"

"That's simple," Stew joked with a chuckle, "I applied for positions in businesses I wanted to be associated with...and then I left it up to God."

"Right," Matt said, not wanting to do any further comparisons.

"Neither of us will care about our surroundings if we enjoy the work."

"I'd like to go to the theatre while I'm here. Will we be able to get tickets this late?" Matt asked.

"We'll check and then stop by the apartment building to leave our hotel address for Miss Landis' telegram."

The two men thoroughly enjoyed exploring the city and surrounding areas. Later in the week, Matt insisted they stop by and check with the apartment manager since they had not received a telegram from Miss Landis. The manager was out of town, and the lady in charge insisted no telegram had arrived.

Matt was concerned and believed they should contact the sheriff immediately, but Stew, expecting it might have taken longer than anticipated for Miss Landis to locate the uncle, wanted to wait. Although Matt strongly disagreed, he relented since Stew had been selected to make the decisions on Billy's behalf. Besides, it was time to head for Albany, and he wanted to part on good terms after having such a great time together.

Just before Matt boarded the train, Stew confronted him. "Matt, in all the time I've know you, we've never talked about your relationship with God. So, I'm going to come right out and ask if you know where you will spend eternity."

Matt answered honestly, "No, I don't know where I'm going when I die, and Jesus is not my Savior, but I've heard you talk about it. I know the routine. I know what I'm supposed to do. I understand death is part of life, but I can't ignore all the issues I have with God."

After Matt's reaction, Stew hesitated, but realized if he didn't speak now, there might never be another opportunity. "Matt, will you hear me out...as a friend?"

Matt took a moment to think it over. "It's against my better judgment, but because I value our friendship, I'll listen." Even though he was serious, Matt made the statement lightheartedly.

Stew would have preferred a more enthusiastic response, but he was glad to have the opportunity before him. He breathed a quick prayer as he led Matt to a quieter place and then stepped out in faith.

Once Stew's testimony was completed, Matt shook Stew's hand, slapped him on the shoulder, and boarded the train.

18

BEING PERFECTLY HONEST

Before reaching the Jacksons' front door, Adel and Mandy caught a glimpse of Bethany sitting alone in the gazebo. Adel immediately turned the buggy around to park close by. Both women were relieved to have been spared the awkwardness of being received at the house.

Adel secured the reins and stepped down to join Mandy. They walked through the side yard to where Bethany was sitting. Except for the faint rustling of their dresses, their walk was quiet.

"Beth!" Adel called out, hoping not to startle her. "It's Adel and Mandy. We've come to pay you a visit." Bethany looked in their direction and gave a smile as she stood to greet them.

"I hope you don't mind that we took it upon ourselves to drop by unannounced," Adel explained.

"Of course not!" she answered sweetly.

The two walked up the steps into Bethany's arms. "Thank you for coming," she whispered. "I wasn't expecting anyone. I hope this is an indication I'm not a total outcast within our church family."

"Hush! You know we love you and Stew...no matter what. This is just one of those situations where people aren't certain if a visit is appropriate." Mandy hoped her words had the comforting effect she intended.

"Of course. I didn't mean to sound neglected. This is an unusual circumstance," Bethany admitted.

The conversation stopped momentarily because no one knew exactly what to say next.Mandy and Adel were concerned the hesitation might cause Bethany to feel pressured into mentioning the breakup.

"We've come to see if there's anything we can do to comfort you or, if nothing else, just to sit a while and visit. Still we don't want to impose," Adel explained.

"I'm grateful. I've needed my friends—especially today. One minute I'm drenched in God's peace, and the next minute I'm struggling."

"I'm sure it's difficult," Adel sympathized, "but you've always trusted the Lord for strength. You'll get through this with all of your dignity intact."

"Thank you for your faith in me, Adel," Bethany said with an appreciative smile, "but isn't it a bit too late for dignity?"

"Nonsense. You handled the announcement wisely, and you'll handle anything in the future just as well. Now, is there anything we can do?" Adel restated.

"To be honest...I need to talk," Bethany answered hesitantly. "I don't want to burden my parents any further by discussing what happened. I've created enough turmoil for them by canceling the wedding".

"I'm certain your parents don't see it that way," Mandy gently encouraged.

"Yes, even though they are troubled about the situation, they understand there are certain indiscretions I won't abide. Anyway, the relationship is over, and there is nothing that can be done to restore it."

They were both surprised to hear she held such strong convictions.

"Bethany," responded Adel, "we didn't come here to get the particulars, but we're willing to listen. However, before you begin, we want you to know that we saw Rica at the party."

"You know about Rica?"

"Yes, we did see Rica lurking around in the bushes."

"Did everyone see her?" Bethany started to panic.

"Don't worry, Beth. We believe she wanted to be seen by the other guests, but the candles around the perimeter were too bright for anyone to see beyond them. As it turned out, we stepped outside of the lighting. That's how we both caught sight of her." Adel was hoping the information would calm Bethany.

"It's a relief to know that the other guests didn't see her. The breakup *alone* was so hurtful and humiliating. And I don't want to say anything about Stew that would injure your relationships with him, but I need to be completely open."

Adel and Mandy sat quietly.

"Honestly, I don't know how to explain what happened!"

"Bethany, you don't owe us or anyone an explanation. But, if you do tell us, it doesn't necessarily mean we'll agree with the way you see things." Adel wanted to make certain Bethany understood her clearly.

Mandy nodded her head in agreement.

"I certainly understand. I'm not sure where to begin. I...I guess I need to start with a confession...and I hope you'll both accept my apology. You see, for quite some time, I've kept a slight distance between the three of us. You're unaware of it, but something you once said hurt me deeply," Bethany admitted shamefully.

"What?" Mandy and Adel replied in unison.

"Neither of us would want to do anything to hurt you. What have we done?" Adel was horrified at the thought.

"It was when Stewart and I first started seeing each other. I heard you both discussing us in the church sanctuary."

Adel interrupted, "I think I remember the conversation."

Bethany continued, "The two of you didn't understand why Stew was showing interest in me when he could have had his pick of several young ladies."

"That wasn't what we meant. You mistook our meaning. I'm so sorry if it hurt you. I wish you'd come to us about it," Adel responded.

Mandy jumped in to rescue Adel, "I was the one who initiated the conversation, but we weren't referring to you in a negative way."

"I'm certain I misunderstood." Bethany wanted them to know she held no resentment.

"The conversation wasn't about you personally, but it was out of concern *for* you," Adel explained. "We love Stew. He's like a brother to us. He loves God and serves Him with a true heart. Stew is a good man but unique in some respects. He stands out wherever he goes.

"I'm sure you remember Mandy and I were both interested in Stew when we were younger. In fact, it was causing problems in our friendship. His attention made us feel special, and it had the same effect on other girls—as it did you.

"Then one day we both realized there wasn't any reason for us to be jealous over Stewart. He had no real interest in either of us. At the time, Stew wasn't romantically interested in any *one* girl. In his mind, we were all just friends."

Mandy jumped in, "We just assumed his attention toward us was romantic. Once we realized it wasn't, we decided just to enjoy him as a Christian brother. I don't believe he had any idea the effect his attention was having on us—or other girls, for that matter."

"Bethany, you were young when Stewart started showing an interest in you. So naturally, knowing how he felt about girls, we were concerned that you might be hurt," Adel explained.

"Obviously, I was being petty. I should have been more trusting," Bethany admitted,

Then Bethany became serious. "I do understand your point about Stew, and until last night, I never believed I had a reason to consider his attentiveness toward other young ladies to be an issue. I'm not the jealous type.

"Stew was loving and attentive. Not only was he my fiancée, but I felt he was my best friend. Our relationship seemed perfect. I trusted him. But during the engagement party, I was given reason to question his true personality.

"If you'll recall, early in the evening, a maid brought me a card while the three of us were talking."

"Yes. Mandy and I remember."

"The note on the card told me to meet Stew at the garden shed. I assumed he wanted to be alone with me before we greeted our guests, but when I walked into the shed, I saw Stewart embracing and kissing... Rica Adams." Bethany broke into tears.

"You poor dear!" Adel grabbed Bethany and held her tightly out of compassion. The two were immediately joined by Mandy enfolding them both.

They wept together for her pain and disappointment. Yet the two friends found it difficult to believe Stewart could have been part of anything so scandalous.

Mandy finally pulled away, wiped her eyes, and asked the dreaded questions, "Bethany, are you positive in what you saw?"

Bethany nodded and wiped beneath her tear-filled eyes. "No mistake. They were clearly visible."

"I can't think him capable of anything so...so unchristlike. There must be more to this. Stew would never intentionally hurt you like that."

"He tried to persuade me to forget it, but I could never—" Bethany trailed off.

"Beth. That was not the Stewart Jefferson that Adel and I know. Something has gone terribly wrong. You must believe that." Mandy defended Stew, hoping to keep Bethany's heart open toward him. "What he has done seems inexcusable, but I can guarantee you Rica was behind this."

"Bethany, we're not prepared to believe the two of you aren't meant to be together," Adel stated earnestly. "Let's go over this story once more. Surely there's something you've missed."

19

A PASSIONATE PLEA

As Bethany sat under the willow with her hands clasped around her knees, her thoughts were interrupted by a butterfly that fluttered up and landed on her index finger. The insect was beautiful, and Bethany was immediately intrigued by its perfection. She studied the fascinating little creature and wondered what determined its flight. Then, as suddenly as it had appeared, the butterfly flittered away. It was such a delicate little creature, yet it confidently flew out into the world totally unaware of its Creator's protection. If God cared about the flight of one tiny butterfly, then He understood and cared about the sorrow in her heart, and He would direct her path as well.

"Bethany, are you here?"

"Yes, Mama," she answered pleasantly.

"I love it when you call me "Mama". I think it must be one of the most beloved words spoken to a mother by her children. All mothers secretly long to turn back the clock to those times," Helen reminisced.

"Are you saying you wished I'd never grow up?" Bethany kidded.

"Guilty!" her mother confessed. "However, I'm here to let you know it's time to leave."

"I'm ready," Bethany replied. "I just had a few minutes. It's such a lovely morning but go ahead. I'll be right behind you."

"I believe I'd prefer to have you as company beside me while I can." Mrs. Jackson stopped to wait for her daughter to catch up and hooked her arm in Bethany's.

"God has allowed us to have you for a short time longer, but someday you will be whisked away from us—that is how it should be. Parents do struggle with letting their children go," her mother sweetly confessed.

"I don't see myself marrying for years—if ever," Bethany sighed.

"But you're so wrong, sweetie. There's a good Christian man waiting and praying for his lovely, young bride. And, my beautiful daughter, God will someday bring you together."

"I suppose God has confirmed these new wedding plans?" Bethany joked, not wanting to get into a serious conversation.

The church was full and the service was just beginning when the Jacksons arrived. Bethany appreciated that her father had intentionally driven slower than usual. He understood the awkwardness she felt in attending church for her first time after the breakup.

As Bethany walked with her parents to their usual pew, she received many supporting smiles from her brothers and sisters in Christ. Even Stewart's parents smiled at Bethany lovingly to let her know they still adored her. She took time to hug them, and their reception of one another was a blessing to those who witnessed it.

After service while she was speaking with Adel and Mandy, the pastor asked Bethany to meet with him. She consented and followed Pastor Strong to his office where they were joined by his wife. He asked Bethany to be seated before offering a very peculiar prayer.

"I'm sorry to detain you so unexpectedly—especially after the trial you've experienced of late. My wife and I wouldn't be putting such an overwhelming proposition before you if it wasn't an emergency," Pastor Strong apologized in hast, not giving Bethany time to interact.

"So, I'll get on with the reason I've asked to meet with you. You see, my cousin, Pastor David Goodry, is the new minister of a small church and orphanage out west. We believe strongly in this ministry and support it. At present there are few supporters, so it's a struggle to keep the doors open. David has to work at a mill to help with the finances. Originally, a seasoned missionary was hired to help him, but her arrival had been delayed because of her elderly mother's health. For a short time, his sister, Janet, agreed to help him at the mission, but she recently married her childhood sweetheart.

"Here's the problem. Due to these circumstances, David has sent a plea for a strong, hardworking woman who has teaching credentials, is well-versed in the Word, and has a deep relationship with God. She will need to fill Janet's position until the missionary arrives. Only the Lord knows when that will be."

"Oh, your cousin is in a desperate situation!" Bethany agreed.

"Bethany, my wife and I have considered every available person in our congregation who might be eligible and willing to take on such a challenge. You're the only one qualified to fill this urgent need. We believe you're the one the Lord has chosen."

"Me?" Bethany questioned.

"Janet's replacement will have to be willing to work in several areas. The position involves being a teacher on Sundays, teaching school half days during the week, and working as a nanny in the evening to get the children ready for bed.

"There are older women who do the cooking and some of the child care. They're dependable and dedicated but limited in what they can do. Janet ended up having to supervise the help, so I assume the replacement will have that responsibility too."

"Oh, I don't know!" Bethany was stunned.

"There's more.... Not so long ago, Pike City, where the mission is located, was a thriving town. Cattle were brought there to be bought and sold. Unfortunately, the town suffered a devastating blow when the railroad decided to go through a town just north of there.

"As it turned out, the cattle business moved to the rail town, and many people in Pike City lost their money and good paying jobs. The mission church members do what they can for the orphanage, but most of the congregation is young mothers who make their living scrubbing floors to feed their own children."

Then he haltingly added, "Bethany...this is volunteer work...so the temporary replacement will also need to take a part time job to help support the mission—"

"This is very complex," Bethany interrupted as she shook her head in disbelief.

"—and you would need to leave tomorrow morning if at all possible."

"Tomorrow morning?"

"As I mentioned, this is urgent. We don't want to lose this ministry. There are little lives depending on it, and David doesn't want to turn any child away."

"Pastor Strong...it's so much to comprehend. I'm not sure I can measure up to it."

"Bethany, you can do this! Your parents never allowed you or your sister to sit idly just because you're privileged. You've been exposed to hard work. You have the skills."

With that, the pastor closed his argument, knowing he had presented the facts as vividly and passionately as possible. His wife could not speak for fear of crying.

"Frankly, I must speak with my parents and pray. If I do take this on, there must be no doubt in my heart it's God's will. I don't want to fail God or the children."

"We understand...but, Bethany, it's imperative we have your answer by this afternoon. Will it be acceptable if we visit your home around four o'clock? I don't mean to be so insistent, but, as I've said, this is urgent." Then he rose to conclude their meeting. "Thank you for your time."

"You're welcome, and I'll be ready with my answer when you arrive." Bethany left the office deep in thought.

20

BITTERSWEET

On the way home from church, no one spoke. Helen wiped her eyes and Mel wore a somber expression. Bethany's face told them all they needed to know at the moment—something was amiss—it was very serious—and it involved her. They both secretly hoped it had nothing to do with the struggling mission their friends had been discussing.

This time, her father let the horses trot instead of walk, so it seemed only moments before they pulled to a stop in front of the house. George, the groundskeeper, sensed something was wrong and offered to take the buggy to the stable. Mr. Jackson gave him a pat on the back out of gratitude

Bethany and her parents walked slowly up the steps. Once inside the parlor, her parents sat together on the couch; she sat across from them in a wingback chair.

No one spoke as her parents prepared themselves for the news.

"Bethany, should I get another handkerchief?"

"Yes, Mother, I believe so," she answered honestly.

"Then what do you have to tell us, sweetheart? How much time do we have with you before you leave us?" her father asked.

"I must do some praying, but it appears I should leave as early as tomorrow morning."

Not wanting to show their true feelings, both kept calm and did not react. There was no doubt the decision was already made. Bethany would follow God's leading, and they must let her go—even if it meant sending her away with a broken heart.

Bethany then poured out the entire story as it had been relayed to her by Pastor Strong. Each took turns praying out loud over their concerns about the assignment. Then they separated to spend time alone with the Lord. It was the Jacksons' way of handling serious matters.

In the end, Bethany knew what she must tell the pastor on his arrival.

At exactly four o'clock, Pastor and Mrs. Strong knocked on the Jacksons' door. Mary led them to the parlor where the family greeted their guests with the good news.

The pastor handed Bethany the travel information and a long list of the items she would need. Mrs. Strong advised Bethany that the living quarters would be small and primitive.

As soon as the Strongs left, Mary and the Jacksons reviewed the list. Everything packed would need to be useful. Each was given a portion of the list to fill, and the articles were to be taken to the study.

Later that night, the women checked the inventory: several practical dresses and aprons, bed clothing, medical supplies, toiletries, and towels were only a few of the items stacked around the room. To help out, George brought down the trunk from the attic while Mel collected a bag of small hand tools and other paraphernalia. They had to work through the night in order to complete the packing.

Mary prepared a huge breakfast of sausage gravy and biscuits in honor of Bethany's venture. Not long after, the carriage was brought around for their departure. The ride to the station was made memorable as they recalled some of Bethany and Tanna's childhood antics. Then, more quickly than seemed possible, Bethany was waving goodbye.

21

I CAN'T DO IT

Bethany's nap was interrupted by the loud, obnoxious snoring of a heavy gentleman seated beside her. Although he was dressed well and looked like a decent man, she was not pleased he had taken it upon himself to share her seat without asking for permission. After being up all night packing, she was in desperate need of rest and did not appreciate being robbed of it. A sleeping berth would have felt wonderful, but such comfort would not be available for several hours.

Her only hope of getting rest was to find a way to move to another seat without disturbing the man beside her. Bethany heard the sounds of closing books, folding newspapers, and disgusted sighs as other passengers decided to find seating in another car away from the horrible sound. That was fine for them, but she was tightly stuck in her seat with no obvious way to escape.

Exasperated, Bethany stood to her feet hoping to slide through the narrow space in front of him, but the man had scooted down and his knees were pressed tightly against the seat. So she delicately placed her hand on his shoulder and gave a gentle shake which caused no reaction. The next shake was a bit harder but had no effect. She finally gave him a rather violent shaking, but he only shifted in his seat. It appeared she was imprisoned.

Just before being seated, a handsome, older man—looking amused—stopped in the aisle and offered her his hand. His eyes revealed he was overly tired from a day of hard work.

"Sweetheart, may I be of some help?"

"Yes sir. I most certainly could use some assistance," Bethany answered with a smile.

"How 'bout you step up on your seat, and I'll help you over?"

Following his directions, she grasped the back of her seat and stepped up. In a few seconds she was free. The remaining passengers clapped, and she profusely thanked the man for coming to her rescue.

The circumstances had lifted her mood and seemed to give the other travelers a little reprieve. She gave a little wave to them and then went to find another seat.

As Bethany sat for a long while thinking about the assignment ahead, she was suddenly overcome by loneliness and doubt. Yesterday it seemed so clear the Lord wanted her to take the position, but, at the moment, it seemed silly and naive. *What do I really know about children or teaching? Is God truly directing me? I was wrong about Stewart. Am I making another mistake?*

I can't do it! I'll get off at the next station before making a fool of myself...again! But deep inside she knew a lot of people were counting on her, and she could not let them down. It would be irresponsible to turn back without even trying.

In response to her fears, Bethany opened her Bible to 1 Corinthians 14:33—*For God is not the author of confusion but of peace....*

It reminded her that doubt is a product of confusion, and God's Word is a source of comfort to correct the Christian's spirit and mind. With these truths in her heart, Bethany retired to her berth. Once there, she bathed in God's Word until a gentle breeze drifted through the window and helped carry her into peaceful slumber.

22

LONNIE AND THE DOWNTRODDEN

The view from the window gradually became more interesting as the green of the Midwest and the sway of the prairie grass was replaced with sights of red soil, tumble weeds, cactus, and far away mountains, while countless rock formations speckled the landscape. Bethany could tell her lifestyle was in for a drastic change.

As she continued to watch from the window, the distance between towns became greater, and the communities became smaller with less to offer. Since Pike City was near the orphanage, she wondered if the comforts and conveniences she was accustomed to having would be found there. Nonetheless, watching the scenery change was entertaining and made the trip tolerable.

Eventually, the train did pull into the unfriendly station of Tally. As soon as she stepped onto the platform, the kindness received on the train was traded for sharp replies and uninformative information. To make things worse, there was not a soul in sight to take her to the mission.

After several futile attempts to hire a ride, she finally came across a man who agreed to take her to Pike City—but only within six blocks of the address she had given him.

Originally, she had been harshly informed by him that he was there to pick up a load and was not for hire. After being reprimanded for the mistake, she quickly begged his pardon. Then for some reason, he changed his mind and told her to be ready when he returned with his load or he would leave without her.

Fortunately, he arrived within a few minutes and motioned for her to get in while he loaded her trunk. She politely thanked him as he whipped the horses and drove away making her feel as if she had done something terribly wrong. He did not acknowledge her or say a word for almost an hour, but when he finally did speak, he was so offensive she wished he had not.

The ride was long, hot, and tiring, and by the time they reached Pike City, the foul man had indulged her in a very unpleasant conversation. "Ah don't usually have anything to do with ya lowlife's from down that way! As fa' as I see it, ya aught ta be burnt out. Nothin' but scum down thar!" he spewed angrily.

"I'm sure I don't know what you're referring to. I've just arrived here as an assistant at the orphanage until the missionary arrives," She was a bit hesitant to correct him but was tired of his hateful attitude.

"Wahl, as fa' as I'm concerned, that makes ya one of the filthy lot!" he shouted at her.

"I don't understand your attitude toward me or the downtrodden of the area, sir," Bethany returned.

"Well, maybe you'll unnerstand nis! Gimme ma money and git out a ma wagin, ya hateful li'l thing!" he bellowed. Then he stood up and toppled her trunk onto the ground without leaving the wagon.

"Most gratefully, sir! Here's your money. I wouldn't want to be beholding to someone who behaves in such a manner. You might contemplate attending church. God can free men from their poor attitudes." Bethany managed to get the statement out before he pulled away in a cursing rage.

Suddenly, she was left standing in near darkness, wondering what she should do. Bethany did not have a clue where the map was, but it would be of little use since she had no idea where *she* was. Still, she was glad to be rid of the wagon driver and was too upset with him to be frightened.

"What on earth is a pretty little thing like you doin' out here all alone?" a kind feminine voice asked.

Bethany turned and saw a thin woman in an overly flashy dress moving toward her.

"I'm afraid I was just kicked off the only ride available from the train station. He doesn't seem to think much of the side of town I'm headed for."

"Honey, I hate to tell you, but I have a notion you're already on the side of town you're headed for. You shouldn't be out here on your own—especially when you don't know where you're going. But maybe I can help you," the lady with the soft voice and heavily painted face offered.

Bethany would not allow herself to imagine what the woman might do for a living, but right now she seemed like an angel sent from heaven.

"I'm expected at the mission here in town," Bethany answered.

"Well, sweetie, I'm headed that way myself. Sorry to say I can't go all the way with you because I've got little ones to 'tend. But I can tell you how to get there without being noticed. It's only a short distance from where I'll leave you. Come on." She seemed more than happy to help, and Bethany was more than grateful for it.

Then the lady grabbed one side of the heavy trunk and Bethany's largest bags. "I'll help you hide your things when we get to where we part. Sorry to say it, but you'll have to make at least two trips to get all your stuff hauled to the mission."

They had only been walking a couple minutes when Bethany began to hear babies crying and adults arguing and screaming at one another. Soon after, the rundown shacks came into sight. Most of the yards had trash and junk strewn about. Men, women, and even children walked the streets or sat idly on broken-down porches. One man threw a women out a front door and called her horrible names; the children followed crying after her. Another group of men rolled dice in the street, while a drunken, young man lay sprawled beside them. The whole area reeked of garbage being burned in poorly lit fires.

"My name's Lonnie James. What's yours?" Lonnie wanted to distract Bethany from the horrible things they would see along the walk.

"I...I'm sorry. My name is Bethany Jackson. I'm filling in at the mission until the assigned missionary is available. I should only be here a month or so." Bethany tried not to sound too apprehensive about her surroundings since she did not want to insult the lady.

At that moment, they came upon two huge rats scavenging in rubbish scattered on the street. The rodents made no effort to run and even stopped to watch the women pass. Bethany was frightened, but Lonnie picked up a long stick and threw it at them.

"Nasty critters! They'll eat somebody's little one if given a chance," Lonnie warned, causing Bethany to shiver at the thought.

About that time, they walked by a couple of drunks leaning against a dilapidated house, where two very young children with filthy clothes and dirty faces crawled about unattended on the hard-packed ground. They, too, stopped to stare at Lonnie and Bethany. The dim light shining from the open door of the house exposed the children's faces enough for Bethany to see the sadness and hunger in their eyes.

"You'll see a lot of that. You might as well face up to it...but it wasn't always this bad," Lonnie informed her.

"I reckon you don't think much of me. You probably already sized me up."

"Why, yes, I guess I have. You're a very nice lady with a kind heart who's willing to help someone in need. And I appreciate it." Bethany's response brought a smile to Lonnie's face.

"You know I'm a saloon gal, don't you? But not long ago, I was a respectable woman with three kids and a husband. We came from the East and built a home here. This town was booming with everything from fancy shops to livestock. The hotels were filled, and most of the streets were safe to walk down.

"Then one day, everything was ripped away from us. The train didn't come through Pike City as supposed. All the cattle business went with it. Not long after that, many of the businesses started closing down. Some people were smart enough to leave town before they'd lost everything. The rest of us tried to stay, thinking things would turn around."

"I'm so sorry to hear it," Bethany sympathized.

"We lost our farm and, soon after, the horses and wagon—

which meant the loss of any type of work for my husband. He couldn't even get a job sweeping floors. Then one day my Dan was found hanging from a tree just outside of town. I guess he didn't feel like a man anymore since he had no way to support our family. You see, I'd already gone to work in the saloon.

"My kids will soon be old enough to realize their mama's no good. I hope someday they'll understand I didn't want to live this way."

Lonnie's touching story pierced Bethany's heart.

"That last papa back there has given up—like most of the men. The guy usually spends what little he makes on liquor—even at the expense of his kids going hungry.

"I've heard the mission takes in children when the parents abandon them or pass on. God bless that minister for his efforts. There isn't much kindness like that left around here. There are several wealthy families in town, but even some of the rich take advantage of the poor when the opportunity arises.

"I'm sorry. I didn't mean to bear my soul about all this. I just got lost in my thoughts, and it came pouring out. I don't get a chance to talk to women much."

"No, please don't apologize. I have to admit I've had no experience outside of my own perfect, little world. It's not that I've never known sorrow, but I've had a very nice life.

"Before I left, my pastor gave me a little history on what happened to the people in this area, but seeing it and hearing the story first hand has helped me understand the devastation. I suppose it could happen to any family if the right circumstances took place. We hear of things like this happening to people, but it always seems so far away."

Lonnie had no idea how much her story had already changed Bethany's attitude toward the people of the area.

"I don't mean to sound flippant, but God has the answers to all of our problems. Have you ever turned to Him for help?" Bethany asked cautiously.

"Oh, believe it or not, back home I was quite the church goer. But my Dan was treated badly when he was growing up. His parents were overly pious and beat their kids. He swore he'd never make his children go to church, so I never bothered him with it. I guess it was wrong," Lonnie shamefully admitted. "But God wouldn't want me now—with men hanging all around me. Don't get me wrong—they have to keep their distance. I'm not *that* sort... but it's too late for me."

"Lonnie, it's never too late with God. He knows the circumstances of your life. If we had to wait until we're good enough to come to God, none of us would ever be saved. It's not possible to earn forgiveness through the good things we do. That's why Jesus gave his life. He paid for all our sins. Maybe we can talk about this again sometime...if you wouldn't mind."

Lonnie only shrugged her shoulders.

Just then a man ran right into Lonnie and sent her flying into a pile of junk. He was being chased by a big, burley man shouting profanities and carrying a piece of wood that he meant to use as a club.

Bethany helped Lonnie up and checked to see if she was injured. As Lonnie brushed off her clothing, Bethany looked around and wondered how life could possibly be any worse than what she had observed on this walk. She was thankful there would be a clean, safe place to sleep tonight.

Lonnie turned her attention to Bethany and said, “Well, here’s where I leave you. We’ll hide the trunk here in the brush. I’ll look around before you go, and if I don’t see anybody coming, you need to take off down *that* way.” She pointed down a dark path with the only lighting coming from the widows of homes.

“The mission’s straight up that road. The homes thin out fairly quickly. Mostly old folks living up that way. Just stay in the shadows and walk fast...run if you can. Don’t stop for any reason, and you should be fine.” Lonnie did her best to put Bethany at ease.

“I have to learn to be brave sometime. Now, go on home to your children. Thank you for your kindness, and God bless you.”

Bethany gave Lonnie a quick hug and ran.

23

UNWELCOMED

Bethany was glad when the mission came into view. She had never been truly afraid before tonight.

Not wanting to leave the shadows, she quickly dropped her baggage on the steps of the mission. Then after taking several deep breaths and gathering her nerve, Bethany ran with all her might back to where the trunk was hidden. Knowing it was too heavy to carry, Bethany lifted one end and tugged. The road was sandy and the trunk moved.

Once all her belongings were at her new home, Bethany took time to scan her surroundings and catch her breath. She was surprised to find the facility in such good condition. The main structure was an impressive building with several surrounding barns and sheds.

Bethany had no idea what time it was when she knocked on the mission door, but, when no one came to greet her, she decided to push the door open and go inside.

She walked around until she found a hallway with children sitting along a wall. Almost all of them were in tears, and her unexpected appearance frightened several of the little ones, causing them to cry aloud.

The noise caused the thin and haggard, young man, who was down on his knees washing a child's face, to turn and look up at her. "Miss Jackson, I assume?" he shouted. "If so, grab that pan of water and give a good scrubbing to that row of children you're standing next to. It's way past their bedtime, so they're tired and hate being bathed all the more. When you get done, take them upstairs and put them to bed. Then come back down, and those three little ones sitting beside you need their diapers changed and a good bathing. They go in those crib-looking things upstairs. We've had our evening prayer. And before you take any of the children upstairs, grab that bucket of water and let them all have a small drink. The less they have to drink, the fewer wet beds we'll have in the morning. Now that you're here, we'll be able to take in the infant."

The man was attired as a minister, so she assumed he was Pastor Goodry. It took only a moment to see why he needed someone's help immediately. The place was a mess and quite dirty. All of the little bodies and their clothing were covered in dust from the day. Even the slightly older children were assigned chores to help get everyone in bed.

After she had done as the pastor had instructed, Bethany returned to find him talking to a little boy about six years old. The child was crying, but she could tell it was against the boy's will to do so.

"I understand you're having a hard time, but you'll eventually get used to it here. You'll soon make friends, and with Miss Jackson here, things should be much better. Now, go get in bed. I must speak with her." The minister was attempting to console the boy, but the pastor's heart was not in it.

She watched and followed the minister's lead as he picked up the area and put things away. Finally, the minister turned to her and said, "I'm Pastor Goodry. I hope you remember your assignments because I don't have time to keep repeating details. You're to go sit with the children to keep them quiet until they fall asleep. A lady will arrive soon, and she'll remain with them for the night. When she takes over your watch, you'll find me in the dining hall. I do my paperwork there because it's somewhat cooler at night. Anyway, at that time I'll show you where you'll be staying." Then the exhausted, young man turned and walked away, giving Bethany no further information.

Bethany was disappointed in his attitude and could not understand why he had been so unwelcoming and abrupt.

24

A HOSTILE ENVIRONMENT

The leathery skinned woman entered the room and tapped Bethany on the shoulder. The old woman put a crooked finger to her lips, so Bethany smiled, rose quietly, and left the room. This was not the time to get acquainted.

Bethany found her bags and went to look for the pastor; the trunk would have to be seen to later. It took a while to find which corridor to take, but she eventually found him sitting at a table in the dining hall. The pastor was much younger than she had expected. He was tall, somewhat handsome, and had dark brown hair which was parted and combed neatly to one side. She assumed his extreme thinness was due to the stress he was under currently.

"Excuse me, I didn't hear you come in. Let me have your bags, and I'll take you to your quarters." His face and manner indicated he was doing the task out of expectation and not out of politeness.

Outside, the night air was still and offered no relief from the heat. Unable to keep up the pace, she trailed behind, and he did not offer to slow down on her behalf.

"I need to make it clear to you that nothing here comes easily. You'll have to figure out what's expected of you on your own. I'm sorry this was forced on you so suddenly," the tired, hollow-eyed minister informed her. "Expect hard work for your entire stay."

Once they reached what she thought was a small, adobe shed, there was not even a brief conversation between them. "This is where you'll be living. Get up when the rooster crows and be in the dining hall shortly thereafter. Good night." As promised, he left her to fend for herself.

It was a dark night, but Bethany did not need a light to know the place was filthy. Even more disheartening was the pastor's attitude. She was insulted by his lack of gratitude and by the fact he had left her standing alone, in the dark, in a dangerous and unfamiliar area. "At the very least, the man could have left the lantern and put my bags inside the door," she mumbled.

Stew would have ... Bethany stopped mid-thought, shook her head, and pushed open the wooden door. The hinges screamed from lack of oil, but the little hut greeted her with a hint of unexpected coolness.

Uncomfortable in the dark, Bethany reached down to feel for her bags and found the one that held the candles and matches. She grabbed a candle and struck a match on the side of the building to light it. She then pushed the candle through the door and guardedly followed behind.

The candle offered only a dim light, giving her little cause to relax. There was no reason to consider unpacking, so she pulled her bags inside and lined them up to make a bed—at least she would not have to sleep on the hardened ground. She reached outside the door for the leather strap and hooked it over a peg on the wall. It was far from secure, but it made her feel better.

Fully dressed and exhausted from the trip, she collapsed on the makeshift bed. Unfortunately, the heat made it nearly impossible to sleep and the concern about missing the rooster's crow—not to mention thoughts of unwelcome creatures—added to her restlessness. It was not uncommon for Bethany to rise early, but to do so at the command of poultry had evaded her thus far.

Bethany *did* hear the wakeup call when it came. It was still too dark inside the hut to see much of anything, so she stepped outside to find the facilities and the well.

When she returned, the hut was light enough for her to see faintly. She quickly bathed, changed into a lightweight dress, tied her hair back, and left to find her place at the mission. Knowing she would receive little instructions, Bethany stepped inside the dining room and stood out of view to watch what was taking place.

The first thing she noticed was the children sitting at long tables. They all looked sad, and almost every child wore tattered and badly laundered clothing. Several were not even attempting to eat the meager meal in front of them.

Bethany then saw the minister taking his place at the far end of the first table, so she decided to get her food and join them. She walked over to a bony, worn-out looking lady standing in front of a large pot.

"Hello! I'm Bethany Jackson—Janet's replacement until the missionary arrives," she said, to introduce herself.

"Ma name's Aggie. I'm in charge of the cookin'. Glad to meet ya." With that said, the women plopped a large spoonful of gray matter into a bowl and handed it to Bethany.

"I look forward to getting to know you. Thank you," Bethany said politely, trying to keep her eyes from looking at what she assumed was oatmeal.

She turned and walked to where the children were sitting, taking her place at the opposite end of the table from Pastor Goodry. She assumed she had done the right thing since he ignored her.

"Hey, pretty woman!" one of the younger boys yelled out.

"Lewis! We do not address a lady in that manner," the pastor corrected.

"Children, this is Miss Bethany Jackson. Most of you saw her last night. She'll be taking over Miss Janet's duties until the missionary arrives. You're to address her as Miss Jackson at all times, and you're expected to listen and obey all she asks you to do. School will begin as soon as the morning devotion is over. Now, please finish your breakfast."

"Miss Jackson...we have already prayed over our meal." The pastor mentioned it to let Bethany know she was considered late.

Bethany instantly bowed her head to bless the food and then leaned over the bowl to peer at the revolting clump. She was thinking of going without breakfast but saw the pastor eyeing her while he encouraged one of the orphans to eat. Assuming he expected her to set an example, there was nothing to do other than try to eat it.

She grabbed the spoon and quickly scooped the stuff into her mouth, and that was where it stopped. The lump was cold, slimy, and felt like it was doubling in size. She started to gag but fought the urge. Bethany had never eaten oatmeal that was not served perfectly cooked, covered with cream, and sprinkled with a nice coating of brown sugar.

Then she noticed the children looking at her. She tried to smile, but her mouth was occupied with trying to keep the oatmeal inside. Finally, she forced a couple of chews and let it slide down her throat. Bethany prayed it would stay down. With that done, most of the little heads turned back to their bowls. Bethany did manage to complete the meal but agonized over each bite.

When breakfast was over, everyone found seats facing the front of the room. Pastor Goodry led them in a song and gave a short devotional while the children participated obediently.

Upon dismissal, the ones too young to be schooled were taken outside by an older woman and her daughter. The school age children moved to the back of the room to sit in what apparently had been their assigned seats when Janet was teaching. The pastor left without offering any type of instructions to help Bethany get started.

Bethany was totally unprepared. It had never occurred to her that she would be expected to fend for herself immediately without any information about the children's learning skills or what Janet had taught them up to that point. She hoped the children did not notice she was more than a little perturbed.

She started class by reintroducing herself and then had each child stand to state their name and age. It was a relief to find a few pieces of writing paper, which allowed her to take notes on what she learned about each pupil. Next, the children were asked to recite the alphabet to begin the process of assessing their capabilities. Later, Bethany spotted some slates and asked each child how far they could count. Those who could write were told to write their numbers as far as they could. The more advanced students were to stop at one hundred unless they wanted to go higher. Since most of the children preformed their numbers adequately for their age, she assumed Janet had been a good teacher.

Bethany asked how reading was done, and one of the girls pointed out the primers and a few upper class books which probably had been discarded from another school. She did math drills with the older children by having them sit down when they could no longer figure the problems given. Bethany found some skills lacking, yet all of the children seemed reasonably intelligent and teachable

Wanting to bring the morning to a good conclusion, she ended class with a spelling bee of very simple words. The younger children seemed to be encouraged by being able to spell words correctly in front of the older ones.

Bethany dismissed the class for lunch and picked up the pages of information she had gathered from testing. Her goal was to review what was recorded and memorize their names by the next morning.

Lunch was not much better than breakfast. It was a bowl of watery soup beans and a piece of dry cornbread. Bethany felt guilty for the abundant and well-prepared meals she had taken for granted throughout her life.

Looking into the dejected eyes of the orphans made her wonder what tragic circumstances had brought them to the mission. She almost hoped none of them could remember better lives; she felt it might be easier that way.

The children were very quiet during lunch, except for the new boy who would occasionally sniff and wipe a tear from his eyes with the back of his hands. He wore nice clothing, but they were in need of a good washing. She assumed his sorrow reflected what the other orphans felt most of the time.

The children were told to go to the bathroom and get ready for their naps; evidently, it was expected for all ages. Bethany decided to take the time to unpack and start setting up the little hut. She was on her way there when Pastor Goodry stopped her. "You'll need to use the afternoon to find a job, Miss Jackson. As you can see we need your financial support as soon as possible," he stated matter-of-factly.

"But I haven't had a chance to unpack. I've not even had a clear look at my living quarters, and surely you don't mean for me to leave as I am. I would need to freshen up and change into something more suitable."

"You look fine for hunting the sort of job you'll find in this town. But it wouldn't matter much if you did clean up. By the time you get to town you'll probably look the same as you do now—hot, sweaty, and tired. Put on a bonnet," the minister commanded.

"I'll get it," Bethany said begrudgingly—but still submitting to his authority. "However, since I'm not from this area, could you possibly give me directions to town?" By this point, she was extremely irritated with the man.

"Yes!" he answered, then jerked his head to the side to direct her. "See that path right there. Stay on it! Be back by five...with a job." After the sarcastic remark, he started to leave.

"Excuse me, *Pastor*!" Bethany wanted to remind him of the position he held. "Is there anything I should be concerned about such as reptiles, insects, animals, or *people*?"

"Probably...so, stay on the path and away from anything that scares you." He gave her a disgusted look, and then walked away.

Bethany stomped off, and it was a full fifteen minutes before she realized she had left without even a bonnet. It was too hot to turn back since she had no idea how far she had to walk.

She thought it must have been, at the very least, a twenty minute walk before the path ended in a clearing behind the downtown area. She walked around the side of a building and stepped onto a wooden walkway. There she propped both hands on her back to take a moment to cool down and see what the town had to offer.

Bethany found it very charming—in a cowboy sort-of-way—and she was delighted to see saddled horses tied to hitching posts. It was all very romantic to her and just as she had imagined the West to be. She was disappointed her first experience in the West was under such circumstances, but she had agreed to come as a servant and not for her own pleasure.

Bethany shielded her eyes while looking up and down the street as far as possible. Most of the stores looked reasonably new and appeared to be turning a profit; however, she *did* notice some were boarded up.

About then, a sophisticated looking woman in a beautiful green dress walked by and stopped directly in front of her. The lady surveyed Bethany up and down and had the audacity to say out loud, "Honestly!" Then she proceeded down the walkway.

If Bethany had not been a Christian, she would have chased the woman down. Never had anyone judged her in such a manner.

Just then, she spotted a mirror displayed in a store window and went to take a look at herself. Bethany was embarrassed to see her hair had fallen and her face was smudged with dirt. Although her dress was of nice quality, it was full of dust from the walk. She realized the woman must have mistaken her for one of the poorer locals, yet knew it was no excuse for the lady's poor conduct.

Bethany suddenly realized she had never been judged as being lower class. She did not like the feeling and supposed the downtrodden did not care for it either. Recalling how quickly she had formed a negative opinion of the poor on the streets last night, she wondered how many times in the past she had mistakenly assessed others unfairly.

Bethany slipped back onto the pathway to find the trickle of water she had noticed dripping from some rocks just before the path ended. After beating the dust from her dress, she removed the handkerchief tucked in a sleeve and placed it under the water.

The cool, damp cloth soothed and toned down the redness in her complexion caused by the brisk walk and the blistering heat. Bethany then removed the ribbon from her hair and combed it with her fingers before tying it back.

When she returned to the street, she glanced in the mirror and was satisfied with her appearance. It was then she saw the *Help Wanted* sign and stepped inside the store.

A middle-aged man with a receding hairline stood behind the counter busily stocking the shelves. He turned to offer a greeting when the doorbell jingled. His polite and gentle smile was warm and sincere. "May I help you, young lady?" The kind voice was music to Bethany's heart.

Bethany smiled and walked over to the counter. "Good afternoon, sir. My name is Bethany Jackson, and I'm here to inquire about the position you're wanting to fill."

"My name's Burt." He reached out and shook the small hand which was offered. "I'm sorry, but the job is for a man experienced in woodworking. It's one of our side businesses. My nephew ran it for a few years, but he had to return to South Dakota to care for the family's farm. His dad fell through the hay loft about a week ago.

"Sorry, miss. I wish I did have a job for you. I believe I'd hire you in a minute! You have honest eyes. This town has taken a change in character lately. Kind of hard to know who can be trusted these days. Wasn't like that too long ago," he spoke with regret.

"Why, thank you kindly. Actually, I'm new to the area, but I have heard of the misfortune the town has suffered. I understand it was quite lovely before," Bethany responded politely.

"Yep! It was. So, may I ask what brought you here? We don't have many young ladies coming into town—unless they're from wealthy families." It was clear he had spoken without weighing his words and instantly felt bad for what he had carelessly implied. "Sorry, sweetie. I didn't mean to let on like you were—"

"Oh, of course not. Please, don't feel you need to apologize on my account. I do normally dress like a lady, but I had a difficult morning at the mission. I'm a sight to see, I'm afraid."

"You look just fine. You needn't make excuses on my account. I don't know why women want to fool with all that fixin' up anyway. Now, did I hear you say you came from the mission?"

"Yes, I came in on the train yesterday and arrived in Pike City last night. I'm here to fill in for a missionary for a short time.

"I have to find a part-time job to help support the orphans who live there. That's why I had to hurry off after lunch. The mission is struggling because there are only a few supporters so far. Even the minister holds an outside job." Bethany wondered why on earth she had just unloaded all the information on this busy man. "I'm sorry. I'm keeping you from your work. I should be going. Thank you for your kind words."

As she started for the door, an attractive lady with blonde hair entered the room. She looked at Bethany and smiled, "Well, who might you be, young lady?"

"This is my wife, Lena. Lena, this is Miss Bethany Jackson, a volunteer at the mission."

"The mission! The one behind the mercantile?" Lena questioned. "It reopened? I didn't know. We usually hear everything that happens around here."

"Yes, she just arrived last night. She's lookin' for a job."

"I sure hope you find one. What kind of work are you looking for?" Lena was truly interested and did not mean to be nosey.

"I haven't had time to give it much thought. I'm expected to take anything I can find. It's that urgent. I can do about anything if I put my mind to it. My mother is a remarkable seamstress, and she's taught me well. I suppose *those* jobs would be taken.

"Well, it's been wonderful visiting with you. Thank you both for your kindness, and I wish you a good day." Bethany slid out the door as she gave them a grateful wave.

The next sign was at a laundry house, but the job was filled while she waited to speak to the clerk. She wondered why the streets were so empty but supposed people did most of their shopping early in the morning and stayed inside during the afternoon heat.

One of the livery stables needed someone to shoe horses and

not someone to clean stalls. Later, she came across a restaurant that needed a cook. Bethany asked about the job, but the hours were all wrong. However, the dishwasher had just quit. The owner offered the job for a next to nothing salary, but the hours would work. She decided to think it over and went down the street to see if something better was available.

Bethany soon learned she had no alternative but to go back and ask if the dishwashing job was still open. She accepted the position and started back for the mission, glad the task had been accomplished in such a short time.

25

A PLACE TO CALL HOME

Since Bethany had quickly found a job, she hoped to use the extra time to make her little hut habitable. After all, it was still within the time limit the pastor had given her.

She was able to slip through the door of the hut without being noticed. To her relief there was not much rubble inside the building. There were old packing crates, a stack of wood pieces, a discard pile with a few rusty tools, and a bag of rags. She found the bucket she had used that morning and sneaked out to fill it with water for cleaning. Other than having a place all to herself, the well and the small outhouse were the only provisions available to her. Having the hard-packed ground for a floor was a disappointment, but the place could easily be made livable in the time she had.

Leaning against the wall was an old broom which she used to brush off the dust and knock down cobwebs. She was not fond of spiders, but it was good she was not overly frightened of them since there was every indication the little pests would be paying regular visits. Soap and water were put to good use, and every item which could be washed was quickly scrubbed.

Then she pulled the long packing crate to the middle of the

back wall, turned it over, and propped each corner up on a block of wood for a little more height. The trunk had been brought over during the day, so she placed it at the end of the bed.

Before Bethany left home, Mary had explained how to make a mattress by stuffing the tick she had sent. Fortunately, Bethany had been able to find clean straw in the barn. After filling the tick, she stitched the small opening closed. It was such a pleasure to think of sleeping on a freshly made bed. Her snow white sheets were already pressed to perfection, and a quilt of pastel colors made a comfortable-looking bed. Mary had also included a goose down pillow which fluffed up nicely.

The barred windows were small and open, with shutters on the outside for storms. Bethany did not like the idea of open windows, so she rummaged through the bag of rags and found a roll of finely woven cheesecloth. Remembering a container of nails and tacks, she delicately hammered the cheesecloth over the windows, while running hair ribbon along the edge to aid as a seal. The tacks did chip out the adobe somewhat but held well enough. It would do for protection from most insects and small reptiles. The cheesecloth would allow air flow with the extra advantage of still being able to see outside.

In the bottom of the supply bag Bethany found several matching pillow cases tightly rolled together. Evidently, Helen thought the cases might be of more use than pieces of material, and they could be easily reconstructed. They also matched well with the quilt. Bethany had a flash of creativity the instant she saw them. She quickly ripped out the stitches of one side and the bottom seam of four of the cases. Using a needle and thread, she sewed a hem at the top of each one, running it parallel to the bottom hem. Then she ran twine through the top hem. Next, using a tack on each side at the top of the two windows, she tied the twine to hold the cases tightly between the nails.

The pillowcases would do fine as curtains, and she would hem the sides later and put another stitch across the top for a little detail. She grabbed some more ribbons, pulled the curtains to each side, and tied them back to allow air flow and light. They could be untied at night for privacy.

After that, she pulled the largest crate to the front of the building, in the opposite corner from the door, where she would stand it against the wall. Bethany had seen leather used for hinges, so she nailed old leather strips to one side of the crate and to the lid to create a door. Then, on the inside she attached a thin board and added a row of nails. The latch was made of a piece of leather with a nail as a hook. The crate would be used as a closet to hang clothing.

Time was running out, so she hurried and moved a small crate to the side of her bed and covered it with a pillowcase. She sat last night's candle holder and her Bible on what was now an end table. Another crate was placed beside the door for a wash stand. The wash pan she had brought was set on the stand with the bucket. Bethany laid out a candle and matches to take to the mission to light the way back to her little home.

On the other side of the bed, she turned the last small crate over and attached the lid to one side with the rest of the leather. The lid was leaned against the wall. Then she grabbed two more pillowcases and filled each halfway with the remaining straw. The rest of the case was tucked inside to form a square, and the open side was whip-stitched closed. One was laid on the bottom of the box for a seat cushion and the other was leaned against the lid to pad the back, making a chair.

Bethany sat down on her new chair and looked around. God had provided. Even though she was not completely finished, the place was neat, clean, and functional.

She needed to unpack, but she could do that after the children were in bed.

Just when she thought there might be enough time to do something about her appearance, the dinner bell rang.

26

DOMINEERING AND INEXPERIENCED

When Bethany entered the dining hall, she stopped just long enough to put the candle and matches on top of an old cabinet where the children could not reach them. While looking around to see where she might be needed, she noticed that the pastor was walking toward her with a very dissatisfied expression. Instantly overcome with guilt, she swallowed and waited for the reprimand.

"Miss Jackson! We need you to help the smaller children with their plates, I hope you can spare the time," the pastor stated sarcastically.

"Yes, Pastor. But if you are suggesting I am late, then there must have been a misunderstanding. I'm sorry on my part, if there was. I was told to be here by five. I assumed the time remaining *after* finding employment was mine to do with as I wished. I used the time to set up my sleeping quarters while it was still daylight. The place was *filthy* and *unsafe* as it was." Bethany was not about to allow the man to intimidate her.

"Miss Jackson! It's been a difficult day with the children. I need you to carry your weight. Please, get to work!" he ordered.

Bethany had to physically bite her tongue to suppress the

strong desire to give the man a good scolding. She had not come west to be abused by this domineering and inexperienced minister.

"Yes...sir," Bethany answered slowly as she considered her willingness to submit. Relenting, she walked past the parson and took the hands of two younger children.

Once they were in the food line, Bethany looked down at the two toddlers. Their sweet faces and hollow eyes stifled her desire to pack for home. She filled their plates and led them to a table.

After a meager meal of boiled beef, a hint of cabbage, and dried fruit, the older children and staff cleaned up while the little ones went outside to play until the church bell rang for service; everyone was expected to attend.

As Bethany entered the chapel for the first time, her eyes were drawn to the front of the church where the evening sun, streaming through a large, stained glass window, illuminated a breathtaking image of Christ on the Cross.

Bethany then counted twelve more arched, stained glass windows. The six windows to her left portrayed scenes leading up to The Crucifixion, and those on her right displayed scenes which took place after The Crucifixion.

The walnut pulpit, high-backed chairs, communion table, and pews all possessed the same intricate carvings. On the communion table were a golden goblet and a plate. Six golden, lantern chandeliers lit the center aisle to reveal many other lovely features which indicated the church must have originally been Catholic. Bethany felt blessed to worship in such a place and struggled to keep her mind on the message since the chapel was so mesmerizing.

The service was touching, and the acoustics emphasized the sweet harmonious voices of the children and workers as they sang praises to God.

Afterward, she took the youngest orphans inside for their nightly scrubbings and made certain the older children bathed properly. Two of the younger toddlers cried continuously while she worked, but the new boy tried to comfort them—even though an occasional tear trickled down his own little cheek.

Bethany sang softly while tucking the children in bed. Her clear, velvety voice was sweet and soothing, and a few of the children even smiled. In time she hoped to include a story in the nightly routine to add at least one small comfort of home life.

She watched a few of the little ones wiggle and squirm while hearing others whimpering out of loneliness. It was a sad experience, and she wished she was still at home and unaware of such a hurtful existence.

Before long she felt the motherly-like tap and stood up to give the chair to the wrinkly-faced woman to whom she had never officially been introduced. The lady smiled and gave her a wink; Bethany smiled back in appreciation.

Bethany expected to find the minister working at a table in the dining hall, but, to her relief, he was not there. Grateful for not having to come into contact with him, she lit her candle and cautiously walked to the little hut. She was glad to get inside and hook the leather strap over the peg. Even though she knew the Lord was watching over her, she could not keep from being a bit apprehensive. Most definitely, she would stop by the mercantile to purchase some sort of lock to make the door feel more secure.

While unpacking her clothing, she found two new books her mother had sent as a surprise.The unexpected luxury of relaxing with a good story brought tears to her eyes, especially after such a difficult day.

Utterly exhausted, Bethany pulled the curtains shut and got ready for bed. She had never realized how delightful crawling into her own big, soft bed had been. Tonight, however, even sleeping on top of a crate would feel good to a tired body and mind.

After spending time with the Lord, the book on the night stand was put to good use until she drifted off into a much-needed sleep.

It didn't mean anything! Stew's hurtful words brought her out of a restful slumber, and, even worse, the rooster crowed shortly thereafter. She put on a robe and went to pump some water; Bethany was not the type to start a day without bathing.

While straightening the hut, she made several mental notes of what must be accomplished during the day. Teaching and holding a job would be difficult enough without the extra burden of finding time to develop lesson plans. Still, she wanted to do her part to make certain the mission children received a good education. She knew the Holy Spirit would show her how to keep up the pace.

But those thoughts faded when she entered the dining hall and saw the toddlers who needed their breakfast. Each of the children received a dry biscuit and a cup of warm milk, fresh from the cow.

Once the children and minister were served, Bethany found a place at the table and reminded herself that the food was for nourishment and nothing else. A meal at the mission was a privilege, and she must keep that in mind. After having witnessed children who needed the basic necessities so desperately, Bethany wondered if she could ever again take pleasure in the finer things of life.

The second day of teaching was a rough sketch of a normal school day, but the children did not seem to notice or care. She did give the class a fifteen minute break but felt it was too hot for them to go outside. As an alternative, the children were allowed to stay inside and play tic-tac-toe on the slates. Bethany also used the time to get to know the children on a more personal basis.

Lunch was unrecognizable, and, after tasting it, Bethany decided she preferred it that way.Leaving for work was not easy because a few of the youngest children clung to her. Out of guilt, she took the time to help put them down for their naps. The task drained her energy and made her late on her first day.

"You've got yer nerve coming in here late yer first day!" a hateful voice accused as she entered the backdoor of the restaurant. "I won't have any trouble replacing ya in this town, and ya might as well come to terms with that! You come strollin' in here late again, don't bother comin' in a'tal...miss high and mighty in yer fancy duds! Now git the water a boilin' and git to work on them dishes! Don't expect no pay for doing nothing, neither!"

The woman was furious, so any reply from Bethany would have been futile. She was in the wrong and was too weary to exert the energy to explain—especially after seeing the mounds of dishes awaiting her. Fortunately, the hateful women was needed elsewhere and never returned to the kitchen for the rest of the day.

A few times, Bethany came close to fainting from the heat but splashed her face with cool water to avoid it. She vowed every dish would be completed by the end of the shift, or she would stay until it was. She must not give her employer any reason to complain. The orphanage needed the income, and it was part of her Christian upbringing to always do her best—and more when possible.

After leaving the restaurant, she stopped by the mercantile to purchase a lock. She so wanted to visit with Burt and Lena, but, hoping to have the next day's lessons completed before the dinner bell rang, she needed to hurry back to the mission.

Not having decent school supplies made it difficult to find ways to reach the children. Since the morning's games seemed to have had a positive effect, she decided to keep it simple by mixing fun with learning. Once a routine was established and she understood how each child learned best, she could switch to a more traditional teaching method.

It seemed only moments before the bell sounded for the evening meal. Being greeted again by the critical eyes of the pastor caused her spirits to plummet. This person was nothing like the man Pastor Strong had described, and why Pastor Goodry disliked her from the start was a mystery. Still it was her Christian duty to do as the pastor asked; on the other hand, he had never *asked*...just *demanded.*

Once again Bethany took charge of the youngest children by helping them get their food and seeing they were properly seated.

Then she fed the new infant the pastor had mentioned when she arrived. Bethany wanted to cuddle and rock the baby for a while, but time would not allow it. Following a strict routine appeared to be mandatory at the mission.

That night, Bethany retired to her quarters much later than expected since she had insisted on holding baby Betsy until she fell asleep. Rocking Betsy to sleep had been the only gratifying experience thus far.

27

MAD AS A WET HEN

Stew woke early and went down to the lobby to check the morning paper for apartments near his office. He was pleased to find three listings which might meet his needs, so he sent a boy to set up appointments for that afternoon.

It turned out all three were nicely furnished and conveniently located, but after some consideration he decided on the somewhat smaller one. It was a sublet with a short term lease. The arrangement would get him through the winter, and by then he would have a better idea of where and what he might want in a permanent home.

The apartment was immediately available, so he made arrangements to have his things delivered later in the day. He was relieved to have his own place and to have time to look for a local church which shared his convictions.

Stew did find a church within walking distance, but he was disappointed after attending the following Sunday. The reverend's sermon was excellent, but he found much of the congregation to be of high society and very distant.

Stew had little experience in being ignored and was offended by their reception. Still, he decided to attend there until spring. It was near his apartment, and the unfriendly congregation gave him no reason to believe there would be a problem in breaking ties when it came time to leave the church.

The days passed quickly, and he was soon addressing the doorman at the entrance of his new workplace. He stopped at the information desk to check in, and the receptionist immediately accompanied him to an office on the top floor. She found Stew extremely attractive, even compared to the handsome businessmen who constantly made advances toward her.

After introducing him to the snobby secretary behind the desk, the receptionist turned and gave him an interested smile before leaving. Stew was embarrassed by it but thanked her for escorting him. The executive secretary did notice the exchange, but let it slide for the time being. Then she promptly ushered Stewart into Mr. Lance Derby's office.

"Well! Mr. Jefferson, glad you've arrived. And not a moment too soon, I might add. I've had my secretary see that your office was set up so you can begin work immediately. I trust you *are* in the frame of mind to start work, that is. I hope you've found Bay City to your satisfaction," the older businessman rattled off. It was obvious his new boss's life was consumed by his occupation.

"Good morning, Mr. Derby. It's good to be here. I'm most certainly prepared to begin working, and I have found Bay City very much to my satisfaction. Thank you for asking, sir," Stew pelted back his response as he reached out and shook the hefty employer's hand.

"Oh, I almost forgot you were recently married. Am I correct?" his boss brought up in pretense of being interested in Stewart's personal life.

Stew was caught off guard by the question, but he managed to answer, "Actually we've parted company but have decided to remain friends."

Stew detected a faint smile under the thick mustache, and Mr. Derby cleared his throat to reveal his true thought. "Good. Nothing to distract you.

"So, Jefferson, I have no choice but to get down to business. I have five accounts for you to deal with—preferable as soon as possible. We sized you up as a man with the talent to deal with individuals who are difficult to handle. That's what singled you out from the other applicants. As I was saying, these accounts are in trouble, and the problems are compounded because of the clients' stubbornness. I'm going to be honest with you, Jefferson—how you handle these first projects will decide if you have a future with our company. I trust you're up to the challenge?" Derby asked point blank.

"Yes sir!" Stew gave his most confident smile. "I welcome the opportunity." He could tell by his boss's continence, he had answered correctly. However, Stew's mind faintly touched on some recent difficult situations he had handled badly. Fortunately, the most painful memory was swept away as his boss continued.

"Then I will turn you over to my secretary, Mrs. Mock. She will show you to your office. In the future, any questions you have for me should be addressed during the morning meetings. I'm a busy man. Please take as little time as possible in familiarizing yourself to your office. I trust you're a self-starter and pick up on things quickly. We have no time for mollycoddling our employees, and there's no time to waste on these accounts. Do you understand?"

"Absolutely, sir!" Stew replied enthusiastically. Once again, he could tell his answer had pleased the boss. He was certain the man had tried his best to intimidate him, but Stew had met the challenge.

Mrs. Mock was as direct and business-minded as her boss and had no intention of cutting him any slack. On the contrary, Stew would not allow Mrs. Mock the satisfaction of acting as if he cared.

Stew was pleased to enter the newly decorated office suite which he would apparently be sharing with another employee by the name of Clarence Perry. Perry was some sort of an accountant from what Stew could gather from a quick glance at the plaque on the door. He also noticed his own nameplate had been installed.

Unexpectedly, a nice looking, middle-aged redhead stepped out of his office. If she had been unnerved by their presence, she covered it well. Mrs. Mock's stare indicated she did not approve of the woman.

"This is your secretary, Mrs. Lillian Grey. She also is secretary to Mr. Perry who shares this suite. You'll find Mrs. Grey performs her duties adequately and is obliging when need be." The sarcasm was intentional, but Mrs. Grey smiled pleasantly and nodded courteously in Stewart's direction. It was plain to see Mrs. Mock did not receive the reaction she had anticipated from Mrs. Grey.

Stew was very impressed with his secretary's fortitude and immediately noted Mrs. Mock was one to be handled. He was fairly certain he and Lillian Grey would be allies from this point on.

Mrs. Grey led them into Stewart's office where he immediately stepped behind his desk to let it be known he was taking charge.

He was positive Mrs. Mock, as Derby's secretary, had planned to put him under her thumb. However, he made it clear he was not about to succumb to her tactics, and the surprise of it was reflected on her face.

Stew looked up at the woman and said, "By the way, Mrs. Mock, that is a lovely suit. You look very professional."

The statement was made with a dominant air which stumped the woman who was accustomed to frightening new employees into seeing her as their superior. Stew had shaken her confidence, and the woman could only reply in the most business-like manner she could muster. "Th-thank you, Mr. Jefferson." His simple comment had immediately put her on a secretary's level.

Then she tried to carry on as if she was not flustered. "I assume you have several questions concerning your responsibilities here," she stiffly stated, trying to regain control.

"Thank you, Mrs. Mock, but I don't see the need to impose on you further. You are, after all, the secretary to the highest ranking executive here in the company. I'm sure Mrs. Grey is more than capable of handling anything I might need. Now, if you'll excuse us...according to Mr. Derby, I have work to do.

The secretary did not move. She had never had a new executive take over their position at once, nor had she ever been dismissed by one. She was outraged.

Stewart and the executive secretary remained in a standoff stare until he decided to reaffirm the dismissal. "Have you forgotten something, Mrs. Mock?" Stew questioned her firmly.

"No. Very well, then. I see you believe everything is under control," she snapped in compliance, since there was nothing else she *could* do. Mrs. Mock was as mad as a wet hen when she left the office, and Mrs. Grey appeared amused to see someone finally had the nerve to ruffle the old hen's feathers.

It was then Stew turned to his new secretary and said, "Mrs. Grey, I'm looking forward to a long and productive working relationship with you."

"And I with you." She started to leave, but stopped and said, "You catch on quickly. You'll do well here"

"I plan to," he replied with a knowing look.

Stew left work late that afternoon, feeling satisfied in knowing it had been a very productive day. He had cleared up three of the accounts and was fairly positive the problems with the other two were due to oversights. If his assumptions were correct, he should have them rectified early the next day. When this news reached the front office, Mrs. Mock was wise enough to see it might be to her advantage to befriend Mr. Jefferson.

As the days passed, Stew realized upper management *had* tagged him correctly. He did have a way with difficult clients, and his talent was already resulting in huge financial gains for the company. He was pleased with his successes but knew the skills he possessed could only be attributed to God's grace working in his life.

Since his new position had demanded his constant attention, Stew was still agonizing over Billy's welfare. Although the telegraph office had confirmed the telegram from Andrea Landis *had* been sent to Stew's original apartment building, the manager continued to deny having received it.

It was not until Stewart resolved a lengthy, on-going dispute—which would have dealt the company a devastating blow—that Mr. Derby *finally* insisted Stew take the afternoon off for work well done. Stew had done as his boss requested and went to speak with the apartment manager about the telegram. He was reasonably certain Billy was fine, but he had to know for sure.

When the manager again denied receiving the telegram, Stewart, using his most authoritative voice, threatened to go over the man's head. With his job possibly on the line, the manager enlisted his staff to conduct a thorough search of the office. To the manager's relief, the telegram was found where it had been absentmindedly laid in a pile of expired contracts. Stew, although angered, was too relieved to berate the manager for his previous lack of cooperation and concern over this crucial matter.

28

MORE FRUSTRATION

Stew was relieved to find Miss Landis had been true to her promise to send the message.

He grabbed the telegram from the manager's hand:

Arrived safely. Uncle no longer living. Sheriff to find Billy a home.

Stew felt ill. *What have I done? What has become of Billy? I thought of everything else. Why didn't I remember to get Miss Landis' home address?* He immediately went to the telegraph office and wired the sheriff out west.

Stew was wild with worry. Matt had begged him to check with the sheriff's office at the time, but he had felt it unnecessary. He had been certain the arrangements would go well for Billy. Now, there was no telling where the boy was or if he was even alive. He might have been adopted to a good family by now, but, if not, would the sheriff put him out on the street?" Stew badgered himself.

Once he started to wire Matt but decided it might be better to wait until he had heard from the sheriff. He reasoned that Matt had not inquired about the boy since leaving Bay City, so there was no need to trouble him at this point.

Regrettably, more interference took place to delay Stew's efforts in finding the boy. The telegrapher out west became ill and had to leave early that particular day. He was hard pressed to find someone as a replacement and left the office in the charge of a young man who lied about having worked in a telegraph office. When Stew's telegram came over the wire, the boy botched the transmitted message and threw it away rather than be found out.

Stew frantically waited for the return answer but received nothing.

Finally one day, he mentioned his problem to Mrs. Grey, and she kindly composed a letter to the sheriff requesting an urgent response. Unfortunately, the sheriff was the lazy sort and even though a self-addressed, stamped envelope and paper were included with the letter, he laid it aside, planning to take care of it later. Therefore, several more days passed with no word.

29

SETTING HIM STRAIGHT

The days came and went with hard work from sunrise to late night, just as Pastor Goodry had warned. To make things worse, her restaurant employer's demands mounted each day, and the woman continuously found something to blame on Bethany. Most days she left work in tears, which was embarrassing when Burt and Lena waved to her as she passed.

In addition to the already gruesome agenda, she had to find time to prepare a Sunday school lesson each week. The increasing schedule left no extra time to do any deep cleaning at the mission or time to spend loving on the children—especially the tiny baby. And without proper respect or support from the pastor, the volunteers ignored all instructions or suggestions Bethany made to help the mission operate more smoothly.

As conditions continued to decline at the orphanage, the new boy—whom they called Pete—took on the parental roll of Baby Betsy. Bethany often found him sitting on the hard ground rocking back and forth as he fed Betsy a much needed bottle. It was distressing to realize that, without Pete's care, Betsy would experience little love during the first crucial months of her life.

"Miss Jackson! What are you fooling around with now?" The insulting question came from out of the dark dining hall one night. "Don't you have any idea how to use your spare time effectively? The children need a teacher not an artist!"

"Excuse me, sir?" she returned as respectfully as possible. "As their teacher, it is my responsibility to find ways to help the children learn. If I can teach in a way that puts smiles on their faces, I see it as an *excellent* use of time." Bethany laid aside the colorful map which he had handed back to her after looking it over.

"Obviously, you have no idea what it takes to run this mission. Since you were raised as a princess, conserving money or time is beyond *your* grasp. I have apparently made a mistake in trusting my cousin to find a suitable replacement for my sister. Clearly, you've had little experience in the hardships of life—although I'm certain you *could* plan a shopping trip or lawn party quite nicely. You can't seem to get a grip on what is needed when it comes to working among these poor children. You've been of little use to us here." The young minister had no problem making the harsh accusations.

Bethany was shocked at his sudden attack but managed to categorize the accusations in her head.

"May I ask...for what reason do you feel justified in treating me in this manner? It's insulting and uncalled for." Bethany made the statement with as much respect as she could muster but was prepared to speak her mind.

"I need assistance and support to run this mission! I need

someone who can care for the children and direct the volunteers! Something *you've* not managed to do since your arrival!" he stated without batting an eye.

"Pastor, I have been respectful and patient with you since you are a servant of the Lord in authority over me. *However*, I will not allow you speak to me with such disrespect.

"You've not spoken a kind word or made a cooperative gesture toward me since my arrival. You've not even pretended to offer me guidance in *any* form—professionally *or spiritually*.

"I may not be an asset to this mission in many ways—but *not* from lack of trying.

"I also recall being informed of *your* background. I believe *you* were brought up in much the same lifestyle as *I* have been. Yard parties, traveling, and shopping are not beyond *your* station in life. *And* judging from the way you're directing this ministry—when it comes to the care of the children— *you, sir*, are the one who seems to exhibit the least amount of experience. The mission is *appalling* in its current state."

In response, Pastor Goodry folded his arms and gave her a cold stare.

Surprised the pastor did not retaliate, Bethany continued, "These pitiful, little children are wearing dirty clothing and eating food not fit for a dog. They cry at night and receive little attention or compassion from you or the staff. In these two areas alone, they're treated worse than most farm animals. Fed...but not acknowledged."

Bethany took a deep breath. "On occasion, you could at least show up to share a few kind words or say a prayer with them before bed. And it wouldn't hurt you to take a few minutes to compose a letter to ask for support from other churches.

"This establishment is a wonderful idea, but, as it is, the children are the ones suffering. You and I can walk away, but they can't. I have seen you hard at work...but you don't seem to have a clue as to how to *manage* this mission."

Having completed her reprimand, Bethany was pleased she had stated her mind with a calm but firm voice.

"Miss Jackson, it's amusing to listen to you proclaim your superiority, even though you've probably never been in a position of authority. What little work you do here— Well, I suppose it's better than *nothing*!" the young pastor snapped in retaliation and out of embarrassment, since he knew Bethany's summation of him was true.

This spurred Bethany on. "I *refuse* to put up with anymore of your unjust accusations. Rest assured, if I'm subjected to such treatment *again*, I will pack my belongings and leave immediately. *Then*, I will report your unqualified attempt in managing this establishment to Pastor Strong. And *he* will believe me!

"By the way, being the pastor, have you even considered letting go of your pride and allowing God to guide you in ways to make a difference? Would you rather continue running the mission ineffectively rather than to accept me as the assistant God has provided?" Bethany questioned truthfully.

"Miss Jackson, you are totally out-of-line!" With that, the young pastor turned and left the room.

Bethany was in shock as she watched the minister abruptly walk off. The exchange left her feeling even more disheartened.

She hadn't planned to express her feeling so forcefully, but he was being unfair and unreasonable.

30

CHANGE IS COMING

After their confrontation, Pastor Goodry seemed to be avoiding Bethany, and the mission routine continued as it had been. However, working at the restaurant was becoming nearly unbearable since the owner, like the pastor, seemed to take pleasure in harassing Bethany each day.Unfortunately, she was at the woman's mercy since the mission needed her salary.

Finally one day, out of frustration, she sat down on a bench at a nearby cemetery and broke into tears. Bethany just wanted to go home.

Amid the sobbing, a kind voice asked, "Goodness sakes...what are ya carrying on about? Surely somethin' as sweet lookin' as you don't have any problems that can't be fixed. Now you look up here and tell Sandra what's goin' on. Maybe I can do somethin'."

Bethany was not able to speak until the crying subsided, but finally she looked up into the beautiful, brown face. "I-I'm sorry. I didn't mean for anyone to find me acting so defeated. You must think I'm terrible for crying in a public place where I can be seen," Bethany apologized.

"Well, you *were* goin'at it. I guess I won't think too badly toward ya if it makes ya feel better. But if ya don't feel better, I suppose I'll have to think ya shameful," the lady teased. "Now tell me what the problem is."

Bethany wiped her eyes as she confessed, "I want to go home to my family. Things aren't working out at the mission. The pastor isn't happy with me, and I can't please him. I finally stood up for myself, and now he slights me. I'm supposed to manage the workers, but they ignore my instructions. I'm praying, but I haven't seen anything change for the better. I'm tired—" Bethany could say no more.

"I'm sorry ya don't feel things are working out just now. But could ya tell me what mission you're talkin' 'bout? Surely ya don't mean the one on the other side of town. I thought it was shut down."

Bethany's head popped up as she explained, "No, it's still open. I'm filling in until the full-time missionary arrives. I was convinced God wanted me here." Bethany had to stop before she burst into tears again.

"Well, I guess I have the gist of it," Sandra chuckled. "Now settle down and let's think this through."

"I shouldn't be speaking to you about the issues I'm having with the pastor. Christians are supposed to work problems out amongst themselves. And you may not even be a believer.... I'm making this worse with every word I speak, aren't I?" Bethany wiped her eyes.

"Now, now. It's fine. Sounds to me like ya *need* to be speakin' to somebody. We all have our moments. Calm down and don't worry. I'll keep it to myself. But I am a born again Christian and a devout servant," Sandra assured without a moment's hesitation.

"So, you and this preacher had words, did ya'?"

"Yes...a great many...and most of them were mine," Bethany answered in a low tone. "I spoke the truth...or at least the way I see it. The man needs help...desperately! Though I did step over my bounds. The words just flew out, and I wasn't of a mind to stop them. Still, I believe they needed to be said, but we haven't spoken since.

"You see, he is a good man from what I understand. But he's *a man*, and he doesn't have a clue about domestic things. Yet I'm sure he loves the children. I did shame him severely."

"And just how old is this preacher?" Sandra asked.

"A few years older than myself, I guess...why?" Bethany questioned.

"Oh, I think that 'bout sums it up. But never mind that. You're just worn out, and I 'spect the preacher is too. It sounds like the two of ya were dynamite sittin' by a ragin' fire." Sandra's eyes glistened with understanding. "Now just what is it ya want to change at this mission?" Sandra questioned sincerely.

"It's filthy! The place needs to be torn apart and given a good cleaning. The children need a good, daily bathing and new, clean clothing—not to mention the bedding. The food is unfit for humans. There's no consistent affection because there aren't enough dependable volunteers. The children's needs are barely met. *And* we should be trying to find loving families for the children. Not one child has been adopted since I've been here.

"It could be such a lovely place for children. Right now, we can't even improve on the basics. A few of the children are even wearing wool. They need simple, cool fabric to help them endure the heat. What I have in mind for uniforms would be easy to make and care for.

"I'm ashamed to tell you this...but I took it upon myself to do something without the pastor's permission. I wrote my mother and asked her to consider making some of the things the children need. I also sent her my ideas for making inexpensive bedding which could be easily stripped and washed. Since the pastor and I are at odds, I'm sure he wouldn't approve my ideas," Bethany confessed.

"It sounds like the pastor may be tryin' to run that mission on his own. We hafta give our problems to the Lord 'fore He can move. When a child breaks a toy, he takes it to his father to fix. But, if the child won't let go of the toy, it can't be repaired. *Then* the little one must be willin' to wait and trust until the repair is done. I've certainly had to learn *that* lesson more than once in my life."

Bethany nodded her head in agreement.

"I'll tell ya what...I'm off on Saturdays, and I'm very picky when it comes to cleanin'. Mr. and Mrs. Kenny—the people my husband and I work for—always get after me for workin' too hard, but I'm not happy unless I'm workin'.

"If you don't mind, Elmer and I will come on Saturday and dig in. And I have a bunch of friends that'll want to help too. No sense the little ones livin' that way. We may not be able to help *all* the children in this town, but we can do a little somethin' for the ones at the mission. And I'll speak to Mrs. Kenny. She'll want to help in some way. She's a good Christian woman and has an awful tender heart." Sandra's eyes were wide with excitement.

With that said, Bethany stood and gave Sandra an appreciative hug.

"And writin' your mama was just what you should've done. God may have planned to use her all along. This isn't 'bout the preacher. It's 'bout those children. You meant no disrespect to the man. He's young and just learnin'.

"You're there to do the Lord's work, and I believe He's callin' me to do somethin' too. I'll be there early mornin' with some decent food for the little ones. Now, what other thoughts do ya have on the things that need to be done?" Sandra's face was filled with enthusiasm, because she liked nothing more than a good challenge.

So the two ladies shared ideas and planned their strategy to take on the needs of the mission. Unfortunately, it was during that time when a nicely dressed couple drove away from the mission, disappointed they had missed the opportunity to speak with Bethany.

31

A DISAPPOINTING LETTER

Stew wondered why he had allowed himself to get so involved in the life of a child he had only known a few hours. Still, he *had* accepted the responsibility, and he did care.

Out of sympathy for her boss, Lillian Grey spent several breaks searching for a professional to help find Billy. After much research, she located a highly recommended attorney—Randall Stone. Lillian felt a young, eager lawyer would be more likely to take the case seriously and might not mind the legwork involved. A letter was immediately mailed to request his services.

Out of gratitude for finding the attorney, Stew made plans to take Lillian and her husband to dinner at one of Bay City's most exclusive restaurants.

The thought of dining alone with the Greys made Stew uncomfortable, so he invited Alicia Hamilton, a young woman to whom he had been introduced at church, to accompany him. The next day at the office, Lillian—realizing that Stewart was young and inexperienced with Bay City high society—warned him to beware of girls like Alicia who were known as social climbers looking for a wealthy husband. Stew currently had no desire in establishing a relationship with *any* girl, and he could not chance angering a father who might be a potential business client. He concluded that he must tread lightly when it came to young ladies.

As the weeks passed, Stewart *did* find himself bombarded with party invitations from overly forward girls who wanted to have a good time and from ladies of the social graces who were trying to acquire a wealthy husband.

Keeping his Christian convictions among society had not been difficult since the men and women of wealth were willing to tolerate almost anything if it meant bettering their social standing. It was their culture, so Stew's high morals were accepted.

Stew found many of the young, society women boring and shallow. Even the young ladies from his church seemed to know little about their faith and lived according to the world's standards. Stew could not escape making a comparison with Bethany.

He continued to delve into his work where his skills became so profitable for the firm that the board started increasing his salary and catering to him long before necessary. Because of rumors that other establishments were planning to lure Stew away, the board had felt such precautions were needed to establish his dedication to the company.

On the other hand, Stew began to notice his rising success and popularity did not set well with some of his male colleagues. To remedy the situation, he was more than happy to have a reason to attend fewer parties and spend time developing friendships at work.

He was not as happy living the big city life as he had expected.

Once Attorney Stone's reply was received, it required payment up front before he would begin working on the case. Stew, willing to do anything necessary to locate Billy, immediately complied. At last, the search for Billy could begin.

It was a good while before Stew received a letter from the attorney stating he had come across some information concerning Jake Black. Unfortunately, the sheriff had been fired for neglecting his duties and drinking on the job. Piles of important paperwork had been left undone, so each case was currently being dealt with according to the date it was received.

It might have taken months for the inquiries about Billy to be uncovered, but the wise attorney had asked the right questions and found the sheriff had not kept *any* records. That immediately ruled out the sheriff's paperwork as the main source of information.

The lawyer had started questioning people in the area and found a saloon girl who remembered hearing the sheriff and a young lady arguing over her need to leave a small boy in his care. The bartender recalled that the former deputy had found Billy's uncle dead in his home, but Stone was unable to locate the deputy. Stew was extremely disappointed by the news since it meant more waiting.

Disillusioned with city life, Stewart started looking for an estate which might appeal to him as a permanent residence. Due to the newly invented promotions and his inheritances, Stew could afford to purchase almost any home he desired.

During the search, he found himself wondering if Bethany would care for certain features in a property or location. Bethany and he always had similar tastes in such things, and it was hard to break the habit.

There was a time or two when he was ready to make an offer—only to back out at the last minute. He never seemed to know exactly why. Yet Stew continued the search and hoped he would be making the purchase before the holidays.

32

CHRISTINE

During his first months in Bay City, Stew was introduced to a young woman he found intriguing. She—as compared to Bethany—was tall, willowy and extremely fashion conscious. The one thing which set her apart from the other women of Bay City was that she and Stew seemed to share the same Christian convictions. He did give leeway in some areas; since her family was extremely wealthy, she could not *completely* escape the world's influence. Optimistically, he believed her faith would develop into a closer relationship with the Lord.

It was a beautiful fall evening when Stew turned into the driveway leading to the stately home where Christine Stanwick lived. He was not in the least intimidated by the mansion since he planned to own a comparable residence in the future.

He was met at the door by a maid dressed in black and wearing a white apron and cap. "Good evening, sir," she said politely as she curtsied.

"Good evening, my fair lady." Stew offered a kindly smile which brought light into the young maid's face. "I'm Mr. Jefferson. I'm here to call for Miss Stanwick."

"Yes, sir. Miss Stanwick is expecting you. She asked that you be seated in the parlor to our left. Please follow me." She opened the door and directed him into the room. "Please make yourself comfortable. Miss Stanwick will be with you shortly." After taking his hat, she gave another curtsy before leaving the room.

"Thank you, miss," Stew responded with a bow of his head in acknowledgement of the maid's proper care. The home was not to be rivaled by any in the area, even though the Stanwicks were not the wealthiest family of the Bay City area. Mrs. Stanwick obviously had a flair for decorating and was willing to spend her husband's money to keep the décor up to date. Judging from this home, Stew was certain the Stanwicks owned more than one estate.

The room was graced with two elaborate chandeliers, but the focal point was the enormous, gilded mirror hanging above the mantel. The furnishings were obviously the finest, and the room glimmered of gold. Stew felt as if he had entered a palace rather than a home. Many would have been honored to be invited into such a room, but Stew was not the type to be impressed by an overstatement of wealth. If the Stanwicks were willing to spend such money on only one room, he could only imagine what type of investments they had made in their only child.

To his surprise, Stew did not have time to take a seat before Miss Stanwick entered the room. "My father believes one way to judge a man's character is by his ability to meet his commitments by precise timing. You, Mr. Jefferson, have met your commitment... at least for this evening, that is," she teased to break the ice.

Christine stood demurely before Stew. He found her stunning. Her dark hair was severely pulled back to emphasize her beauty. She wore a long, black, beaded dress which was more form-fitting than most, but it accentuated her fine, slender figure in a most ladylike manner.

"Miss Stanwick, you look lovely." This was an intentional understatement. Most other men would have used the word "breathtaking", but Stew was not ready to offer extravagant praise to just any woman. In his thinking, such words should be saved for someone special.

"I have to admit I struggled with the time issue. I wanted to arrive *much* earlier in anticipation of the evening." Stew made this comment without a moment's hesitation. He could be quick with clever lines; yet he felt uncomfortable having made the statement. Stew wondered if she knew the effect her appearance had on others.

"Thank you. You look very striking yourself. One can always appreciate a compliment or two from time to time. May I offer you some refreshments before we leave?" she asked, not dwelling on the intimacy of the compliments.

"Thank you, but I believe it is in our best interest to start for the city. I hope you don't mind, but I chose to bring an open carriage. I think there's something to be said for a leisurely ride. It's unusually warm this evening."

"It sounds lovely," she answered sweetly. The maid brought her cape, and Stew placed it on Christine's shoulders before leaving the home.

"Oh, aren't the trees lovely with the sun shining on them! The first of the fiery reds with the gold...I love the gold!" Christine stated as they stepped out the door.

Several thoughts ricocheted through Stew's mind, but the thought that settled was how lovely her eyes sparkled when she said it. He was impressed.

He took her delicate hand and carefully assisted her into the carriage. Stew was surprised by how comfortable he felt with her, and, if he was not mistaken, they were already enjoying each other's company. Stew and Christine were both aware this would be only one outing in many to come, and it pleased them both.

He gave the reins a light snap and off they went to enjoy a delightful evening together.

"You don't strike me as the type of girl who would enjoy riding in an open carriage," Stew commented to get the conversation going.

"Well, if that's the case...Mr. Jefferson...why did you bring one?" she asked to force him to come up with an answer to the witty question.

"I suppose to find out if you *were* the type of girl who would enjoy a ride in an open carriage," he quickly came back.

"Very clever of you. Naughty, perhaps...but clever," Christine answered with a sly smile. "And does this evening promise to be a battle of wits?"

"I guess it remains to be seen. But I am a bit worried I may have met my match." He thought it might be wise to soften his last statement a bit.

"I may strike you as being fragile, but what you must consider is...I *am* my father's daughter, and just in case you haven't heard... *he* is a tough old bird," Christine returned with a mischievous air.

"I see. Then I believe I'm glad your father *is* away on business."

Stew gave a playful smile, ready to move on to another subject. Then the two laughed and tossed light conversation back and forth until they arrived at their destination.

The restaurant of choice was The Bay View Inn, which was Stew's favorite for fine dining. The room offered seclusion for private conversation, and tonight the lights were low—and Christine was beautiful.

As Stew escorted Christine to the table he had reserved earlier in the week, every available head turned to view them as they passed. It was easy to hear the whispers referring to Christine's extreme beauty and the remarks which indicated they made a striking couple. The analysis pleased him.

Stew could not help but imagine how wonderful it would be to go through life with this magnificent woman as his companion. She was like a ship easily parting the ocean water, unaware of the turmoil created by its wake.

Even after Stew and Christine were seated in a very private corner, others seemed determined to try to catch a glimpse of them. Stew could not help feeling proud of being the man accompanying her.

They carried on pleasant conversation, and her laugh was like the gentle tinkling of chimes. She was dazzling. Stew could not keep his eyes off her, so he did not expect anyone else to be able to do so. As far as he was concerned, her beauty could only be surpassed by one other.

After dinner they went to the theater where Christine created yet another stir. Stewart proudly escorted Christine with her hand placed gracefully within his arm and his masculine hand laying protectively over it. He was pleased to find they were already on a first name basis.

"The play was outstanding. Don't you agree?" Christine's eyes lit up as she waited for Stew's reaction. "I wouldn't know...I was looking at you," he spoke softly. It was a line, but he meant to be sincere—yet he wished he had not said it.

"You know I've heard that line before," she stated.

Stew shrewdly defended himself. "That doesn't come as a surprise to me. I can't speak for the other gentlemen—but as for me, the statement was meant as a true compliment."

"Very impressive, but I do believe you've spoken those words before. Am I correct? Don't fib. I can see it in your eyes," she sweetly interrogated to draw it out of him.

Stew's face darkened. He understood that the feeling of betrayal toward Bethany was evident and had spoiled the mood. "Yes, I guess you're right. I *have* spoken those words before when I meant them. But that was *then* and this is *now*." He felt Christine might as well know there was nothing more to discuss.

"I see. I didn't mean to dredge up sad memories, but you must understand that I do not want to become involved in a relationship where I am not first priority."

"A man would be a fool to—" Stew started to answer but stopped, "I tell you what...I agree with and respect your position... and I have no such ties. So, let's move to another subject before I make the mistake of using another line you've heard before." He wisely brought the conversation to an end, not wanting to do anything else which might spoil the evening.

Amazingly though, they were able to go on as if the touchy subject had never happened. Being with her made Stew realize that—having been denied a future with Bethany—he might as well yield to Christine's charm.

The carriage ride home was all too short, and neither wanted the night to end. After making plans for another outing, Stew left her with a tender kiss on her lovely hand. To him it appeared to be a wonderful, new beginning.

33

AN UNEXPECTED BLESSING

When Bethany arrived at the restaurant, the boss met her at the door with a list of demands. Again, the woman had no problem expecting her to wash the dishes and do the cooking for the afternoon crowd—without an increase in pay. It was the third day in a row the fulltime cook had not shown up for work, and the owner was determined to force Bethany to fill the gap.

"Mrs. Haskell, I've filled in for the cook and washed the dishes for the last two days, and you've refused to pay me the correct salary. If I'm expected to do both jobs, then I must insist on the cook's and dishwasher's salaries. You're aware I have other demands when I leave here. The additional work makes it difficult to fulfill those duties." Bethany tried to be diplomatic but meant business.

According to the customers' reactions, it was obvious Bethany was a fairly good cook, and the restaurant could profit greatly if she was promoted. Bethany knew her cooking skills were acceptable since she had spent many hours in the kitchen learning from Mary. Not only had she enjoyed it, but her mother had insisted she learn.

Nonetheless, Mrs. Haskell was a greedy woman, and, being aware of the mission's financial situation, she thought Bethany could be intimidated into doing both jobs for the dishwasher's pay. "Yer the dishwasher! I told ya when ya hired on that you might have to fill in here or there! You'll either cook for the same pay or hit the road. Ya kin be replaced easy an'uff! "

"Very well then. You may pay me for the last two days," Bethany answered with determination in her eyes.

Mrs. Haskell pulled a roll of cash from her apron pocket and planted two day's wages in her hand. Bethany removed her apron and promptly walked out the door without another word. The owner followed her through the door shouting threats and accusations in hopes of bullying her into returning, but Bethany kept walking.

A few blocks later, Bethany realized what she had just done on an emotional whim. She had hoped taking a stand would have worked on Mrs. Haskell—as much as Mrs. Haskell had hoped *her* bluff would have worked on Bethany. She ached to run back to the restaurant and beg for the job, but it was too late; the despicable woman would only revel in turning her down.

Bethany stepped into an alley and leaned against a building for a few minutes to regain her composure, but she refused to despair. The best and only thing she could do was to keep the needs of the mission before the Lord in prayer. There was nothing to be done at this point, so she started back to the orphanage while deep in thought.

Trying to support the mission with two meager salaries and a few donations was man's way of providing; it was a lack of faith in God's provision by the pastor. While they slaved away trying to make ends meet, the children suffered with most of their needs not being met, and she hated being part of it.

The pastor and she could never successfully manage the ministry unless the Holy Spirit was leading them. Unfortunately, they had never had a civil conversation—much less prayed for the welfare of the mission together.

She was walking slowly on the boardwalk in front of the last few shops when Lena burst through the front door of the mercantile and blocked her path. "Bethany! I'm so glad I caught you! Burt and I came to visit you at the mission yesterday. Did you get the message?"

"Why, no!" Bethany was flabbergasted by Lena's unexpected appearance and in finding out they had been to the mission. "Was there something you needed?"

"Yes! *You!* I have an offer I'd like you to consider!" Lena was so excited she could barely catch her breath. "I've always felt sorry there were no seamstress jobs available for you. But a few days ago, it hit me! I've considered opening a dress shop for years. I never have because I was afraid it might interfere with the mercantile. But when I mentioned the shop to Burt, he thought it was a wonderful idea and felt he could manage the store on his own. Burt believes a dress shop could be a very profitable business and a blessing to the town.

"So...would you be interested in coming to work for me as a seamstress? We'd start out with sewing readymade dresses for the rack and do alterations, but in time, I'd like for us to start designing.

"Doesn't it sound like fun? We can set our own hours. Do you think you might be interested?" Lena did not intend to pressure Bethany, but she could not keep from asking again.

"Seriously? You want me to work for you as a seamstress?

How wonderful! Well, yes! I'm very interested as long as we can work out the details and time involved. Although...I may not be here much longer.

"Have you considered there must be several, experienced dressmakers in town who'd love to work for you?" Bethany wanted to be fair to Lena but was honored to be asked.

"I want *you*, Bethany Jackson, so don't concern yourself! I've given it a lot of thought.

"That first day when you came in the store and mentioned you'd like a seamstress position, I just couldn't get it out of my head. It breaks my heart to watch you pass on your way to Haskell's restaurant every day. It's no secret that it's a horrible place to work.

"We've already started working on the shop. So come inside and let me show you what I have in mind." Lena led her through the mercantile to the adjoining shop.

Bethany followed Lena like an excited pup. She was certain the offer was an answer to prayer.

"Right in here," Lena said as she opened the door and began going over the plans. "This room has been used as storage for years, but we've already moved the stock upstairs. Burt is going to install a door for the ladies to enter from the walkway. It will be much more convenient than walking through the mercantile.

"He's already started building dressing rooms, and I've ordered dressing screens to use for fittings. Then there is painting and papering. You get the idea. We could be ready to open in a couple of weeks, if not sooner. Do you think I could persuade you to give up the dishwashing job and start sewing? I have several dresses ready to be cut out. I hate to ask you to quit so suddenly, but we'll need dresses on the rack when we open." Lena was ready to bargain. "I'll pay you after each dress is completed."

"Wait, Lena. I need to explain something before you go any further."

Lena looked a little apprehensive as she waited for Bethany's explanation.

"You see, I just left...I mean...I just walked out on my job at Haskell's. So, it's not a very good recommendation for someone you're thinking of hiring. It was very irresponsible of me," Bethany explained honestly.

"You don't say!" Lena said, taking a breath of relief.

"I've never believed it was God's best for me to work there," Bethany added.

"That's wonderful news! We've been worried about your health." Lena yelled to her husband in the mercantile, "Burt! Bethany has quit the dishwashing job!"

"Praise the Lord! It's about time! So, young lady, can I assume you'll be working for my wife?" Burt called back.

"Yes! I believe you can count on it!" Bethany returned. Then she and Lena grabbed each other and hugged as if they had been close friends for years.

"Come over here behind the counter. I need your opinion on the curtains. We had better give some thought to seating too. Regular chairs can be so uncomfortable. Don't you agree? I have some thoughts for the name of the store too!" Lena rambled on in lighthearted excitement.

34

TAKING CHARGE

Bethany had another sleepless night, but this was the first time she was happy to wake up since she had been at the mission. It was Saturday and Sandra had promised to be at the orphanage early. As she hurried to dress, the words from the note found tacked on her door yesterday came to mind.

The note was to inform her that the pastor had been unexpectedly called out of town due to a death in the family. He offered no further details but requested Bethany take charge of the mission until his return. The key to the money box was also included in the envelope. While Bethany was deeply sorry for the man's loss, his absence would certainly make overhauling the mission much easier.

About then there was a tap on the door, and one of the volunteers told Bethany a large crate had just been delivered. He handed her the letter which came with it. The letter explained that The Ladies' Aid Societies of Faith Chapel, Pine Creek, and Longley had voted to assist Mrs. Jackson in supplying the orphanage with the *entire* list of items Bethany had wanted.

Bethany was shocked. It would have taken Helen Jackson months to complete the work, but it had only taken a few weeks with the women from the three churches working together. Evidently, the groups viewed the work as the most worthwhile project they had ever attempted.

Unfortunately, she needed to hurry over to the dining hall and did not have time to finish the letter. She arrived just as the cook was lighting the kitchen stove.

"Good morning! I'm glad I caught you before you started breakfast!" Bethany sounded as lighthearted as she felt. Fairly certain the cook had been informed of the pastor's departure, Bethany wasted no time in giving Aggie an option.

"In the pastor's absence, I've decided on a few changes to make the orphanage run more smoothly. Today is as good as any to get started, so I have a surprise for you! You may take the day off...or... spend the day helping watch the children. The choice is up to you. Which would you like to do?" The offer was made in a way to let the woman understand Bethany was taking charge. Aggie and the rest of the staff had been allowed to ignore all of her instructions in the past, but *things were about to change*.

At first the woman looked offended, but then her stooped back seemed to straighten a little. "I don't mind if I'm ta haves the day off. I love dem kids...but I'm terrible worn out."

Bethany was relieved to hear Aggie agree to a day off. This way the old cook would not be hurt when Sandra showed up with the well-prepared meals she had promised to bring for the children. It worked out fine with Aggie leaving only a few minutes before Sandra walked in with several fully loaded baskets and an *army* of friends prepared to work.

Sandra only took a moment for a quick introduction before

instructing several of the ladies to attend to the little ones and take their time in getting the children ready for breakfast. Then she began pulling supplies from the baskets while shaking her head and carrying on about the filthy kitchen and dining room. "This is no fit place for roaches, much less little children! My...my, those poor little things! It sure will take a lot of scrubbin'. It surely will. It's too far gone for one or two people to take on. My goodness!! Ya did the right thing, little Miss Bethy. Ya sure did do the right thing tellin' me. The Lord's hand is in this. It surely is."

Bethany loved to listen to Sandra carry on. She knew how to put things in perspective. Sandra did not mean to be critical, but she was an extremely clean person who loved caring for others.

Before Sandra started the final preparations of the meal, she ordered four huge pots of water to be put on the stove to heat so they would be ready for cleaning when breakfast was over. She then put Bethany and some others to work scrubbing the tables and benches from top to bottom with strict orders not to stop until they shined.

Next Sandra gave the kitchen counter and serving table a good scouring. She made certain all the cleaning was being done to her satisfaction.

"Their breakfast might be considerable late this mornin' but at least they won't be eatin' it atop of filth. Nothin' but filth...just the plain and simple truth! That's all!" Sandra continued to carry on.

It was after eight o'clock before the orphans were led into the dining hall for the long awaited meal. Bethany barely recognized the children since they had been scrubbed from head to toe and given proper haircuts.

To her surprise, the crate had already been opened, and each child wore clean, new clothing.

The boys wore short pants with pullover shirts, and the girls wore longer pullover shirt-type dresses. Each child had a special appliqué, such as a horse or a dog assigned to their clothing with their name embroidered above it. The appliqués would make it easier for the younger children to recognize their belongings. Everything was made out of cool, durable fabric.

Each little face brightened when they saw the appetizing food awaiting them. All of the workers were delighted in seeing the little neglected ones treated to the pleasure of a full and satisfied tummy.

Once the children had their fill, there was a short devotional, and then they were taken for a long walk.

Sandra and some ladies started scrubbing the kitchen and dining hall while Bethany and several women went to the bedrooms to start tearing out the sleeping areas. Most of the furniture and supplies were taken to a discard pile to be burned. Then by using Sandra's famous cleaning solution in buckets of hot water, the ladies scrubbed the walls and floors until they were clean and fresh smelling. Later, the walls were given a coat of whitewash to help brighten the rooms.

A few of the men fitted screens in the windows and repaired the broken shutters on the outside of the building. Then pretty curtains were hung and pictures were put on the walls to give the room a homey feeling.

When they had finished cleaning, Sandra's husband, Elmer, and a crew of men brought in bed frames they had made from scraps of donated lumber. Next large pillowcase type sheets were put onto new, straw mattresses to complete the beds. This way each child's bedding could be easily stripped and replaced on a regular basis or when necessary. Elmer had painted two old pigeonhole cabinets to give the children a place to store their belongings. Bethany was amazed by Elmer's genius and hard work. When the men were done there, they went outside to work.

The other ladies moved on to the next area to be cleaned while Bethany put a nightshirt, towel, washcloth, comb, cup and toothbrush in each child's section. In the bottom of the crate, she found a rag doll for every girl and a bear for every boy. They were only sewn in the basic shape of a doll or bear, but they were cuddly and had a few features embroidered on them. One of the workers painted each child's emblem and name on the pigeonholes so the children would know which one was theirs.

By the time Bethany was finished in the bedroom, all the little ones had a new top sheet, knotted quilt, and feather pillow. Before moving on to another project, she breathed in the freshness of the room and pondered the effects the cleanliness would have on the children.

Bethany was surprised by what the group of ladies had accomplished downstairs. Everything in the kitchen area had been pulled out and was polished to a spit shine. Sandra had inspected every item from top to bottom before it was put back in place. Unfit food supplies, a broken table, a worthless cabinet, and a set of shelves were removed, making the kitchen more spacious. Cooking pots and utensils were hung attractively and conveniently.

Once the work in the kitchen and dining area was done, Bethany paired the children with the adults to share lunch. The orphans freely accepted the special attention, and Sandra's delicious chicken salad sandwiches, cubes of watermelon, and sugar cookies were a heavenly treat for the orphans and the hardworking adults.

Immediately after lunch, the children were taken outside to play. Since they were too excited to sleep, all the children, except for Baby Betsy, were excused from their naps.

Elmer sent a few of the men outside to build a simple frame with a tin roof on the side of the mission where the children most often played. The structure would allow shade from the blistering sun on extremely hot days.

He then took Bethany to the pump to show her how to use the new trough to fill the wash tubs for bathing the children and doing the laundry outside. The trough was long and forked so two tubs could be filled at the same time.

Elmer and his friends also had used junk parts to mount tubs on wagons so the tubs could be pulled away from the yard and easily dumped. He had even made oval curtain frames above the tubs. The curtain encircled beyond the tub to give the children enough room and privacy to bathe and dress. The entire setup would make bathing and wash days much easier during the many hot months. Sandra was extremely proud of the huge, thick dressing curtains she and her friends had designed.

Later in the day, one of the volunteers noticed there was a stream a short distance from the mission. The stream had an area where it pooled, and as long as they were careful, he felt it would be a safe place for the children to play in the water. Bethany was thrilled by the possibility. Other than the well, fresh water of any type was scarce.

The men stayed outside to burn the discard pile and pick up the junk strewn throughout the mission lot. The women decided it was time to clean the minister's sleeping quarters and office.

The pastor was very neat and organized, so his belongings were easily removed and the area was given a good scrubbing. Fortunately, screens and shutters were already in place. The women quickly whitewashed the walls, put up new curtains, and replaced the old tattered bedding. A few pieces of useless furnishings were taken to the burn pile, and the rest were repositioned in a more accessible and comfortable arrangement.

Bethany brought the children inside for games while Sandra and a few ladies fixed the evening meal. A small team of men pulled weeds and finished up the yard work. The rest of the workers cleaned and whitewashed the foyer, main receiving room, halls, and closets. The ornate, antique furnishings were then returned to their original locations.

Sandra rang the bell for the evening meal of fried chicken, mashed potatoes, green beans and chocolate cake. Squeals of delight came from every child.

Once the orphans had their fill, the ladies used washcloths to remove the dirt from their busy day and refresh them for a good night's rest. Then each child was surprised with their new night shirt and cuddly toy. Afterward, they were tucked into beds and given a warm hug. Sandra was asked to offer a goodnight prayer in celebration. Bedtime stories were told by volunteers who watched over the children until the sweet lady with the wrinkly face came to take the night watch. She, too, was surprised with a nice, new chair and cot.

Earlier that morning the mission had almost seemed too rundown and dirty to be brought back to life. Yet God had used only *one* woman to gather a team of workers who were willing to put forth the time and effort to convert the unfit orphanage into a clean and safe home.

Many of the town's residents had thought the mission was no longer useful, but it had been easily revived for the Lord's work. God's love would continue to go out from the mission to comfort the needy—whether in body or spirit—for many years to come. All who had taken part in the restoration were blessed by the opportunity.

35

UNEXPECTED

Over two weeks had passed since Sandra and the volunteers had taken on the project of cleaning and repairing the mission. Everyone was pleased by how well the orphanage was operating with Bethany as acting director.

Bethany was content with her work as a seamstress and had already completed several simple dresses. Sewing was much more fulfilling than standing over hot dishwater for several hours a day.

When Lena saw the output and quality of Bethany's work, she had more sewing material delivered to the mission. A respectable salary and a note were attached to the dry goods to encourage Bethany and compliment her talent. Lena was certain the dresses would sell within a few days, and she expected requests for designing original dresses would begin soon.

The children still were not accustomed to having healthy, good tasting food on a regular basis, so each meal was like a surprise party for them. It was a blessing to see the children wearing smiles and engaging in conversation at the dinner table.

"Miss Bethany," Sandra paged, "I'm growin' more and more worried about Baby Betsy. She just doesn't seem to be perkin' up like she should, even though she's bein' fed proper. I'm half a notion to take her home to Mrs. Kenny and see what the two of us can do for her. That is, if you'd allow it?

"We'd be awful careful with her, and I just know Mrs. Kenny would be all a jitter to have her there. We've never had a little one around," Sandra explained, hoping to convince Bethany the request was just out of concern for the baby's welfare.

"Oh? Are you saying the infant isn't thriving as well as she could be? Perhaps I should send for a doctor instead?" Bethany could not help quizzing Sandra for the fun of it.

"Oh, I don't believe she's hardly that bad off, as far as I can tell, but it wouldn't do the babe any harm to have some care all to her own. With two of us to coddle her and then Mr. Kenny home in the evenings—I'm thinking she'll perk up in no time!" Sandra smiled slyly when she realized Bethany could see through her plot to entice Mr. and Mrs. Kenny into adopting the baby.

"I can see what you're thinking, and I'm concerned Pete is spending too much time caring for her. He's only a small boy, but he hovers over the baby as if he were her father. He really does need to have more interaction with the other children. I hate to separate the two, but I think it might be best for both of them," Bethany analyzed.

"And since I was left in charge with no instructions as to what power I have in making such decisions, then...yes. I think it's a wonderful idea. By all means, take her home to Mrs. Kenny for a few days." Bethany was more than happy to agree with Sandra's little scheme and thought it quite ingenious.

Sandra quickly packed up Betsy and toted her off to Mrs. Kenny. Bethany giggled as Sandra began entertaining the baby with a medley of songs before she even left the building.

Once they were gone, Bethany hurried off to the kitchen to help with dinner but was taken by surprise when she was forced to step aside to allow two men to pass by. It took a few seconds before she realized one of the men was Pastor Goodry. She was glad to see the men were too engrossed in a conversation to notice her.

Bethany, being caught off guard, felt a surge of anxiety since she was unprepared to be taken to task for the extensive and unauthorized modifications within the orphanage. However, she was proud of the changes and planned to be respectful—but unapologetic—to the pastor if the need to defend the changes arose.

After all, the pastor had accused her of being incompetent and useless. Just recalling the harsh accusations made her cheeks flush. Even though it was her Christian duty to forgive, forgetting was not as easily done. Still, she hoped the pastor would approve. Bethany breathed a prayer, asking God to handle the inevitable confrontation, and decided not to worry about the pastor's reaction.

The dinner bell rang, and the thoughts vanished as she arranged the food for serving. It was a pleasure to bring out the huge bowls of vegetables, plates of roast beef, and trays of baked potatoes. Bread and butter were also placed on the table with pudding for desert. The meal had been lovingly prepared by two new volunteers brought in by Sandra. The children's eyes gleamed with excitement when they saw another tasty meal waiting for them.

Once everyone was seated, Bethany noticed Pastor Goodry and the distinguished looking gentleman had returned to the dining hall and were starting through the food line. From that moment on,

Bethany would not allow her eyes to drift in the pastor's direction.

When it came time for the evening devotional, Bethany made a point of sitting among the volunteers instead of upfront with the children. Immediately after service, she gathered her assigned group and hurried them off to get ready for bed. She was thankful it was her night to help with bedroom duty.

Hoping the pastor would retire before she was done, Bethany turned each chore into an unnecessarily long task. She was not prepared to deal with him tonight and prayed she would not be required to do so.

Regrettably, a note was handed to Bethany by the dear, wrinkly lady who still took the night watch. Bethany unfolded the paper and moved closer to a lantern. As she suspected, the message was from Pastor Goodry, requesting her to come to his office as soon as possible.

Bethany could do nothing to avoid the meeting with him, so she gave the older woman a polite nod of acknowledgement and left immediately in reluctant obedience.

Each step echoed in her ears to match and magnify the pounding in her heart. She knew his door would be open, so she could not stop outside to catch her breath and gather her nerve.

It was obvious by the light shining into the hallway that the pastor's lamp was turned up high, so eye contact would have to be maintained—no matter how uncomfortable the encounter was. She breathed another prayer for the Lord's leading and entered the room.

Up until that moment, Bethany had not allowed herself to imagine what the pastor's reaction would be concerning the changes in the mission. Regrettably, as soon as their eyes met, she suddenly became breathless.

While trying to conceal that she was gasping for one tiny breath after another, Bethany took into account how young the pastor looked and thought his hair was a bit mussed. It was also the first time she had even considered how handsome he was. She assumed a few home cooked meals must have put some meat on his bones and color in his cheeks. Then she wondered why she even cared about his appearance.

At that moment, Pastor Goodry looked up from the stack of paperwork and spoke, "Miss Jackson, I'm sorry. I didn't hear you come in, but I'm glad you could meet with me. Please have a seat. I sent a note to ask you to stop by my office since it seemed you weren't aware I'd return." He wanted her to know he had noticed she was intentionally ignoring him.

"I wasn't informed of your expected return or of your arrival," Bethany replied. She did not like his insinuation—even though it was true.

"Well, the acknowledgement would have been appreciated just the same."

His remark did make her feel ashamed of the way she had acted toward him.

"But you're right. It's just that I had a chance to save some money by riding with a friend partway. I came the rest of the way by train, and I *did* have trouble finding a ride from the station. There wasn't an opportunity to get a message out. I'm sorry if it was an inconvenience."

"It may have slipped your mind, but I *do* recall how difficult it is to find transportation from the station. However, your arrival wasn't necessarily an inconvenience, just unexpected." Bethany's reply was very stiff, and she had intentionally used the opportunity to chastise him for not providing transportation for her the night she arrived at the mission.

"Well, judging from the condition of the mission, I see you've managed quite well in my absence."

Bethany did not know what he meant by the statement, so she just stared at him and waited.

"I would like to compliment you on what you've accomplished in such a short time. I was totally taken by surprise, and I must admit I was praised for the way the establishment is being managed. The observation came from the gentleman you saw me with earlier. He caught up with me at the door as I was returning from my trip.

"Anyway...to be perfectly honest, I owe you a humble apology, and I would like to explain my previous behavior to you...if you will allow it...please."

Bethany could tell the request was sincere, and to be honest, she was almost sorry it was.

"Of course," she relented. But her short answer was to let him understand she was not ready to let down her guard.

"First of all, I want to explain that I had every intention of apologizing to you *before* I was called away."

To her surprise, she found Pastor Goodry did have a very disarming way.

"I would have asked for your forgiveness for the way I spoke to you and for the undeserved accusations. To be perfectly honest, I didn't mean a word of it.

"What I should admit to you is...everything I accused you of... was what I *actually* felt about myself. Believe me, I'm perfectly aware I have completely botched the job of running this place."

Bethany sat motionless and offered no reaction to his comments.

"You see, when my sister and I first arrived we'd planned to get the place cleaned up before taking in children, but there wasn't time. Children started appearing almost immediately. Then, when we were barely getting the place up and running, Janet's fiancée showed up and talked her into returning home to be married. She was in charge of the decisions with the children and running the home. I didn't have a clue how to take care of children or run the place, and I'd already taken a job to bring in money to support us. Most of my extra time had to be spent on preparing weekly church services and doing visitations. I had planned to gradually learn how to care for the children, but, when Janet just up and left, it was all dumped in my lap. And to make things even worse, several of the volunteers left when she did.

"I'd only had one assignment after seminary, and it was in a very small church. While there, I was asked to consider starting the mission. I'd never worked with children in any capacity, but I believed it was the Lord's calling. After all, I was told I'd be working with a missionary who was well-trained in this type of work. A few days before I was scheduled to arrive, I was informed the missionary's mother had taken ill and she wouldn't be free to come for some time. That's when Janet agreed to help out. You're aware of the rest of the story.

"Things deteriorated so fast after Janet left that I just couldn't keep up. I had to contact my cousin, and I expected him to send an older woman. I assumed it would be someone who had been a mother or at least had some experience in managing children. So when I saw how young you were— Well...I became even more frustrated and angry, and I convinced myself you were a spoiled, lazy, rich girl.

"Still, even before you came here, I was second guessing my calling. With everything falling apart...I don't know...I just wanted to blame someone besides myself.

"Please believe me. I'm truly sorry. Can you forgive me for the way I've acted toward you *and* for leaving you here to run the mission alone?"

Bethany still gave no response.

"When I left I just wanted out, and I was glad to go. I didn't want to think about this place or even return.

"Please understand, when I first arrived...I prayed...and I worked...and at the start I had faith. But week after week nothing changed. By the time you arrived, I felt like the doors of heaven were closed. There seemed to be no answer."

Bethany was surprised by his words and still had no answer. She opened her mouth but could not speak.

Pastor Goodry nervously continued, "I left you here...a young, defenseless woman...and not a strong woman at that."

Suddenly, Bethany—recalling everything she had endured—stood to her feet to defend herself. *But* instead of speaking out in her the typical, clear-thinking, intelligent way, she sputtered in childish indignation, "I *am* strong! I'm *very...very* strong!" As soon as the words were out, Bethany knew how foolish her reaction sounded.

The blundered statement and the wildness in her eyes were too much for the road-weary minister.

At first, a faint smile came to his lips; then his shoulders began to shake ever so slightly. He could not contain the buildup and burst out in laughter. For the first time, Pastor Goodry found Bethany's reaction adorable and refreshing.

Bethany remained standing in utter disgust and drew a deep breath ready to speak her mind. She placed her hands on her hips for effect with every intention of reprimanding him again. "Well, I...if...you..."

Finally realizing how silly she must look and sound, her stern face gave way, and she had no choice but to laugh along with the pastor.

It was a liberating breakthrough for Bethany—for Pastor Goodry—and for the mission. As it turned out, the two talked well into the night as Bethany explained how God had moved within the mission during his absence.

36

GETTING TO KNOW HER

I was in love with the man you portrayed yourself to be! I don't love you, Stew! The haunting thoughts had caused Stew another restlessness night, and he was glad when a loud knock roused him.

He jumped to his feet, grabbed his trousers, and got to the door just in time to catch the young man with a telegram. The message was from a retired member of his company informing Stew of an estate that had just come on the market. Being intrigued with the short description of the place, he immediately made arrangements to see it that afternoon.

When the time came, Stew had his horse brought over and hurried out of town, eager to explore another road he had never traveled. The route was fascinating with twists and turns over rolling hills. The surrounding acreage was covered with huge blue spruce, spotted white sycamores, strong oaks, and an abundance of shaggy pines, creating a pleasant ride during any month of the year. Yet the scenic route did not compare to the lane that led to the impressive home.

Huge weeping willows swayed and swished as he passed. Even though the leaves were gone, he was impressed. The newly built, stone mansion was the perfect structure for the landscape. *It's just the way we'd envisioned.* Stew was unaware he had included Bethany in his evaluation of the place.

Stew was met by a thin, but friendly, middle-aged man who explained why the home was on the market and had never been occupied. It seemed, several years earlier, the original home had been destroyed by fire after falling into disrepair. A wealthy, older couple had purchased the estate and had built the home as one of their retreats. However, before it was completed, the elderly man's health failed, and they could no longer travel from place to place. Making a profit was not the issue; the owners just wanted it taken off their hands.

The estate was within Stewart's price range, so he signed the contract to purchase it before leaving. The deal was finalized within a few days. He was more than ready to begin making plans to move but decided it would be best to wait until sometime after the holidays.

Christine was away when the transaction took place, and, by the time she returned, Stew could not seem to find the right time to mention it to her—although he did not know why.

Stew received a letter from Randall Stone stating he had come across a shopkeeper who had overheard a conversation which might help locate Billy.

The man recalled overhearing the former sheriff arguing with the deputy about taking a boy to an orphanage. Although he could not pinpoint the exact date of the incident, he was fairly certain it would have been around the time Billy had disappeared. The lawyer felt the situation was worth exploring.

Stew's job became more demanding as each day passed, but the long hours seemed worth it when a complaint was solved in a way that spared the company's reputation and ended with the customer being satisfied. Since his arrival in Bay City, he had made great strides in reconstructing the image of the business by using a friendly, honest approach. Stew's name appeared in many news articles within business and social columns.

Christine and her parents were very impressed with Stewart's accomplishments, which meant the young executive was a welcomed and frequent guest in the Stanwicks' home. Of course, it was to his liking since he thought highly of their daughter.

Matrimony was becoming a pleasing thought to Christine and her parents.

Stew could not have envisioned a more extravagant Thanksgiving than the one he shared at the Stanwicks' home. Considering the guests in attendance, it seemed more like a large dinner party. Seated around an enormous and elegantly decorated table were a few local and out of town family members, the reverend and family, several wealthy friends, and various business acquaintances.

Prayer was offered by the reverend, and then a turkey was placed in front of Mr. Stanwick for the traditional carving ceremony. Once the carving was completed, joyful clapping rang out to note the occasion. This also signaled the parade of servants to enter with the multiple dinner courses which included several other choices of meats.

The conversation and festivities were to continue late into the night since many of the guests were spending the rest of the holiday with the Stanwicks. The Thanksgiving dinner was one of the most interesting Stew had ever had the privilege of attending.

"Are your Thanksgiving dinners always so extravagant?" Stew asked Christine as they took a short walk just before he left. "It was quite remarkable, and thank you for the hospitality. I was even introduced to a couple of new games I don't own. That surprised me a little."

"My parents fancy themselves as being connoisseurs of entertainment, so no stone is left unturned when it comes to finding the most current games. They find many of them when they travel."

"I see. Well, I do travel occasionally, but I've never thought to include games among my purchases. I'll add them to the list." Stew could barely complete the statement as he looked into Christine's beautiful, dark eyes.

Christine then tucked her hand into his arm and leaned her head on his shoulder while they strolled the grounds. After they walked for quite a while, he noticed her shivering, so he gave her his jacket and escorted her directly to the front door. "I'm sorry I was so thoughtless in keeping you out so long. I should leave. You need to go inside—although I will be thinking of you until our next time together." With that, he hugged her warmly and gently kissed her on the forehead.

Christine had expected to be swept into his arms and kissed passionately, so the conservative kiss was a terrible disappointment which left her feeling romantically cheated.

Stew, on the other hand, felt it respectfully proper not to rush their relationship.

Two weeks later Stew sat tapping his fingers on his desk, contemplating what might be the perfect gift for Christine on their first Christmas together. About then Lillian entered his office with some paperwork for signing.

Stew stopped the tapping to sign and then inquired, "Lillian, I wonder if you might be able to help me?"

"Certainly, I'll be glad to help if I can."

"I don't know if I've mentioned it before, but I've been seeing someone. And with Christmas coming up, I don't know what to buy for her. I'm not sure what's appropriate at this stage of the relationship." Stew felt foolish asking his secretary, but he was stumped and had no one else to advise him.

"I see. Would you mind if I ask a few questions?" The secretary took pleasure in his embarrassment.

"Well, I guess that would be necessary," he answered, knowing he was at her mercy.

"Does this young lady come from money and is she stylish? Is she spoiled? Does she seem to care about others? I'm sorry to be so direct, but those traits do make a difference in what you should select as a gift," Lillian explained.

"I understand completely. I guess the answers are...yes, she comes from money ... yes, she is stylish and spoiled...but I feel she *is* caring. She's well educated, and we share similar Christian beliefs. In addition, she is tall and beautiful." Stew could not help bragging.

"Is the young lady Christine Stanwick, perhaps?" the secretary questioned with a knowing smile.

"Why, yes! How did you know?" Stew was astonished by her guess.

"Mr. Jefferson, I *am* your secretary. It's my business to keep on top of your affairs. I do read the newspapers, you know." She then gave him a rather sheepish look. "Besides, many of the girls who work here are jealous over the fact that Miss Stanwick is the only woman keeping your attention. So I have to admit...office gossip was my main source of information."

Stew just rolled his eyes and gave a little laugh, "I don't doubt your sources, so you're in the clear. But as for Bethany...Christine, that is...I find her lovely and highly intelligent.

Lillian tried to act as if she did not notice the mistake in names.

"So what's the answer, miss executive secretary...on top of my affairs?" Stew loved to see Lillian scrunch her face when a problem needed to be solved.

"Well, how serious is this relationship? Might the lady be expecting a ring?" Lillian asked guardedly.

"Hardly, Lillian! Nothing of the sort! We haven't been seeing each other *that* long." Stew did not mean to protest so strongly at the suggestion.

"Are you certain she isn't?" Lillian felt he should give the situation some serious thought.

"Yes!" He was not about to consider the suggestion.

"If you say so." Lillian ignored the outburst. "Well then, have you considered jewelry? I'm afraid it would have to be very expensive. It's what she's accustomed to wearing. I'm not certain, but I believe more than one gift might be expected in such circles."

"I don't mind the expense. My concern is determining what's appropriate. Of course, I'd like the gift to be something special." The discussion was becoming more uncomfortable for Stew.

"What about mink? Maybe in a hooded cape and muff? It would have to be completely lovely and impractical. Most likely she already has at least one mink of sorts...if not several." Lillian's face crinkled again with the suggestion.

"Alright. I'll keep it in mind in case I get desperate. What type of jewelry?"

"I'm afraid you must be careful in your choice there. All women have their own taste in jewelry. Have you noticed if she wears any particular style?" Lillian's attitude had grown more serious by this time.

"Yes. It's always large. Christine is a tall, gorgeous woman. She can easily carry off large and extravagantly designed pieces," Stew boasted.

"Then I suggest the gems you choose for Miss Stanwick should be large, colorful, and include diamonds. The piece must be elegant and have a romantic appeal. It would have to be at least a large pendant with matching earrings...maybe even a bracelet. If you want to go a little farther, a musical jewelry box might be a nice touch. I've seen several well-to-do women admiring them when I pass the jewelers. Maybe consider giving the gift in a romantic setting. It might make the holiday seem more special. You're a very creative thinker, sir. I'm certain you can come up with something."

"That's it! I have a plan! You've been a tremendous help. Thank you."

Stew was so excited about the ideas that he gave the secretary a bear hug and a big kiss on the top of her head. He did not realize the kiss was much bigger than any he had given Christine. After releasing Lillian, he grabbed his coat, donned his hat, and walked out the door completely unaware he was leaving work two hours early—although, there was not an executive in the building who would have questioned Stew's early departure—not even his boss.

As he took to the street, Stew was determined to push away the memories of Bethany which plagued his thoughts constantly. He wanted nothing to spoil this shopping spree.

He recalled passing an elegant display of jewelry boxes at Hendrix's. When he walked in the door, there were several customers studying the boxes. Fortunately, Stew was tall enough to easily view the boxes from where he stood, and he spoke up as soon as he saw the one he wanted. "Pardon me, sir. I'd like to have the rosewood jewelry box taken out for purchase, if you please." The man behind the counter removed the box and set it aside while Stew stepped over to the jewelry cases.

His eyes were immediately drawn to a large, oval, ruby pendant surrounded by small diamonds; it shouted "Christine". But Stew ignored it and selected a smaller, emerald cut diamond with brilliant clarity. Small aquamarines adorned the top of the pendant to give the gemstone a more elegant look. The matching earrings and bracelet were equally splendid.

He assumed Christine loved sleigh rides, so the next part of his plan took him to a prominent furrier. There he purchased a hooded cape, matching muff, and a throw trimmed in mink. Christine's Christmas had already cost a fortune, but there was more to come.

Once he had made arrangements for those gifts to be delivered, he stopped at a little shop known for packing romantic baskets for special occasions. He ordered an imported non-alcoholic wine, specialty cheeses, gourmet crackers, and several delicate chocolates. A red and green blanket was also added to the basket. Stew hoped the Christmas picnic would help create a special memory when he gave Christine her gifts during a surprise visit to his new estate.

A few weeks later, Stew stood waiting at the door of the Stanwicks' mansion. He was there as Christine's escort for the yearly holiday party for friends and business associates. The home had been lavishly decorated for the occasion with every detail meticulously in place—down to Mrs. Stanwick's and Christine's expensive Christmas gowns. Again, Stew felt Christine had never looked lovelier.

This night, however, was dedicated more to business associates than friends or family, and the conversation had nothing to do with the reason for celebrating the holiday. Stew often found himself standing alone while Christine was escorted about or speaking with guests.

It was on this night when Stew realized how truly intelligent Christine was. As a matter of fact, several times he found her engaged in conversations with groups of men discussing various economic and political views. Stew was indifferent and bored by much of the discussion and sometimes disillusioned by Christine's opinions on important issues—especially those dealing with ethics.

Stew and she did have a disagreement during the party, leaving him in a foul mood, and she seemed to gloat once he backed down. He tried to rise above it but struggled to let it go.

The party was in full force when something about the Stanwicks' home began to bother him. It was entirely made of stone, granite, marble and the like. It felt more like a courthouse than a home. Even with the beautiful décor, it was uninviting and cold. A chill ran down his spine. There was no true feeling of a home; it seemed to be only a display of wealth.

Even though Christine seemed to have forgotten their little spat, Stew was disheartened by it and used spitting snow as an excuse to leave the party early.

On the way home he chastised himself for acting a fool over a little misunderstanding. Having had time to give the situation some thought, he realized it was *not only* the disagreement and her views on the subject that had upset him—it was the attitude of superiority she used while engaged in the conversation.

Stew appreciated that Christine had a brilliant mind, but he had the distinct impression she would have continued the argument with him until she won. She seemed determined to drive home the point that she was extremely intelligent and more informed on the subject. He felt like she wanted to put him in his place.

Then again, Stew questioned *why* he would harbor such an opinion of Christine? Most likely, the whole affair was from her being overzealous due to the pressure of being a hostess. Certain he had misread her intentions and had overreacted, he would extend an apology at the earliest opportunity.

37

A PERMANENT ADOPTION

The day after the party at the Stanwicks' home, Stew was feeling guilty for allowing his pettiness to ruin a memorable evening. Convinced Christine had been innocent in the dispute, he chose to bare the entire blame and had flowers delivered with a card stating how much he was looking forward to spending the rest of the Christmas season together.

With the season nearing its peak, Stew felt Christine more intriguing with each encounter. He was beginning to wonder if it was Christine—and *not* Bethany—whom God had intended for him all along.

Yet *another* occurrence had taken place the night Christine agreed to attend the Christmas office party. Stew, having to work late, had sent a message asking Christine to meet at his apartment. He had left Christine alone to wander the apartment while he dressed. Walking back into the room, he had found her holding an elaborately framed picture.

"I assume this is someone special?" Christine asked in a rather peeved tone.

Stew was caught off guard. "Um...let me see" was the only response that came to mind.

Christine stared at the picture long and critically before releasing it. "Well, I suppose one *might* find the girl attractive in a quaint sort of way. Blonde...petite...feminine...Bethany?"

"The housekeeper must have placed it there when putting the apartment together. The photograph should have been returned." Stew was relieved to have come up with a convincing response.

"Of course. No need to remind yourself of past mistakes," Christine replied dryly as she reached for another photo of him and Bethany together. "She looks short standing next to you...a *mere* child." Christine made the judgmental comment before setting the picture aside.

"She's older now, Stew said as he picked up a *third* picture of Bethany from a shelf.

"*Another* picture of Bethany you were unaware of?" she asked sarcastically. But Christine had too much confidence in herself to let the matter upset her beyond the moment.

Stew was glad to have the incident dropped, but the *over-confidence* did bother him. Nevertheless, he made a mental note to put the photographs in storage.

"Mr. Jefferson...Mr. Jefferson," Lillian said, raising her voice just a bit to get Stew's attention.

"Yes!" Stew was obviously startled.

"My goodness, where were you? If I didn't know better, I'd think you were in love," Lillian teased.

"And why wouldn't you know better?" he asked with a smug smile.

"Oh. Are you owning up to something you denied only a couple of weeks ago?" Lillian mused.

"Alright, Lillian. What do you have for me that is so important you had to call me back to reality?" Stew admitted without hesitation.

"It's a letter from the lawyer out west. I thought you would want to see it right away." Lillian handed it over to him.

Stew did not bother to reply but took the letter from her hand and gazed at it for a moment. His face grew serious as he ripped it open and began to read. Lillian waited anxiously with no pretense of not being interested in its contents. Even though she had not met Billy, his welfare had become a concern of hers.

Stew took his time reading the letter and then sat back to study it before saying anything.

"The attorney has found Billy. The sheriff had sent the boy to an orphanage, and Stone has been to see him. Billy appeared to be reasonably content, in good health, clean, and well fed. The facility was sanitary and sufficiently maintained.

"He was able to meet and speak to the minister in charge of the facility and took it upon himself to ask if *I* could have custody of Billy. However, the minister refuses to release any of the children unless it is a permanent adoption. He believes Billy's intelligence, attractive looks, and personality will make him highly adoptable to a home with a father *and* a mother." Stew gave a long sigh of relief and handed the letter back to Lillian.

"I don't understand why Stone asked such a question. I told him I would only consider bringing Billy back here if he wasn't in a safe environment. I do care for the boy, but, to be honest, I'm not up to taking on a child at this stage of my life," Stew admitted painfully. "Lillian, do you think I should seriously consider adopting him?"

"Oh, I'm afraid you're asking the wrong person. I wouldn't know what to do if I were in your position. If the boy seems content and is doing well, I don't suppose there is any reason to disturb him. You've fulfilled your commitment. Besides, you aren't *married*. According to the attorney, the minister seems to favor finding a father and a mother for the boy...although, Billy might enjoy receiving a letter from you."

"Well, I guess I need to stop and write Matt about the ordeal. Maybe he will have some suggestions. He became very attached to the little guy. I hope he'll forgive me for not getting in touch with him about the matter before now." The letter had put Stew in a state of confusion, and he had no idea how he should handle the circumstance.

Lillian went to grab her note pad to help her boss compose the touchy letter. While she was gone, Stew's mind drifted to Christine. He would share the story of Billy with her the next time they were together. It would be interesting to see her reaction. He wondered if Christine would insist he rescue the child—as he knew Bethany would.

Stew and Lillian spent a good deal of time deciding on how much information should be relayed to Matt about the matter.

Dear Matt,

I hope this letter finds you and your career doing well, and I apologize for not writing to you earlier.

I did find a nice furnished apartment near my

office. There is a livery nearby, so I can have a horse ready in short order. I assure you I make good use of the service.

My job is going well, and I've had a couple promotions. I do like Bay City and its conveniences, but, if you recall, my true desire was to find a place of my own outside of town. As it turned out, I found the property much sooner than expected and have purchased an estate from an older couple.

Billy, however, is the main reason for this letter, and I hope you will understand my position.

First, I must apologize for my poor judgment in not heeding your warning to make certain Billy was safe when the telegram didn't arrive as promised. Andrea Landis did the best she could under the circumstances.

Regretfully, the situation wasn't as simple as Billy's mother had made it sound in the note. Billy's Uncle Jake had passed away, so Andrea's only choice was to leave Billy in the care of the town's sheriff.

She did send the telegram, as I requested; however, the message was lost, and I didn't receive the information until a much later date.

It was necessary to hire an attorney to track the boy down. He located Billy in an orphanage not far away. The attorney visited the facility and found it to be well kept and described Billy as being in good health, content, and well cared for.

I could possibly bring Billy here, but the minister doesn't want the child to be removed for any reason other than a suitable adoption. He feels the children in the orphanage have had enough trauma in their lives, and he doesn't want to expose them to anything less than the hope of a happy home life. I must agree with the minister's reasoning.

Any input you have on the matter would be appreciated.

Once again, I beg your pardon for not contacting you sooner. May God always direct your path.

Your loyal friend,
Stewart

It was late when the letter was completed, so Stew insisted Lillian go home. He promised to make the necessary corrections and mail the letter.

Before Stewart left, the very forward Sassy Baker stopped in—as she often did when he worked late. Her advances were less than proper, but Stew always acted as if he was unaware of her intentions. He kept the conversation light and offered a respectful goodbye. In return, Sassy put an index finger to her lips, kissed it, and suggestively pretended to blow the kiss to Stew. He reluctantly smiled at her gesture. There were other girls who pestered him in that way, but she was the most obvious.

As soon as Sassy was out of sight, he grabbed his coat and sneaked down the back stairs, hoping to make it to the post office before the evening mail went out. Stew was not aware it was snowing until he stepped outside in the crisp night air. It pleased him to know a sleigh ride might be included on the agenda of the upcoming romantic visit to his new home. He could not imagine a more perfect setting to impress Christine.

38

A STANWICK CHRISTMAS

Stewart was in deep thought and unaware he had taken a wrong side road until one of the curves needed his full attention. The mistake was aggravating since he had to stay on the road until he came to an open area wide enough to turn around.

As he gently coaxed Ebony and Midnight in the turn, the sound of rushing water caught his attention. He glanced up just in time to catch a glimpse of a frozen waterfall—a magnificent sight on such a beautiful, snowy day.

Stew slowed the horses long enough to get a second look. *Bethany would love to see this.* Not even noticing the inadvertent thought, he clicked his tongue, gave a light snap of the reins, and glided safely back onto the road.

Stew stopped the sleigh in front of the Stanwicks' mansion and checked his pocket watch to see how much time the wrong turn had cost him. He leaped from the sleigh, waved to the stable boy to take the horses, and then skipped up the several steps to the front door.

The butler greeted him and took his hat, but Stew barely noticed. He was puzzled to see the home was overflowing with guests.

To make things worse, Christine was so caught up in socializing she had not even noticed he had arrived. When she did come to greet him, she only slipped her arm in his and led him into the parlor to meet her grandparents and join the party.

"I remember very distinctly being told this occasion was to be a *small, family* affair," he remarked stiffly.

"This *is* a small gathering for a Stanwicks' Christmas. We're a very close-knit group," she teasingly laughed.

"Christine! I'm sorry, but I must steal you away from Stewart. I have an emergency which must be taken care of *immediately*. Come with me. Hurry, dear!" Mrs. Stanwick insisted as she swished by in her green satin gown.

"Sorry to run, love, but as you can see, Mother is worked up about *something*. You can entertain yourself, can't you?" Christine cooed, not waiting for an answer.

Once again, Stew was left to mingle among strangers, and it appeared Christine had little intention of hurrying back to rescue him. At least he was spared any introductions for a while.

It was not long until Stew was forced into a conversation with one of Christine's attractive, unmarried cousins who was more than ready to cozy up to him. Isabella was disgracefully flirtatious, and Stew did little to discourage her. She was loud, hilariously funny, and had no qualms over having one drink after another. Fortunately for Stew, Isabella could not hold her liquor and soon had to be escorted upstairs to lie down.

From a distance, he had noticed Christine seemed to be annoyed with him and Isabella, but he felt it was the Stanwicks' responsibility to curb their guest's behavior. Moreover, he was not in the habit of being in a Christian home where liquor was made available, and he was disappointed to find it was allowed by the Stanwicks.

Stew went through the pretense of mingling with the relatives while trying to catch up with Christine. Every time he got remotely close to spending a few minutes at her side, she would excuse herself for one reason or another. Still he remained patient, not wanting to cause any friction.

Eventually, the noon meal was announced and the adults gathered at an abundantly decorated table. Greenery, various colored glass balls, gold ribbon, and hand painted name cards made every place setting gorgeous and special. Stew was grateful to finally be paired with Christine, and she apologized for being inattentive. Although he appreciated the apology, her absence had definitely made him feel belittled.

Then to add to the disappointments of the day—instead of the traditional Christmas dinner he had expected—plates of French cuisine were delivered by the household staff. Christine explained that a gourmet chef was hired each year to prepare their Christmas meals.

Mr. Stanwick stood at the head of the table and offered a short prayer while everyone bowed their heads. Then the family engaged in high society conversation which was of little interest to Stew.

After a while, he leaned over to Christine and whispered, "When will I be able to steal you away from all this madness so we can have some time alone?"

"Time for what? I wait all year for our family Christmas, and I don't want to miss a minute of it. Aren't you enjoying yourself?"

she asked seriously.

"Well, I do have a surprise planned for you. After all, you did mislead me into thinking this dinner was with your immediate family," he whispered back.

"What could be more romantic than having you share Christmas with my entire family? We have so many plans for the weekend," Christine said laughingly.

"Like what?"

"Well, after our late night supper we all gather in the great room to listen to a professional pianist. Afterward, the entire family sings carols. Then father shares a Christmas story—he's an excellent narrator. Then at midnight, we gather around the tree to exchange gifts—first the children, and later the adults. If there is a *special* gift to be given—such as last year when father gave mother her second set of wedding rings—an announcement is made to allow all the family the opportunity to share in the moment. It's such a glorious time!" she gloated.

Stew had never seen Christine act so playful and animated.

"But seriously, Christine, I want to take you away from here for a couple hours," Stew insisted.

"You can't mean it! Stew...I really don't want to go anywhere. There are so many wonderful activities I'm looking forward to." Christine was not in the least interested in Stew's plans.

"We'll be riding to a special destination in the most beautiful sleigh you've ever laid your lovely eyes on." Stew hated to disclose part of the surprise but felt he had no other choice than to make the invitation tantalizing.

"We have several, beautiful sleighs *here*! Our property has any number of lanes with hills and valleys to make the most wonderful rides. My grandparents start things off by taking the first ride of the afternoon. It's not unusual for us to ride until dawn. It's tradition! I do hope it snows in those lovely, large flakes. It's so enchanting when it does."

"It seems there are several things you didn't bother to mention. Why is that?" he asked, trying not to sound angry.

"Well...I'd tell you, but I'm afraid you'll be upset with me," Christine said, trying to sound babyish—which was most unflattering to Stew at this point.

"Go on."

"I didn't go into detail because I didn't want you to go away for the holidays. I was afraid you would go home and leave me here alone. I just couldn't imagine having you so far away. I can be terribly selfish sometimes, and I don't feel the least bit guilty. I wanted you here with me and that's that," Christine admitted, still trying to act cute.

Stew saw nothing *cute* in her actions at the moment; Christine possessed too much confidence to pull it off. He supposed the confession was meant as a compliment, but being told the day's agenda was more important to Christine than his request did not set well with him.

Stew just stared at her and said nothing in return. Her selfish statement brought to mind how neglectful he had been toward his parents since moving to Bay City. Only sending flowers for Thanksgiving and a card with money for Christmas was such a poor offering for his dear parents. Before Christine, he would have lovingly showered them with gifts and never would have considered missing a family Christmas. As an only child, he should have invited them to spend Christmas with him. He envisioned how thrilled they would have been to visit his new estate.

The holidays had always been an exciting time at the Jeffersons' home since they too were accustomed to entertaining and having the house full of family and friends. However, Christmas Eve and Christmas Day were always reserved for their immediate family. Of course, this year Bethany and her parents would not be there.

Now he realized the only word he had received from home lately was a very short note from his mother stating she was getting ready for the holidays in the usual fashion. His parents had household servants, but Mrs. Jefferson always sent the staff home and handled the Christmas festivities on her own.

Stew knew the table would be oversupplied with ham, turkey, stuffing, noodles, salads, homemade desserts, and anything else his mother could manage to squeeze in.

Then it hit him. *Of course! What an idiot I am! My parents will be expecting me to make a surprise appearance for Christmas. They would assume the card and money were decoys. I'm always doing such things to surprise them—"*

"Stewart! What is wrong with you? You're in a daze."

"I...I was thinking of my parents, and I'm afraid—" Stew was cut off mid-sentence as Christine rejoined the lively conversation in which she had been engaged.

He took a good look at Christine's relatives—each dressed in the most expensive and latest fashions. It was apparent their family gathering was more about competition than caring for one another. As he listened to the conversations flying back and forth across the table, he could hear each one trying to outdo the other with a list of references made to country clubs, travels, acquaintances, and even alma maters.

Of course, they were subtle in the way they presented a subject, but it was clear the clan's main purpose for coming together was to give inventory of their accomplishments throughout the year. He wondered if Christine wanted him there only because he was currently considered one of the area's more successful, young businessmen.

Stew was starting to see the Stanwicks presented themselves as devout Christians but lived their lives by many of the world's standards. They only punctuated their lives with faith at their convenience. He did not doubt they were converted and had a love for the Lord, but God's place in their lives seemed to be on *their* terms. The realization kept Stew quiet for the rest of the meal.

Soon after lunch, some of the guests returned to the great room to play games while others prepared for the sleigh rides.

Once more, Stew halfheartedly tried to talk Christine into slipping away for a couple hours, but she ignored the invitation. By this time, the appeal of surprising Christine was lost.

On the way up to his room to get dressed for the sleigh ride, he found Christine engaged in another debate with a few of the men in the family. Immediately, Stew noticed Christine had taken the discussion to an advanced level to prove her superior intelligence, and it disappointed him. Christine became ruthless in the argument. Again she seemed to take pleasure in trapping others into revealing their positions on issues so she could reprimand them for their primitive thinking.

Stew started to leave, but his attention was recaptured when Christine's opinions on the issues became offensive to his Christian beliefs. Her responses did prove she was educated in the Bible, but she had little understanding of how to apply its true meaning to her life. In that respect, he felt badly for her.

Stew recalled having left early on Thanksgiving Day because of a similar arrogant display by Christine. It was not enough to be beautiful, wealthy, and extremely intelligent, but she seemed to relish in humiliating others.

At that point, Stew walked away to clear his head. He tried to picture Christine again as the charming and sophisticated young woman he had admired, but he could not ignore what he had just witnessed.

If she found pleasure in treating family members so rudely, then she might treat the person she married the same way. It would be difficult for a man to keep his dignity when constantly having to prove himself intellectually. He was sure there were men who might enjoy dealing with such a woman—but the thought was *not* appealing to him.

While Christine continued her debates, Stew dressed and took a walk to the stable to make sure Ebony and Midnight had been made comfortable. The stable hands were busy, but Stew was able to strike up a conversation with a man about fifteen years his senior. The man was such a colorful character that Stew stayed and talked until Christine decided to join him.

Although he was in a better state of mind, Stew used this time to let Christine know he was not impressed with the type of conversation for which she *again* had abandoned him. She shrugged one shoulder and made no apology. For the time being, he excused her behavior by reminding himself that most people have more than one side—some are admirable and some are not.

Soon after, the two were gliding through a crystal woods in a sleigh pulled by a muscular, white horse. They laughed and sang until they both felt like silly school children. Unfortunately, the merriment only reminded him of the way Bethany always found pleasant humor in *everything* they shared together.

"Where are you, Stew?" Christine again noticed his mind had drifted.

"Oh, a little bit of everywhere. This brings back memories of my younger days," Stew answered, hoping to avoid going any further.

"Look! It's snowing! The flakes are enormous! Isn't it wonderful?" Christine exclaimed in excitement.

"Yes...as you wished it would be," Stew replied as his thoughts drifted back to the many times he and Bethany had spent riding and playing in the snow. Fortunately, Christine was too involved in admiring the snowflakes to notice the pain in his face.

39

AN ENGAGEMENT RING

After being out in the cold for a couple hours, everyone was ready to go home, so the ride ended in a spirited race across a snow covered meadow.

Once inside, Christine decided it was time to dress for dinner. Stew did the same and used the spare time deciding how to make Christine's unusual gifts make sense; it was a waste of his time. The romantic ride for a private viewing of his estate and a picnic by the fireplace no longer mattered to him. As far as he was concerned, the giving of the gifts would just be a formality, so he turned them over to the butler to be placed under the tree.

As soon as the evening meal was announced, Christine intentionally reentered the gaiety by descending the wide, marble staircase in a beautiful, red, flowing silk gown. Everyone took a breath at her appearance, and Stew *again* felt she had never looked lovelier. She literally seemed to float by his side as they joined Mr. and Mrs. Stanwick to lead the parade of family members into the dining room.

As expected, the table was adorned with another astonishing creation, beginning with the green satin tablecloth, overlaid with green, snowflake lace. Spanning the center of the table was a red satin runner with an elaborate display of holly and red candles. On each green and red plaid placemat was a full place setting of fine china which was painted with a natural looking holly pattern. There were red stemware, golden handle silverware, and red linen napkins which had the name of each guest painted on the napkin ring to indicate the seating arrangement.

Christine's entrance and the elaborate dining table seemed to promise this was to be an extraordinary evening. The sudden hush from the rest of the clan indicated Mr. and Mrs. Stanwick had outdone themselves in extravagance.

For the rest of the evening, Christine directed her attention to Stew in a most obvious way. Demur looks with admiring eyes, a gentle back rub, a reference to his success, and the pretense of removing something from his cheek with her napkin were all done to lead everyone to believe they were a serious couple.

After dinner, the guests were asked to be seated in the great room for the musical portion of the evening. Stew was entertained and impressed. The pianist was well known, and it was a privilege to have witnessed the man's genius.

Soon after the recital, Mr. Stanwick delighted everyone with his talent for storytelling. The session ended with caroling. The crowd then was escorted into another room for the gift exchange.

Children and adults tore open a mountain of gifts, and a Santa roamed the room passing out candy which created even more excitement.

Stew watched Christine and her parents receive package after package, and he was the recipient of several unexpected gifts.

However, he was perplexed by Christine's parents' gift to him—a trip to Europe.

Still, Stew's biggest surprise was when all the relatives grew silent for the opening of Christine's presents from him. The quietness was so intense he began to perspire from the stress. Noticing the entire family was seating themselves to have a clear view, he recalled Christine mentioning special gifts were done in this manner. Stew couldn't understand why they would assume his gifts to Christine should be seen in such a way.

Stew had no idea where to begin; his mind went blank. Christine gave him a nervous look to indicate he should present her with the first gift.

"Stewart!" she finally whispered.

He gingerly picked up a package and said, "I believe I must explain my hesitation. You see, I mistakenly understood this weekend was to be a *small* affair with Christine and her parents. To my surprise, according to the Stanwicks, this *is* a small affair." A few faint laughs were heard. "Anyway, the gifts were selected to be given in another setting."

The first package was large, so Christine put it in her lap to open it. "Oh, how lovely...mink!" She pretended it was an extremely thoughtful gesture.

Stew was concerned since there was no reaction from the onlookers. He reached for the basket with the large bow and reluctantly handed it over. With this gift, she gave him an apprehensive look. She opened the basket and said. "Oh, Stewart, what an exquisite and expensive array of items! The etched, stemmed glasses are simply lovely!" She lifted one up for all to see, but this gift drew even less of a response. It was obvious Christine was not pleased and was getting nervous—although Stew still had no idea why.

Finally, he handed her the last two gifts. "With this, her eyes narrowed on him, but her mouth said the complete opposite. "More gifts, Stewart?" He wondered why his name had suddenly become Stewart.

But when Christine recognized the jewelry box, she gave an approving smile and nodded to her parents. Unfortunately, the smile disappeared and a look of fear came over her face. She looked into his eyes while opening the final gift. Again, her mouth stated the opposite of what her face reflected. "Stewart! You've spent too much!" Then she held up the beautiful diamond pendant with the matching earrings and bracelet.

There were a few claps, along with some sighs, and then the people stood to leave. Stewart noticed the knowing looks which passed between several family members.

"Stewart!" she loudly whispered in desperation. "If there's a gift you're holding back, you had better give it to me...*right now*!"

"What did you say?" he whispered back, thinking he must have misunderstood.

"I said...if there is another gift—and there had *better* be—then you give it to me *right this minute*! Is that clear enough?" she whispered sharply.

"Why...no, Christine...I'm sorry. There *isn't* another gift," he answered aloud, quite bewildered.

"Hush! Someone might hear you!" she demanded with clenched teeth. "Come with me!"

Christine pretended to lovingly take his arm and lead him

through the French doors to another room. He saw the disapproving glares Mr. and Mrs. Stanwick gave him as he left the room with their daughter. Stew felt like a little boy being led away by his mother to be given a good spanking, and, at this particular moment, he would have preferred it.

"Stewart!" she hissed. "How dare you do this to me! You fool!"

"How dare I do *what* to you?" He was truly confused by what had just taken place and by her anger.

"Is this some sort of punishment for not going away with you this afternoon?" she demanded.

"No! What are you talking about?"

"You know perfectly well!" she answered furiously.

"Honestly, I don't!"

"You refused to give me my *ring* because I wouldn't go away with you! You've shamed me in front of all of my relatives! Do you know how much I've looked forward to this?" she questioned.

"An engagement ring?" he asked.

"Yes! After all of the hints you've made about a Christmas surprise, you know I was expecting a proposal tonight. For your information, I *preferred* the engagement take place in front of my family."

"Seriously? I had no idea you would expect an engagement ring at this point in our relationship. Neither of us has confessed love for the other. We haven't even discussed marriage. We've only known each other a short time."

"You didn't think I was expecting a ring after all of your attention? Not every couple discusses marriage before an engagement. Do you know how many rings I've been offered in less time and for less reason?"

"I'm sorry. I didn't realize you felt that way." Stew had no idea how to respond.

"And where *did* you want to take me today?" Christine spat the words at him.

"It's too late now...but it didn't include an engagement ring." He no longer wanted to mention his estate.

"As far as the gifts you gave me...I *have* mink! And the jewelry? *Who* did you buy that for? I've certainly never worn anything so understated. A picnic basket in the winter? I don't want any of it!" By this time, Christine was poking her finger and aggressively walking forward as Stew backed away.

Finally, her shoulders began to heave as she broke out in tears. "This should have been *my* night."

"I must admit...I have been quite taken with you, but I didn't realize you were expecting *a ring*."

"Well, you know now!" she yelled.

Stew felt horrible. "Christine, why did you take such a chance in front of your family?"

"Why would *you* hesitate to give me a ring?"

"Because, if we're truly honest, we *both* know we're not in love." Stew was almost sorry he had said it but felt he must speak the truth.

"You possess many wonderful qualities which I highly admire...but our Christian standards and how we view the world differ on so many important issues....I want God to dictate how I live my life."

"We're not talking about religious ideals!" she stated in a frightened tone.

"Christine, your real concern isn't about our love for one another. You're only irritated because you expected a proposal in front of your relatives. I just fit your mold." He tried to keep his voice low for her sake. "We've enjoyed keeping company for the last few months, but we're not suited for one another," Stew said tenderly.

Christine dropped her face into her hands and cried as she vocalized her rambling thoughts, "How can I face my family? They're all aware the trip was given to celebrate our engagement.

"Stewart, I've turned down several marriage proposals from wonderful men because I was never certain if they loved *me* or my *money*. When I met you, I decided I would accept *your* proposal. You're already wealthy and successful. Money means nothing to you," she admitted.

"But...what about love?" Stew questioned.

Christine took a moment to consider Stew's words. "I don't know...I love you...or I assumed I was in love." She stood quietly for a moment. "Surely, I wasn't willing to settle for a loveless marriage."

Christine covered her face with one hand and reached for the arm of the bench as she took a seat. "Oh, Stew, what must you think of me? Can you ever forgive me?" she asked.

"It was not just you, Christine. We were both mistaken."

As a new understanding of their relationship developed, Stew put his arm around her and gave her a brotherly hug. Just then, several of her family members passed by and saw them together.

"I've made such a mess of everything. I just want to go to my room. How can I face my relatives?" Christine admitted.

"Well, let's really confuse them." He grabbed her hand and pulled her from the bench. "Let's go for another sleigh ride. Go change. I'll meet you in the foyer when you're ready."

Along with most of the Stanwicks' relatives, Christine and Stew had a great time together. After the sleigh ride they laughed and sang, built a snowman, threw snowballs, and played in the snow until dawn. They even held hands and hugged—as friends often do when they are having fun. As a result, the gossip among the relatives was silenced.

Out of respect for Christine, Stew went to his room to give the impression he was staying for the entire holiday but slipped away once everyone retired. Several of the relatives would be leaving for home after resting, so they would not notice his absence.

Because of the snow, the ride back to the city was treacherous. Still, Stew drove the horses hard, wanting to get back to the city to contact his parents. He needed to apologize for not being there for Christmas.

As it turned out, he arrived home to find a telegram waiting for him. It advised Stew to stay in Bay City because of an impending blizzard in their area. They were disappointed but wished him much love and a blessed Christmas.

Stew thanked God for sparing him the sorrow of having to apologize to his precious mother and father. It would have hurt them deeply to learn their son had never planned to spend Christmas with them.

40

CHRISTMAS AT THE MISSION

On Christmas morning, the mission children were fascinated by the brightly decorated tree and the packages beneath it. Excitement rippled through the room as the volunteers passed out the gifts. Clothing, apples, oranges, toys, and many other items had been donated to make Christmas extra special.

All the children joined in the fun, and Sandra had made a breakfast for them to enjoy while they played in the newly renovated social room.

At noon, the children were taken to the dining hall where they were served a traditional Christmas dinner. After the meal, a cake in the shape of a Christmas tree was cut and served to the anxious orphans.

To complete the celebration, the older children acted out the Nativity story to remind everyone of the true meaning of Christmas.

Bethany reviewed in her heart the many changes which had taken place since Sandra and her friends began the transformation. Even the path Bethany took downtown was now being used as a roadway to make reaching the mission easier and less dangerous. The news that the mission was in operation had spread throughout the area, and people from every lifestyle were asking what they could do to help.

Most of the townsfolk had always wanted to help the victims of the railroad reassignment, but conditions had declined so quickly for the families involved that no one knew how to approach the problem. Now that donations were coming in, ministries had been set up to offer relief to those who needed it. A few volunteers had even started doing home repairs for the sick and elderly.

But best of all, the children of the orphanage were now being adopted into loving homes.

Currently, Bethany's main responsibility was to supervise the volunteers, who were now becoming very self-directed. This allowed her more time to work as a seamstress to boost the mission's income. She found both jobs rewarding and now had extra time to spend with the children.

It was a blessing for Bethany to see each adopted child leave with their new parents and become part of a family. The homelike care the children received at the orphanage had helped them blend into their new lives more readily.

Children were coming and going. Almost all of the original children had been placed with families, and Pastor Goodry made certain each child went to a safe and loving home.

However, Pete, the child who was thought to be the most adoptable, still remained at the mission. It saddened the staff since they all had a special place in their hearts for him.

Christmas Day was warm and sunny, so Bethany asked Pete

to take a walk during nap time. The two had become friends since Baby Betsy had been adopted by Mr. and Mrs. Kenny.

"Pete, does it bother you to see the other children being adopted? I know you must be wondering if it will happen for you." Bethany was not sure why she asked such a hurtful question.

"Nope. Don't bother me any. I'm not really ready to be 'dopted. I miss my mama and daddy too much." Bethany believed him, since he was always truthful.

"It's good you feel such a strong love for your parents. I'm sure they were wonderful people, because you're a special boy. That's why I'm certain it won't be long before a nice couple will take you home with them. Your parents would want you to grow up in a happy home. Do you understand what I'm saying?"

"I know someone is comin' for me. It just ain't...isn't time yet. I'm not ready and neither is he. But he's coming for me—sometime. I've known ever since mama died. Me and him, we just loved each other right off. But it's not time, that's all." The little guy answered as if he had been given all the details.

"He? Who's he? And how do you know this is going to happen?" Bethany was touched by Pete's certainty.

"He's a man I met, and Jesus told me in my heart." Pete spoke with undoubting faith.

"Pete! Do you see the bunnies playing over there?" asked Bethany, thinking she should change the subject.

After the Christmas evening service, Bethany took a stroll with the pastor. "It's hard to imagine we got off to such a rocky start. We seem to think alike, and our backgrounds are so similar. Did you really play in a willow tree when you were younger or were you just teasing me?" she asked.

"I do love teasing you, but I *did* do a lot of climbing in a willow. As a matter of fact, I don't consider myself too old to climb it now. Janet was right there with me. She was quite the tomboy in those days. So, were you a tomboy when *you* were younger?"

"Me...a tomboy? No, not at all. I didn't mind getting dirty or helping with the animals, and I did do my fair share of climbing in the willow. But normally, I had tea parties for my dolls under it. My willow is down by the lake where my sister and I learned to swim. Did you have a place to swim, David?" she questioned.

"Nothing like a lake. I learned to swim in a creek. The swimming hole was just big enough for a good dip on a hot, summer day. But I spent a lot of time there when I was a boy. Actually, it hasn't been long since I went swimming there. And it was much smaller than I remembered. I miss home. I grew up in a wonderful area, and I had a great childhood." The pastor had that faraway look in his eyes.

"I did too. I've grown up with every advantage. Coming here has been a good lesson in life. I needed to see what it truly meant to be poor and to know the effects financial loss can have. I've also learned a little about doing without, but I will be grateful to return to my way of life."

It was satisfying to them both to discover they were becoming close and sharing their personal lives.

The walk eventually brought them back to the mission where Pastor Goodry asked if she would like to join him and another couple for Tuesday afternoon visitations. Bethany agreed, grateful to have an opportunity to witness to the unsaved.

41

SAD NEWS FROM HOME

Helen knocked lightly, concerned she might interrupt her husband's train of thought. She was very aware of his work habits, and if he was deep in thought, the light knock would go undetected.

"Come in, dear," he answered in his kindest voice.

"Good morning, hon. I'm sorry I overslept and missed preparing breakfast for you."

"You had a busy Christmas and a difficult parting. I thought maybe you needed a little more rest. You should do it more often." Mr. Jackson was always thoughtful, especially when it came to his wife.

"You shouldn't worry about me. I'm very happy Mary and her family will be moving back home to be near relatives. Although...I do need to write Bethany and tell her the news.

"I'm anxious to hear about Christmas at the orphanage. I can't imagine the holidays without snow, but I'm sure Bethany was too busy to notice," Helen said proudly.

"Yes, Bethany is quite the trooper when something needs to be done. She has always been one to roll up her sleeves and dig in."

"It sounds like the mission is doing well. And if she has anything to say about it, things will be operating even better before she leaves—which I hope is soon. It just never crossed my mind she wouldn't be home for Christmas. But we did fine, didn't we, dear? I'm rather pleased with the way we managed," she chuckled.

Mr. Jackson knew the little laugh was to cover up the sadness in her heart. "Yes, I'm very happy with the way we both handled it. Despite the bad weather, I believe our guests appreciated not having to spend Christmas Day alone."

"I did miss being with Stew's family this year," Helen admitted.

"There is no shame in that. It should be a pleasant memory in our lives. We did enjoy those times."

"Helen, I've been praying about their broken engagement, and I've decided I must believe the best in Stewart. I don't understand what happened at the end of the relationship, but I do believe he's still the same caring, young man who loves our daughter and wants the best for her. I have peace in it."

"I've given it to the Lord too, but it is a difficult matter when your child is hurting." Helen quickly changed the subject. "I can't wait to hear how the mission children liked the things our church sent for Christmas. I believe we overindulged them quite nicely, don't you?"

"Yes, I most certainly do. And it sounds as though there were plenty of people out west eager to do the same. The little orphans should've had a wonderful Christmas. The mission has turned out to be a true blessing."

"It certainly has. Well, dear...I need to get a letter written in time for the mail. Bethany will be expecting all the details of our holiday. I hate to include the sad news of Mary leaving us, but it must be done. Bethany would be hurt if we kept it from her." Tears came to Helen's eyes at the thought of telling Bethany their friend was gone.

I don't relish the thought of you doing all of Mary's work by yourself. We'll hire someone as soon as possible. Don't think for a moment things are going to remain as they are. Do you understand me, missy?" Mr. Jackson said, with a lift of his eyebrows to let his wife know he was serious.

"Oh, Mel!"

42

A WAY OUT

On Tuesday, Bethany was taking a good look at the Christmas presents from home. She had put them aside to open when she had time to enjoy them. Not being home for Christmas had affected her more than she was willing to admit; a tear trickled down her cheek.

The wrapping paper was a hand painted picture of her family riding in a sleigh to their little white church in the valley with huge snowflakes falling all around. Bethany remembered that beautiful, snowy Christmas Eve as being her favorite.

She gently ran her finger across the picture to let the love transfer from her mother's hand to her own heart. With a sigh of contentment, she put the paper aside and carefully removed the tissue paper from around a small, walnut trunk which had been crafted by her father. She held the chest to her nose and breathed in the familiar smells from his workshop.

The second gift was wrapped in a paper with a summer scene of their gazebo and house. It was wonderful to see home in any form, and her mother had tried to add as many details as possible.

The box inside held a necklace with a delicate, pewter cross pendant. What a lovely reminder that her time of service at the mission was nothing to compare to the sacrifice Christ made on the cross. She carefully fastened it around her neck.

The last gift was a pink nightgown with roses embroidered across the front. The gifts brought a sentimental smile to her face.

Then Bethany wrote a letter of appreciation and told of Christmas at the mission.

Later in the afternoon Bethany met the pastor and Mr. and Mrs. Felder in front of the church for the Tuesday visitations. The two couples clipped joyfully along their route, but their conversation was quickly silenced as their buggy entered the impoverished section of town.

Bethany had had little interaction with the area since her first night's experience, but the light of day revealed how horrible the conditions truly were.

Their ride was no longer a comfortable one. The pastor was forced to weave around groups of sneering men who refused to move so the buggy could pass. Bethany could tell many of the men had lost respect for humankind—whether man, woman, or child.

Occasionally, hateful and vulgar comments were shouted out and followed by nasty laughter. Bethany could see David's pained face. It would be humiliating for any man to let the disgusting action and remarks slide, but for the women's safety and as a servant of God, he could not yield to the temptation of retaliating.

Bethany did notice that David's collar must have earned some type of respect because many unarmed visitors who entered the area were beaten and robbed. It was a scary ride, and she prayed under her breath the entire time.

So much had happened since she had come to the mission. Bethany had nearly forgotten how undesirable the area was. It was frightening to look into the hardened, cruel eyes and even more difficult to feel Christian love for those men.

The most disheartening part of the trip was revisiting the effects the hardships had had on the once respectable women who now sat on their porches using foul language to control their children.

Tired eyed children, dressed in rags, watched as the buggy slowly passed. Babies cried as they crawled on the ground unsupervised and wearing soiled and sagging diapers.

Bethany could not comprehend people giving in to such a destructive way of life. She again fought with her conscience to keep from judging them since she had little knowledge of the suffering these people may have endured.

It was a relief to finally turn down a side street which showed a glimmer of hope. The homes were in disrepair, but steps had been taken to help prevent further decline.

Clothing was shabby and patched, but clean. Children were dirty from playing, but Bethany could tell they were scrubbed on a regular basis.

A few women stood in a group, engaged in conversation, but stopped talking as the buggy went by. Suddenly a glance of recognition passed between Bethany and one of the ladies, but the woman quickly looked down and away.

Bethany knew it was Lonnie James, the lady who had led her to safety when she had been left stranded in this dangerous section of town. Bethany was disappointed but understood it would not be wise for Lonnie to speak.

On the next block the pastor pulled the horse to a stop in front of a small shack that looked as though it had once been a neat, little cottage overflowing with beautiful flowers. The men helped the ladies down, and they all walked to the front door.

A little, hunchbacked woman opened the door and let them in. Evidently, the others had been there previously since she greeted them as if she had been waiting for their return. She offered to fix coffee, but they politely refused since they knew it would be a great sacrifice for her.

They were there over an hour and, toward the end of their visit, sweet, little Edna Palmer bowed her head and asked Jesus into her heart. Afterward, she listened closely to the instructions from the pastor and promised to be ready for church on Sunday.

Mrs. Felder handed Edna an armful of used clothing to wear so the older lady would not feel out of place on Sunday. They also had brought some food supplies.

While the others concluded the visit, Bethany grabbed an empty bucket and went out to pump water for Edna.

"Miss!" Bethany looked around but saw no one. "Miss!" She looked around again and saw a woman half hidden behind some dried up vines.

"May I help you?" Bethany walked over to her.

To Bethany's pleasure, it was Lonnie James. They hugged and exchanged heartfelt greetings.

"I know the Lord, Bethany. I'm so happy He saved me and my children. Our relationship has improved since we've come to know

Him. But how can I be an example to my children when I work in a tavern and have to play up to men to keep them buying drinks until they pass out.

"Before I became a Christian, I worked there to feed my children. But how can I live for the Lord and continue to work there? I need to get my children out of this messed up life.

"I was once respectable—a good mama and wife. We had nice things. I worked my fingers to the bones cooking and cleaning for my family. I loved it. We were all so happy. Now look at me. Even with this job, we are practically starving, and my children are dressed in rags.

"Please, pray God will show me a way out of here!" As soon as Lonnie was finished spilling out her request, she did not wait for a response but turned to run away before she was seen.

Bethany grabbed her hand, "God will get you out of here. He will provide. Trust and be patient. It will happen. Find scriptures that speak hope to you. Keep praising and thanking Him for a new life and don't despair."

Lonnie nodded to indicate she understood and hurried off.

Bethany could barely remember what she had told her, but she knew God had a breakthrough waiting for Lonnie and the children.

43

OBSESSIVE AND OVERPROTECTIVE

Stew wanted the foreman off his property, so he watched until the movers turned onto the main road. The man had kept the staff working productively, but it was of little consequence since he constantly ignored Stew's instructions. Why the company kept such a person on the payroll was a mystery.

Actually, Stew *had* been impressed with the rest of the crew. The girls in charge of putting away the household items *were* a little too friendly, but he still took a few minutes to talk and joke with them. The tall blonde had bravely tucked a note in his pocket as she was leaving. Stew had chuckled inside at the immature gesture.

Regardless of the frustrations with the moving company, it was worth it. Stew was finally in the home he and Bethany had always dreamed of having.

With spring approaching, Stew noticed the commute to the city was robbing him of free time. For that reason, he decided to leave the large church in the city to attend a little, stone church located near his new home.

Of course, it did not take Stew long to become an active part of the congregation since he had the knack for making friends easily. Men and women were drawn to him and encouraged him to stay with the church. Stew loved it there and felt very comfortable with everyone—except the pastor.

For some reason, the warmth Stew had received from the pastor when he first started attending had turned cold. Still, Stew chose to ignore it and went on as if he had been among the congregation all of his life. The pastor's sermons touched Stewart's heart, and the beliefs held by the church matched his own.

However, one Sunday after service the minister asked Stew to meet with him sometime during the week. He agreed and assumed the minister was going to ask him to become a member of the church, since that was the usual procedure when someone seemed to have established themselves.

Knowing he would be a permanent part of the community, Stew decided it was time to transfer his lifelong membership from his home church.

On the evening of the scheduled appointment, Stew rode to the church, tied Ebony to the hitching post, and went directly to the pastor's office.

"Mr. Jefferson, thank you for coming. Please step in and have a seat," Pastor Smith gave Stew a firm handshake and directed him to the empty chair in front of the desk. "I know you're a busy man, so I'll try not to detain you."

He nodded toward another gentleman sitting in the chair next to Stew's and said, "Let me introduce you to Brother Arnold, one of our deacons." Stew reached out and shook Arnold's hand before taking his seat and acknowledging they were already acquainted.

"Well...let's begin. First off, I want you to know I intend to be quite candid," Pastor Smith continued in a no-nonsense voice.

Stew was surprised by the statement and quickly realized the visit was not about church membership. "I'm afraid you have me at a disadvantage, Pastor."

"So noted...the matter I need to address is unfortunately of a serious nature. That's why I've requested Deacon Arnold to be present. I want to follow procedure since this involves a personal and a professional situation. Also, do not mistake me when I say I'm most serious. However, you can rest assured nothing discussed in this meeting will go any further than this room—unless you choose to do so yourself," the pastor informed Stew in a no nonsense voice.

"Sir, I don't understand—"

"Save your breath, son. I will have no problem explaining it to you," the pastor cut in.

"Now, let's bow our heads and ask the Lord to join us. Father... we ask you to bless this meeting. Allow me to say what I must and open this man's heart to follow your lead. In Jesus' name. Amen.

"Mr. Jefferson...while I don't doubt your salvation or your seriousness in serving the Lord, it is my duty as a father and as a pastor to confront you on the unacceptable behavior I've witness on your part. It involves my daughter, Clair."

"Clair?" Stew questioned as he stopped to think for a moment.

"Yes. Clair is my daughter. And it doesn't surprise me that you need to stop and recollect who she is. So let me assist you. She's the young brunette you have been sitting and talking with on a fairly regular basis."

"I'm perfectly aware who Clair is," Stew stated.

"Clair is a nice girl. Some may consider her plain, but, being her father, I think she's beautiful. However, she's the daughter of a minister and must live a sheltered life compared to most young people. This causes her to sometimes feel left out and unnoticed.

"I'll get to the point. Other than a cordial greeting...properly made...I'd like you to keep your distance from my daughter. I've been watching you both, and I can tell she's quite taken with you."

"Sir," Stew said, "I have no intention of—"

"That's exactly the point," the reverend cut in again. "You and I know you have no intentions of any sort toward Clair. She's just a girl you feel is unnoticed and, for some reason, feel it's your responsibility to fill in for the neglect of others toward her. Your careless attention is leading her to believe you're interested in her. As a father, it is my duty to protect my daughter, and as a minister, it is my duty to protect the young ladies of our congregation."

"My carelessness?" Stew was shocked.

"Yes, sir. You are being careless. It is unfortunate I must speak of thoughtless behavior to such a seemingly well-rounded, young man as yourself. However, you're a nice looking man with an appealing personality which easily catches the attention of young women. To be honest, you offer more attention than necessary to young ladies. You fail to regard their feelings or note that your attention might lead them to think you are interested in them."

"Sir–" Stew was extremely offended.

"Mr. Jefferson, you and I know you aren't a match with my daughter. You have nothing in common. I've witness the disappointment in her eyes when you turn your attention to other young women. I don't want to see her become envious of longtime Christian friends.

"So let me make myself perfectly clear. You are most welcome to attend our church. However, please restrain yourself from any further reckless behavior of this sort toward my daughter or any other young lady in attendance here."

"Sir! You have most certainly misunderstood me. My intentions are and have always been to treat young ladies with polite kindness. I've never intentionally presented myself in any other way," Stew tried to justify himself and not sound disrespectful—although he was clearly angry.

"Yes, Mr. Jefferson, I understand you do feel you've been treated unfairly. However, we all need to come to terms with our shortcomings from time to time if we truly want God's best in our lives.

"Son, listen...I'm asking you to go home and examine your heart. Look back on your life and pay attention. My guess is you've overlooked this for some time." The pastor reached out and gave Stewart another firm hand shake.

Offended by the whole ordeal, Stew could not speak another word. He rose from the chair and walked out the door. He was fuming inside but did not give in to it.

Stew knew his attention toward young ladies had always been well intended. He was not a flirt or a ladies' man. He concluded that the pastor, most likely, was an obsessive and overprotective father.

44

A LADIES' MAN

Stew did not understand what was happening in his life. Ever since the night of the engagement party, he had experienced one nasty encounter after another. Up until then, life had been uncomplicated with little conflict. Now, a pastor had accused him of being a ladies' man. Stew cared how people perceived him, so Pastor Smith's words had deeply wounded him.

As a Christian, Stew knew he had never been overly interested in women, nor did he feel he had intentionally sought their attention. Stew could not deny he had had his fair share of girlfriends in the past, but none of a serious nature—until Bethany.

He made friends easily throughout his life and had more than his share of compliments on his personality, looks, intelligence, and abilities. But such praise had never made him feel better than anyone else. Many of his friends had done well in comparison to him, and he was always proud of their accomplishments.

Most of Stew's acquaintances were good Christians who attended church with him. He had always tried to be a good witness to those who did not know the Lord.

Even though his parents were very wealthy, they paid no attention to society's standards. They also made certain he never used their financial standing as a crutch to get through life. Any type of conceit on his part would not have been tolerated. However, Stew was raised to be confident in his God given attributes and encouraged to use those gifts in a way that brought honor to God.

There was only one time he could recall being jealous of someone. It was the *night* he had seen Bethany at a party with another man. It was the *night* he had realized he was in love with her.

While reviewing his life, he did have to admit young women were easily attracted to him, even though he seldom tried to catch a young lady's attention.

Stew began to wonder if the pastor could be right.

Suddenly, young ladies' faces and his actions toward them began to filter through his mind. He realized it *was* true; he *was* unthinkingly giving young ladies the impression he was interested in them.

Actually, he *did* feel obligated to put young ladies at ease. He also felt responsible to rescue girls who were upset, left out, or shunned. It had been meant in kindness, but it did set the stage for confusion and hurt. Although he knew there was a time for sympathetic attention—in cases like Clair's—a few kind words from him would have been the correct response.

It did explain some of the young women's reactions toward him, but then there were the pushy and assuming girls like Pearl, Sassy, and Rica.

Being a Christian, he felt it was his duty to be gentle in rejecting their attention; he did not want to hurt or embarrass them. Since he did not take control of the situations, it gave them justification to continue in their forwardness.

By being tolerant of girls who were manipulative and forward, he was demonstrating weakness as a Christian man. His actions had allowed such girls and even others, like Matt, room to doubt the sincerity of his walk with Christ. God had tried to caution him many times, but he had disregarded the signs.

It saddened him to know he had never stood his ground when girls made advances or flirted. He had always pretended to ignore the situation, feeling it was the right reaction as a Christian.

He wondered if that was why he had allowed the kiss with Rica.

The pastor was a very wise man. Stew realized his interaction with young ladies had often been foolish—very foolish.

By all means, he needed go back to the church and apologize to the pastor and his daughter.

45

THE DECEIVER

It was a warm spring day when Rica entered the cool building and walked toward the attorney's office. She was angry with her father for insisting she collect some legal papers. Having to stop and rearrange her packages every few steps made her resent the request even more. For the inconvenience, she had decided to have her purchases and the legal documents delivered to their mansion in the carriage. Since she was not finished shopping, the driver would just have to make a trip back for her. Rica could have cared less if the papers were highly confidential; she felt he should have gotten the papers himself or trusted them to a courier. After all, she *was* the daughter of a prominent, wealthy businessman—*not* one of his servants.

While Rica stood outside the office door shifting packages from one place to another, she overheard a heated conversation coming from inside.

Evidently, Mrs. Parker, the attorney's wife, had sent her personal maid to relay a message to her husband's secretary, and the secretary was annoyed with the maid's persistence concerning the matter.

"Again, it doesn't *matter* if Mrs. Parker is ill and can't make the trip to Bay City on the twenty-seventh! And I *do* understand she is very sick and in the hospital, but I *can't* get the money back! It just *isn't* possible! "

"No, what you *mean* is that *you* refuse to try!" the maid accused.

"Excuse me! If you had *any* knowledge of the business world, you would know reservations prevent other customers from retaining accommodations on that date. Hotels would go *broke* if they began refunding money every time someone wanted to cancel a reservation at the last minute. That would be a *very* poor business practice. I simply *can't* get the money back!

"Besides...*you* travel with Mrs. Parks on occasion when she goes away for a weekend. You're aware it is nearly *impossible* to find a carriage from the station to downtown—not to mention any type of a room—without advanced notice.

"Reservations at The Regal, the city's finest hotel, must be booked *weeks* in advance...which is *exactly* what I did to get Mrs. Parker's rooms. And as required, Mrs. Parker's bill was paid in full. There's positively *nothing* I can do about it!" Gertrude folded her arms in defiance.

"Well, I should think if a room is so *impossible* to get, then the hotel should be more than happy to have a room available for someone at the last minute! Why would a major establishment want to take advantage of a dedicated patron who has the misfortune of having to cancel a coveted reservation because of illness? Woman, you make *no* sense! Double talking! You'll say *anything* to be right!" the maid reasoned. "Nonetheless, you simply *must* try. We're talking about a large sum of money being thrown out the window. You know Mrs. Parker is not one to waste money."

Mrs. Parker's loyal maid, Velma, continued to argue, refusing to allow the snobby, legal secretary to get the best of her. "You work for the Parkers, same as I do, and when Silvia Parker says *jump*...I say 'how high'! And you better, too, if you know what's good for you!"

"Oh! I can guarantee *I, of all people,* know the Parkers don't take kindly to wasted money. They pay my salary, the same as yours," Gertrude stated frankly. "And, I don't appreciate *you* insinuating I'm not dedicated to Attorney Parker's welfare!" Gertrude added in her own defense.

"Now, don't go getting high and mighty with *me*! I'm just as important to the Parkers as you think you are. I was only meaning that you might be gnawing off a piece of trouble if you don't at least go through the motions of trying to get that money back. The Parkers are loyal as can be to trusted employees, but the two of them can be *pretty nasty* if they think someone is short changing them...and, in this case, I'd say rightfully so!

"Mrs. Parker may be too sick to deal with this *today*, but when she gets back on her feet, you can bet she'll trot herself down here to give you what for! And I don't intend to get stuck in the middle! You'd better listen to what I'm telling you!

"Well, I've done what I was told. But mark my word...I'm not taking the blame for *your* shortsightedness!" Velma warned. Then the huffy, little maid stomped out and left the secretary sputtering. Velma's sharp wit and quick exit had won her the argument, and for that she was well pleased.

Rica was so intent in listening to the dispute that she almost did not hear the maid coming. Fortunately, she had enough time to pull off the illusion she was in route to another office, so the maid passed by her without noticing. As far as Rica could remember, she and the maid had never come in contact with one another, so she should not have been recognized.

Nevertheless, she was already scheming to use the information she had gathered from the quarrel to coincide with another piece of information she had happened to hear earlier in the week. She hurried to the exit at the far end of the hall but planned to return later in the afternoon to take advantage of her good fortune.

For that reason, she went directly to the carriage to have her packages delivered home, *without* the legal papers, and then headed for another department store to continue shopping.

To her dismay, Rica saw that Dolman's was overrun with customers because of a dry goods sale. This meant the "commoners" were there looking for bargain fabric. That type of people, as Rica called them, could not afford seamstresses and normally patronized the less expensive dry goods stores. The fabric at Dolman's was meant to be purchased by the dressmakers of the elite, and it annoyed Rica to think the common people had access to the best of fabrics.

Rica hated having the undesirables in the store and was just about to voice her complaint to the manager when she noticed Eloise Meeker standing beside her. She found Eloise terribly plain and boring; yet Rica asked Eloise to join her for lunch since she hated to be seen dining alone in public. Besides, she needed to kill some time before returning to the attorney's office.

Eloise hesitated, but reluctantly accepted the invitation. Rica was aware Eloise was doing her a favor but felt no particular obligation to be polite to her. As it turned out, Rica treated Eloise so rudely that the young lady left before the meal was served. However, before leaving, Eloise did let it be known she would have nothing further to do with Rica in the future and stuck her with the bill. Of course, Rica did not care what the little simpleton thought and even wagged her head at Eloise while wearing an arrogant smile. As far as Rica was concerned, Eloise had fulfilled her purpose since there was no one noteworthy in the tearoom anyway. So she quickly ate a few bites, and then summoned the waiter for the check.

By the time Rica returned to the attorney's office, she was more than prepared to deceive the secretary. She first requested her father's legal papers and then complimented her way into Gertrude's favor. Gertrude was flattered by her praises and never dreamed Rica's appearance was anything more than business.

When Gertrude returned with the legal papers, Rica was wearing a troubled expression. The acting job was brilliant, and Gertrude was completely taken in. Rica was proud of her performance.

"Miss Adams, I don't mean to pry, but I can see you're upset about something. What's wrong? May I be of service?" Gertrude questioned in a consoling manner.

"No...No. I'm afraid I've made a mess of something which can't be undone. It's my own silly mistake for not thinking things through. I have a terrible habit of that." Rica's expression turned to one of regret in order to set the hook.

"What is it, dear?" By this time Gertrude was extremely interested and very sympathetic.

"I'm afraid I've hurt a close friend beyond repair. I don't think I'll ever be able to make it up to her." Rica distressfully fidgeted with the gloves in her hands.

"Oh, no! What on earth could a sweet thing like you do to cause a friend to be so upset? I'm sure something can be done," Gertrude babied again.

"No, not this time. I've made a horrible mistake. You see, my dearest friend is getting married on the twenty-seventh in Bay City. The wedding guests are staying at The Regal. As it turned out, I'd already promised to escort my grandmother to Ireland to visit with her sister who is in poor health. So when I was asked to be in the wedding, I had to decline. My friend was very hurt when she learned I wouldn't be by her side. Actually, she was quite destroyed," Rica smoothly lied.

"As it has turned out, my grandmother fell and broke her ankle, so I won't be taking the trip after all. I know it's too late to be my friend's maid of honor, but I thought I might be able *attend* the wedding. Unfortunately, I haven't been able to secure a reservation at any of the decent hotels in Bay City—much less at The Regal.

"My only hope is that my friend won't find out, but I'm sure I can count on that hateful Bethany Jackson to tell her." Rica was sniffling as she wiped her eyes with the handkerchief Gertrude had quickly provided.

"I never thought the Jackson girl that sort. I'm so sorry you're upset...but...you may not need to be. Actually...I think I might have the solution to the entire problem! Just let me check the dates and times. When did you say the wedding was scheduled?" Gertrude asked as she rushed behind her desk to the books.

"The twenty-seventh at seven-thirty in the evening. Why do

you ask?" Rica questioned innocently.

"Oh! You're not going to believe this. I handle the travel plans for the attorney's family, and I have two reservations which will go unused on the exact date. I even have the train tickets and a carriage scheduled to be at the station to take you directly to The Regal. It may not give you much time to freshen up after the long trip, but I'm sure you can manage. However, I will have to sell the trip at full cost, and it is quite a tidy sum."

"Did I hear you right? You have two accommodations available for the exact time?" Rica pretended to be shocked by the probability.

"Yes! I have all the arrangements ready for the exact weekend and time!" Gertrude was extremely excited to be of assistance to the wealthy girl, and she had not forgotten the sale of the reservations would keep her out of hot water with Mrs. Parker.

"Oh, this is unbelievable!" Rica did not have to fake her delight.

"It's providential, my dear. But, wait! We mustn't get ahead of ourselves. Let's check again to make certain we're not mistaken," the secretary cautioned, returning to her legal-minded senses.

Rica walked over to the desk and leaned forward to be enlightened by Gertrude. She intended to be informed of every detail regarding the already scheduled trip. She listened intently—all the while itching to hand over the money and thinking what a nitwit Gertrude was.

As soon as Rica exited the office door, Gertrude spun a piece of paper into the typewriter and proudly let her fingers fly over the keys.

Velma,

The money for Mrs. Parker's cancelled trip for the twenty-seventh of this month will be delivered by courier later this afternoon.

Due to my own clever thinking, I was able to secure another traveler in need of reservations for the exact time and date. Therefore, the reservations are no longer your concern.

However, do not think for a moment I followed through with your ridiculous idea of trying to get the money refunded.

I wish to have no further communication on this subject.

Gertrude Watts

Gertrude could not remember the last time she had written anything less than a properly constructed letter, but this message would do for Velma. The note was purposely short because she was certain Velma would agonize over not knowing how the reservations were disposed of so promptly.

However, the secretary would have been furious if she had known the maid did not believe the story. Velma had concluded that Gertrude had taken the money out of her own pocket and would write the hotel for the refund.

In the meantime, Rica raced to see an acquaintance who worked for the newspaper. The reporter owed Rica a big favor for a scandalous story she had provided last month, and Rica had every intention of collecting on it.

46

STEW AND RICA

Stew was confident he had hired the right people to care for the estate. His first employee was a cook who was always in good spirits and more gifted than most chefs. Fortunately for him, the cook had worked with a woman whom she highly recommended as head of housekeeping. She was a meticulous and pleasant woman who introduced Stew to an Englishman who was willing to work as butler and valet. The butler knew of a stableman and a groundskeeper who were looking for work. All were outstanding in the jobs they were assigned.

The staff was equally pleased with their positions and their employer. A family-like relationship soon developed between Stew and his employees, and that was just the way Stew wanted it. He considered them friends, and each morning they came together for prayer before starting the day.

Within the first year of his career, Stew had been nominated for several awards to be presented at the Bay City Businessmen's Award Ceremony. Stew had never been one to enjoy being publicly singled out, and it was even less appealing since he had come to terms with a few of his personal flaws.

On the night of the ceremony, the butler noticed his employer seemed indifferent to the whole affair, so he had to be more attentive than usual. Of course, Stew looked strikingly handsome by the time the butler had finished helping him dress.

The sidewalks were packed with pedestrians and carriages blocked the busy streets, but Stew was able to arrive in time for pictures. As customary, the cameras were already lined up for the nominees to pose for the press before the proceedings.

The candidates were soon packed tightly together for group shots and then shuffled around for other pictures. There were smoking flashes going off all around, and the whole ordeal was irritating and confusing.

Stew was pulled aside for a single shot, and while he waited, he felt a hand on his back. He looked around and saw Rica Adams standing beside him.

"Stewart! I found you!" she said with a friendly smile. "I read in the paper you were one of the nominees, so, since I'm staying at The Regal, I came down to congratulate you. You must be proud of yourself!"

Stew held her gaze for a few seconds and then responded, "The last time we met, I distinctly defined my wishes where you are concerned."

He nodded and walked away.

On the following Sunday, a picture of Stew and Rica Adams appeared on the society page of *The Remington News*. The article beneath the picture read:

"WEDDING BELLS WILL SOON TOLL FOR THIS LOCAL COUPLE"

Stewart Jefferson and Rica Adams were seen together in Bay City at last weekend's Businessmen's Award Ceremony, where Mr. Jefferson received the "Young Businessman of the Year" award", along with several other awards. Miss Adams indicated there would be an announcement in the near future.

Rica was thrilled. She had finally found a way to get back at Stew for rejecting her and was able to crush Bethany Jackson at the same time.

However, the following day while Rica was shopping, she ran straight into Gertrude, the attorney's secretary. "Well, Miss Adams, I see you've made it safely back from your *friend's wedding*," the secretary stated sharply. There was no reason for her to say anything further. Gertrude stepped around Rica and proceeded down the street. The secretary did not know why the girl had blatantly lied to her, but she knew Rica was up to no good.

Rica was shaken. She had not considered what the repercussion might be once the article was published locally. She was glad her parents were out of town and hoped they would not hear about the article until she had invented a lie to cover it.

"I know what happened the night of the breakup, but Stewart marrying the Adams girl just doesn't set right with me. You mustn't take that newspaper article seriously, Helen. Stew and Bethany may not be together, but I know he loves her. Things aren't always what they appear. Now, come sit down and relax." Mel was attempting to comfort his wife.

"I just hope Bethany no longer has feelings for Stewart. Otherwise, this will hurt her deeply. Are you certain I should write her?" Helen asked.

"I understand how you feel, but it's possible one of her friends might mention it in a letter. Besides, if the article should turn out to be true, she'll have time to get accustomed to the idea before coming home. I'd hate for Bethany to be hit with the news when she first arrives. And if it should be over between the two of them, then there's no need for concern," Mel reasoned.

"Then it's settled. I'd better mail the letter today. I wonder if Lonnie and the children would like to ride into town."

"I think anything that might bring pleasure to that sweet, little family is a wonderful idea. I never thought we could find anyone to replace Mary, but I believe the Lord has found her twin sister. I'm glad she decided to take the position. Running the house and working as a seamstress was putting too much strain on you," Mel pointed out.

"I enjoyed every minute of it, dear. But, you're right about Lonnie. I can't believe how she stepped in and took over where Mary left off. I haven't had one reason to tell her the same thing twice, and the girls working under her are happy with her as well. She's shared her past with them, and they paid it no heed. Poor thing, she was trapped through no fault of her own and might still be if she hadn't come to the Lord. I must remember to tell Bethany how much we love Lonnie and the children. Maybe it will help distract her from the news in the article."

47

THE LETTER

When Bethany was told her mother's dress shipment had just arrived, she quickly tucked the unopened letter from the post office into a pocket and followed Lena into the shop.

Lena grabbed the hammer and pried open the crate. Inside were three boxes. The first box contained three day-dresses which were very sturdy and made of well-chosen, floral fabrics. The second box contained four dresses which were more fashionable and of outstanding quality. "They're amazing! And, what a relief to have so many dresses for the rack. I'd better take them to Sally so she can get them pressed. She does such a lovely job."

"We needed something for our dwindling racks. Although...I *am* expecting Kate to have a dress or two for us tomorrow. Bethany, I'm so happy you're here to share in the fun. It feels like Christmas every time we open one of your mother's shipments. I don't understand how Helen can complete the work so quickly. She must work night and day," Lena bragged.

"Mother is very dedicated and hardworking but don't shortchange yourself. I get a second Christmas every time I see *your* creations."

"I'm no Helen Jackson, but I'm more confident in my work than when I first started. Are you ready to open the wedding gown?"

Bethany gave an excited nod, and Lena removed the lid from the box.

"It's lovely!" they both squealed with excitement.

"How does she do it?" Lena questioned. "Look at the train! This has to be the most beautiful wedding gown I've ever seen. The bride will be beside herself. She was pleased with my sketches, but I never imagined all this detail."

Bethany did not answer because it was *not* the most beautiful dress she had ever seen. Her mother had made a dress which was at least ten times as lovely, and she hoped to wear it someday.

"You're daydreaming, Bethy. I guess any young lady would daydream when looking at a gown as lovely as this one.

"I mailed the measurements and sketches for the bridesmaids' gowns over a week ago, so we can expect more excitement in the near future," Lena predicted.

"You're doing a great service for the ladies of this area. They finally have a store completely dedicated to their needs. If nothing else, it lifts the spirits for the women who can't afford to buy or have dresses made. At least they're welcome to come inside to see the new styles and the pretty things you stock. Not to mention, the shop will soon provide decent work for a few more of the women in the area. It's a *ministry*."

"Well, thank you for the insight, Bethany. I'd never thought of it in that way. The boutique *could* be considered a ministry. I know God put the desire in my heart, and with a portion of my profits and your salary going to the orphanage, it's a blessing to so many.

"By the way, I haven't had a chance to tell you we're trying to buy the little store next door. It's been closed for years. I want to open a millinery shop. The ladies will be needing hats to go with their dresses. I'm also considering moving the ladies' shoes in there. That way they won't have to go into the mercantile to purchase them—it seems more ladylike, doesn't it? Anyway, I met a new lady in church who used to make hats for a living. She's a delightful person to be around, and we discussed the idea of the hat shop last Sunday.

"And Bethany...another lady stopped in to say she'd like to supply intimate apparel, if I'd be interested. We need a few more lower-priced dresses. We must keep in mind those who can't afford to spend much...," Lena continued on with various bits of information.

Bethany couldn't help but smile as she thought of Lena's exuberance over the possibilities of the new business ventures.

"Good afternoon, Miss Bethany! I hope you've had a lovely day," Mr. Felder greeted.

"I have, and I hope the same for you and your lovely wife!" she cheerfully returned. "Where's Pastor David?"

"He'll meet us at the mission entrance. There was some business with an attorney that needed to be completed. He should be ready by the time we get back to the front of the building. We didn't want you walking in this heat, so we drove to the back to pick you up," he explained with a kind smile as he helped her in.

"Thank you for being so considerate. I am a bit tired."

When they arrived at the front door, the pastor was ready. He hopped into the buggy and took the reins.

Since Bethany started serving on the visitation team, she had noticed a big change in the outlook of the poor. Many of the hurting were beginning to benefit from the mission projects and were very grateful for the help. There were some who had been embittered because they felt the support should have come when the hard times first hit. However, once they saw the impact a few supplies had made on their lives, their attitudes began to soften.

Now, instead of resentful stares on visitation day, they began receiving slight nods or a quick wave of the hand here and there. Each week the reception improved a little. The pastor could finally let Rook trot down the street as they called out greetings to people with whom they had become acquainted. Many of the sad, forlorn, dirty faces were replaced with smiles. Filthy clothing was gradually being exchanged for cleaner and nicer apparel on their well-scrubbed bodies. Some of the people had started attending church and had accepted Jesus into their hearts. They were grateful for the changes the Lord had made in their lives and the hope He offered for the future.

Bethany was extremely tired when she entered her little hut late that evening. It had been a very eventful day, and she was ready to climb onto the crate for a good night's rest. She took a few minutes to freshen up and started to hang her dress in the closet when she found the letter from her mother. Knowing there would be no sleep until she had devoured each word, Bethany tore it open and began to read.

She was pleased to hear Lonnie was such a blessing. Her mother wrote that Lonnie learned quickly, had already gained the respect of the staff, and had grown in her faith. Both parents loved the children and were having the guest house prepared for Lonnie's family to use as their home. It appeared the two families were equally pleased with one another.

Her mother also mentioned that—for some reason—the groundskeeper was now eating with Lonnie in the kitchen on a regular basis.

Bethany was delighted to know the bridesmaid gown sketches had been received, and when completed, the gowns would be shipped with a few more rack dresses.

Unfortunately, *all* the news in the letter was not pleasant.

> *Now, my sweet daughter, I'm afraid I might have a bit of unsettling news. Your father and I have prayed about whether we should share this information with you while you're away, and we feel it is better that you know now. Please understand there may not be a word of truth in it.*
>
> *What you will find in the enclosed article is all we know about the circumstance. We haven't tried to gather any further information since we don't feel it is wise or our place. We pray this information has no adverse effect on you. We know you will trust in the Lord for strength.*
>
> *My darling, we cannot be there to share this in-*

formation, but be assured, we are with you in love, thought, and prayer.

God bless you,

Mother

Bethany unfolded the article, read it, and then looked at the picture of the couple staring into one another's eyes.

48

FEELINGS FOR DAVID

The boutique was proving to be a successful business. Lena found she had an undiscovered talent for designing and, with Bethany's help, was becoming a very skilled seamstress.

"The money from the shop is providing a substantial income for the mission, and it looks as though it *will be* for some time," Bethany told David as they walked together after an evening service.

"I know Lena and Burt will continue to donate, but aren't you forgetting we're losing *your* salary?"

Bethany quickly responded, "Which reminds me. I have a message to relay to you from my parents. Lena made Mother a proposal to continue designing for the boutique as a professional. She asked Mother to label her clothing. Mother is ecstatic, and father insisted she accept the offer. So guess what!"

"I have no idea." Pastor David knew he was about to be enlightened.

"My parents will be donating *all* of her profits to the mission! The mission is a worthy cause, and it will allow Mother to follow her dreams *and* be part of a ministry. What could be more fulfilling?"

"Honestly? They're that dedicated to the orphanage? I...I don't know what to say! It's amazing how donations are seeming to come out of nowhere. It makes me wonder what else God has in store for us here.

"Please, express my sincere gratitude to them. It's appreciated more than they'll ever know. The children will be blessed, and I pray your family will be blessed for doing it.

"Why don't we continue our walk downtown while the streets are peaceful?" he suggested. "We're halfway there already."

They took the new road by the creek where the children often played in the water. The two were in a discussion about the mission when the thought which had been plaguing Bethany's mind for weeks suddenly tumbled from her mouth. "Are you not attracted to me in the least?" Bethany was shocked she had just spoken her private thoughts aloud.

"Please, I-I don't know what came over me!" she apologized.

"Don't feel bad. You're leaving soon, and it *is* something we should address."

After a moment of hesitation, Pastor Goodry bluntly stated, "You are very attractive, Bethany...but I'm not interested in you in *that* way."

"I see," she answered quickly.

"No, I know you well enough to know you *don't* see. I didn't mean to be so straight forward. It was unfeeling of me.... I'm still working on tact."

"Evidently," she responded.

"I wouldn't intentionally do or say anything to hurt you, so please let me explain," he apologized.

Bethany wanted to leave before the redness of her face was

evident. "No. An explanation isn't necessary."

"Bethany! This discussion is long overdue. If we don't qualify our feelings for each other, it might cost us our friendship."

"Friendship" was not the word she wanted to hear. She had used the word more than once to divert unwanted, romantic attention, but it had never been applied to *her*. She had felt the word to be a compassionate way to spare a young man's ego. Now, experiencing the sting of its implication, she knew the word could feel belittling and hurtful.

"There are several things I've never mentioned concerning my feelings toward you...and the truth is...I was immediately smitten when we first met. To be perfectly honest, it was the main reason why I acted the way I did. I had never felt so strongly about a young lady. It embarrassed me, and I was afraid it might have been obvious to you. After all, I *am* a pastor.

"But while I was away...the time I spent in prayer was as much about *you* as it was the mission," he admitted. "Do you want to know what the Holy Spirit revealed to me?"

Bethany hesitated, then answered defensively, "Not particularly."

"Too bad," he laughed and continued for her sake. "God did not intend for us to walk through life together. At first I was disappointed and confused, but, once I had time to think it through...I understood. He brought us together to enjoy doing His work as friends...and that's all."

"But David...we've worked out our problems, and *I* believe God *intended* for us to be together. It makes perfect sense," she argued.

"I understand that. We have both struggled with our emotions, but there's *more* to this," David said boldly.

"Oh, really!" Bethany folded her arms. "I don't know if I'm up for another sermon."

"'I'm going to be straightforward," he informed her.

"More than you already have been?" she questioned skeptically.

"Listen, Bethany...you're still in love with Stewart Jefferson...aren't you?"

"No! I've told you what he did. You know I was in love with the man I *thought* he was, and not the man he *is*. The man I was in love with never existed!"

"Bethany, you have that answer memorized...*I* even have it memorized. But are you being truthful with yourself?

"Look, all I'm saying is...did you mistake your *disappointment* in Stew as a sign from God? You're overly defensive about the breakup, and it makes me wonder if you ever gave the man a chance to explain." The pastor fully intended to provoke her consideration.

"Did you seek the Lord's guidance before you broke the engagement? Was it the Lord's leading...or did you do it out of hurt?

"We both know the answer...you did it on the spur of the moment. Remember...God just led *me* through a difficult time. I *understand* how it feels to be wrong." Pastor David wanted to show her compassion, but, as her acting pastor, he needed to be truthful.

"I've heard all of this before," she said sternly.

"I'm sure you have."

Then Bethany looked at him pitifully with tears in her eyes, "It really doesn't matter what either of us believe. It's too late."

49

THE FINAL GOODBYE

"Hello, miss!" a feminine voice called. Bethany turned from the pump to find a young woman walking toward her. A tan face, sprinkled with freckles, and copper colored hair went well with the enthusiastic smile. She was a slim girl of medium height and wore a neat, blue dress which enhanced her green eyes. *She's quite lovely,* Bethany thought to herself.

"I didn't mean to frighten you. It's just that I've been waiting in the foyer for quite some time, so I finally decided to look for someone who might know where I could find Pastor Goodry.

"I'm sorry, I should have introduced myself. My name is Ella... Ella Jenkins, the missionary you've been expecting. I wired Pastor Goodry a couple weeks ago to let him know I'd be arriving today," Ella explained as she reached out a gloved hand to Bethany.

"Yes, of course! I'm so sorry to hear you've been waiting. I hope you don't think we meant to neglect you, but we were expecting you to arrive later this evening. The Pastor and staff had hoped to be on hand to greet you." Bethany felt her apology insufficient as she took Ella's extended hand and pulled her into a warm sisterly hug. "The first thing you must learn is that we're huggers...and...a loyal and loving family."

"That's wonderful to hear. I could use a loving family," Ella replied with a pleased laugh.

"I'm Bethany Jackson, and it's been a blessing to have filled your position.

"Pastor Goodry is in his office working on some papers that must be completed by this afternoon. We have a young boy who's being adopted, and his new parents will be arriving tomorrow.

"They're newlyweds and had intended to spend a month on their honeymoon, but they changed their plans at the last minute. The new father wants to spend time with his son before returning to work.

"They telegraphed their lawyer to contact Pastor Goodry so he could get the paperwork in order. He just found out about the adoption this morning."

Ella Jenkin's eyes lit up in hearing the news.

"According to the lawyer, the boy had become acquainted with the couple before he came here. We're always happy when our children are placed in a loving home, but this little boy is extra special to us.

"He loves the Lord and has spiritual depth and wisdom far beyond his years. The little guy has a way of putting life in perspective. We call him "Pete". He plans to be a minister someday. The adoption has come as a shock, so the mood around here is bittersweet.

"Please forgive me," Bethany said, catching herself. "You've just arrived, and I'm already bombarding you with details."

"No, please feel free to share anything that comes to mind. We might as well start my training now," Ella reassured her.

"Well, to be honest, you'll *need* the information because I'm leaving for home early tomorrow morning." Bethany thought Ella might as well know she would have to start working immediately.

"Oh, no! I'm sorry to hear you're leaving so soon. Although I'm sure you must be anxious to get home—especially since you've been here much longer than you were led to believe."

"My leaving tomorrow will also be a convenient way to deliver the horse and buckboard to the train station for Pete's adoptive parents.

"I'm very excited to go home. But don't worry about your training. There are plenty of people here to assist you.

"By the way, Pete's already packed. He did it himself. I'd love to introduce you to him and the other children, but they're on an outing and won't be back until nap time."

"So that's why it's so quiet. I was wondering why there were no children around this time of day," Ella interjected.

"I'm sorry serving at the mission was contingent on the loss of your mother. Please, accept my condolences."

"Thank you. I appreciate your kind words, but my mother was in pain and unaware toward the end. For that reason, I feel blessed she's with the Lord."

"I see." Bethany gave Ella another hug to comfort her.

"Now, can I be perfectly honest with you?" Bethany asked, wanting to sound cheerful. "Please don't take offense, but we were expecting someone much older."

"Yes, I've heard there was an error made on my age. However, I *am* experienced. I grew up moving from one reservation to another and took complete charge of my parents' work when my father passed away."

"You must have had an interesting life. Although, you'll find this place comes with its challenges. Your work here will be quite different from what you've been accustomed to, but you'll soon love it here—as I do."

"I dearly loved growing up on the reservations and loved the people who lived there, but I'm ready for a new life. The reservations were my *parents'* calling. This is where *my* ministry begins." Ella wore a contented smile as she looked around.

"And it's easy to see you can't wait to get started. So let's get you settled in. Is this all of your luggage?" Bethany reached down and picked up a large bag.

"No, I don't travel this lightly. I had my trunk put on the front porch."

"That's fine. A couple of the men will bring it around." Bethany grabbed the bucket of water with her free hand and led Ella to the little hut.

"Your space is small, but I think you'll like it. *Of course,* staying with the children in the orphanage *is* an option," she joked.

Bethany opened the sturdy, new door of the little adobe hut to the view of a newly decorated room. The first thing Ella noticed was a high posted bed with a night stand holding an etched glass, oil lamp. In one corner was a free standing mirror, and under the window was a desk which could double as a dressing table.

There was a wingback chair, chest of drawers, a dressing screen for privacy, and a small armoire. Near the door was a washstand with a light blue bowl and pitcher covered with peach colored roses.

The building now had a wooden floor and framed glass windows with screens. A small stove had been installed for cool nights.

The fabric for the bedspread, chair, dressing screen, and windows all matched beautifully. The windows even had lace panels. There was a rug on each side of the bed and at the door. A picture of children playing in a brook and candle sconces decorated one wall.

Bethany had never slept in the updated room since the new furniture had only arrived the previous day. Everything had been donated by a couple who had recently lost their daughter in a riding accident. The furniture was to have been a surprise for the girl's sixteenth birthday. Bethany and a couple of the volunteers had worked late into the night to put everything in perfect order before Ella's arrival.

The young missionary stood mesmerized while Bethany placed the bucket behind the curtain of the washstand as the final touch.

"I never dreamed I'd spend a night in such an elegant room, and to think this will be mine to come to at the end of each day is beyond belief. God is so exceedingly wonderful! I've never lived in such comfort. When Mother passed, she and I were sharing a cleared out storage room in the back of a store."

Until her stay at the mission, Bethany had only known luxury and comfort in every aspect of her life, so Ella's words were deeply humbling. Bethany would not miss the uncomfortable crate she had used for a bed, and it pleased her to know it was feeding the kitchen fire at that very moment.

Both girls had felt a closeness from the moment they met. Their conversation flowed so well that the mission tour took three times as long as usual, but Bethany wanted to share the history and miracles God had performed while she was there.

When returning from the tour of the grounds, they found Pastor Goodry in his office. Bethany, wishing she had sent word to inform him of Ella's early arrival, gave an awkward introduction. She then excused herself, leaving them alone to discuss the future of the mission. It was obvious David was surprised to see Ella was much younger than expected, and Bethany could not keep from noticing the sparks of interest that passed between the two.

Later in the evening, David and Bethany escorted Ella into the dining hall to meet the children and the volunteers.

Sandra and the kitchen staff had made a delicious meal of roast pork, mashed potatoes, gravy, green beans, spice apples, homemade rolls, and caramel cake. David, Ella, Bethany, and the couple in charge of the outreach ministries were placed at a special table in honor of the missionary's arrival.

After dinner, Ella shared the heartwarming story of her life and how the Lord had led her to the mission. Then Pastor David stood by Ella as the children, staff, and guests filed through the greeting line to meet her. Bethany was pleased with their response and knew Ella Jenkins would do just fine at the mission.

While Ella took pleasure in her reception, Bethany discreetly roamed the room telling the volunteers and children goodbye. Moments later as she slipped quietly out the door, Bethany knew in her heart that she would miss everyone, but it was time for her to leave the mission.

Before sunrise, Bethany, trying not to disturb Ella, carefully threw back the covers and slipped out of bed. It had felt wonderful to sleep on a soft mattress for her last night at the mission, but in a short time, she would be home enjoying the luxury of her own bed.

The new rug was soothing beneath her feet, but it was only a fleeting thought as she walked over to freshen up before getting dressed. It was already hot outside, so she was glad she had picked a lightweight dress for her journey home.

As she left the little hut, she turned for one final glance, but it did not tug at her heart since it no longer resembled the place she had known. She grabbed the lantern and her bags, then tiptoed outside, closing the door quietly.

At the stable, Bethany realized Tom had thoughtfully laid out the tack for the horse and had prepared the buckboard to make it easier for her. *God bless Tom. I should have expected nothing less of him.*

Once the rig was ready, she hurried to the kitchen to grab an apple and a slice of bread for breakfast. The heavy door to the dining hall was closed, so she gave it a heave and ran straight into Sandra.

"Now ya didn't really think your mission family was goin' to let ya set out in the middle of the night with that little nothing of a goodbye last evening, did ya?" Sandra asked with a broad smile. Then she stepped aside to reveal the children, staff, and several members of the church family. The children were still in their pajamas but greeted her with sleepy smiles.

"What are you all doing up this early in the morning? But... it's so wonderful to see you one final time!"

"Since there wasn't a reception when you arrived, we wanted to make up for it in your departure," Pastor David shouted from across the room. All the adults understood his meaning and gave a cheerful laugh followed by loud applause.

Then Ella swept her off to a nearby table where a plate filled with scrambled eggs, sausage, and biscuits was waiting with a hot cup of coffee. Sandra always insisted on preparing the meals for special occasions.

Bethany ate quickly so there would be time for a proper farewell. Sandra's final hug came with a packed lunch, and Pastor David prayed for her safe journey. The children stood nearby waving and throwing kisses as she gave a flick of the reins.

"God bless you all for the wonderful send off!" Bethany shouted as she drove away.

Rook quickly trotted into what was no longer the dangerous part of town for Bethany. She was not sure when it had happened, but over time, those from the mission had earned the respect of the people who lived there.

As she drove down the street, she noticed adults and children standing outside. Then she began to hear various calls.

"Goodbye, Miss Bethany!"

"Ya shore will be missed, little lady!"

"Hurry back!"

"Remember us in yer prayers, Miss Bethany!"

"You've been so kind to us. I'm goin' ta start church Sunday, just like ya asked me to!"

"You're a peach!"

"Yep, she a goodin!"

The calls continued all the way to Main Street. She turned Rook and the buckboard sideways at the end of the street and, with the help of first light, gave one final wave.

On the way out of Pike City, Bethany praised God for the miracles He had performed during her time at the mission.

50

THE CATASTROPHE

Rook, out of habit, took the lead to maneuver the streets. Meanwhile, Bethany relaxed and let the memories collected in her heart pass through her mind.

The darkness melted into light, and a gentle breeze made the ride more pleasant. It did not seem long until they were curving onto the road that went directly to Tally. The shade offered there by a grove of trees was a momentary pleasure.

"Giddy up! Go on, now! I wanta get these poor excuses for women delivered for safe keepin''! I'm expectin' a good meal to be waitin' fer me when I get home tonight! " the jail wagon driver shouted to his horses.

Bethany was too caught up in her daydreams to notice Rook sensing something was wrong. She clicked her tongue and gave the reins an encouraging lash, but, instead of Rook gliding gently onto the main road, he made a drastic swerve to the right.

The driver of the wagon yelled to warn the team as he pulled with all of his might to get his horses to turn hard left. The attempts made by Rook and the driver were not enough.

The man had driven the road for years and had never met anyone at the fork. Unfortunately, the cedars on the corner, a cloud of dust, and a slight hill had blocked both of their views.

"Is he dead?" The redheaded prisoner asked.

"No, I can see him breathin'. He'll be comin' around soon," the blonde answered.

"Hey! I think I can reach the keys!" the redhead told her partner. Even though she was extremely dizzy, she lay down to stretch far enough to reach them. "Got 'em! Move over here and lean in!" the redhead ordered.

The blonde did as she was instructed and with one click she was free. "Good job, Red!" the blonde said as she took the keys and unlocked her ankles. "Now lean to the side so I can unlock you."

"No, Melva! There's not time! My leg is hurt bad, and the driver is startin' to stir. Is the women dead?" Red asked in a lower tone.

"I don't know about her, but I saw *him* move!" Melva whispered.

"You might have enough time to switch clothes with her! Get movin! You've gotta give it a try!" Red told her.

"Why?" Melva replied, unbuttoning her dress.

"Think about it! The driver didn't get a good look at us, and the sheriff ain't seen us. I'll pass her off as you, and you can get the money and the boys. If we don't do it, it'll be a long time before the boys find us this far south. They can break me out if I'm still at the jail. Since the prison's full, I should be in there a while. It's a sure thing. Just get the money before anyone else finds it and bring the boys for me," Red instructed.

"You want me to leave you here?" Melva replied.

"Listen, you idiot! I'm hurt and I'd hold you up. I ain't got no decent clothes either. They'd spot us. We can both be free if you just get the boys. Hurry up! It shouldn't take but two or three days. Besides, it looks like she's goin' to be out a while—if she don't die. If she don't come to, it'll be a long while before they figure out you escaped. I'll make sure of it!" Red declared.

"Mess her hair up, so it won't give us away! You can get that little buckboard untwisted. Back it onto the road with the horse. It's a good thing it righted itself after dumpin' her out. Now, get outa here! He's about to come to!" Red instructed as quietly as she could.

"Don't forget to doll yourself up before you get to town. You'll need to look as good as pretty girl here. Be careful you don't draw too much attention. Someone might be expectin' her in Tally," Red added with a little laugh, pleased with her cleverness."

The buggy was damaged, but it was road worthy. Melva was not even half dressed, but climbed in and gave the reins several slaps to let Rook know it was time to move out. She never replied or even looked back.

Melva had no intention of going for the boys. She was free and going for the money.

Red's man, Bart, and her brother, Yancy, had no idea where the money was since it had been handed off to the girls after the robbery.

The girls had dressed as men during the holdup, and all four of them had exited the lobby back into the front foyer where they had entered. However, instead of going out the front door with Bart and Yancy, the two women exited out a side door and into another foyer. They removed their cowboy hats, masks, and long coats, which had made them appear to be men, and threw the clothing into a carpet bag planted behind the stairs. Next they let down their skirts, put on hats, and quickly entered the boardwalk. Since the folks outside the bank were focused on the two robbers with the money, Red and Melva walked down the street unnoticed, just behind the boys who had left gunning their way out of town.

Bart dropped the money in a washtub as they passed down a side street. The girls followed close behind, grabbed the money, and slipped it into the carpet bag in one slick move. The women were to meet the boys ten miles to the north of town with the cash.

Unfortunately for them, the Boyer Gang never anticipated the witness who watched the entire robbery played out from an upstairs window. Nor did they consider there might already be wanted posters in circulation that would speed up the process of identifying them.

Red and Melva were caught not long after the robbery but had time to stash the loot once they realized they were being chased. Both refused to reveal the location. Red refused for the love of her *man* and Melva for her love of *money*.

There was enough cash hidden to pay for Melva's ticket out of the country and to live comfortably for quite a while. She planned to change her name and buy a wig. The rest of the Boyer Gang would never figure out what happened to her.

Melva and Yancy had hit it off a couple years ago, and she took him up on the offer to ride with them. Anything was better than the lifestyle she was living at the time. Melva had no romantic interest in Yancy but tricked him into thinking so. She had helped the trio pull off a few small jobs, and it had paid off.

Now there would be no more working in saloons or fraternizing with drunken lowlifes. A trip to the other side of the world, a few fancy clothes, and a little finishing school would provide a new way of life for her.

Melva drove Rook to the point of heat stroke, and the older horse would have collapsed if she had forced him to go much further. Fortunately for the horse, when Melva neared Tally, she drove the horse behind a clump of bushes to make herself presentable for the trip. She rummaged through Bethany's things to find what she needed and even came up with a purse that contained a substantial amount of money and a few makeup items. Afterward, Melva dumped the unwanted stuff into the trunk and repacked the bags with the items needed for traveling. Melva was ecstatic to have stolen an entire wardrobe and all the necessities. She would take the first train east with only one planned stop...and it would be to get the stolen cash.

Melva slid into town and abandoned the rig near the railway station. She jumped from the seat, grabbed the bags, and hurried off, not even taking time to secure the horse.

"Well, that puts the wagon out of commission for a while. I reckon the old nag *had* to be shot. I feel real bad about it, sheriff. I couldn't take a chance of waitin' 'til someone came along. I tried to make it here with her, but I didn't have a choice. The blonde was knocked out, and the redhead had a bad leg. I had to make the decision. The horse had to be sacrificed. That redhead cussed me every step of the way, actin' like she was worried about the blonde." The driver was extremely shaken as he relayed the story to the sheriff in Liver.

"It sure is hard to believe that sweet looking, little blonde could be partner to that redhead. I've heard neither one of 'em is worth the price of the bullet it would take to shoot 'em."

"What happened to the other driver?" the sheriff asked.

"They took off! I caught a glimpse of a horse and a buckboard just before we hit. Thank goodness the prisoners were injured, or they'd gotta way. Not that I wish anyone harm, but the keys *were* laying near the blonde one. I suppose the other driver could've gone for help, but I doubt it. Isn't that somethin'?

"Well, guess I'd better head out. I sure don't relish ridin' that big ol' horse home. My head's a bustin'." He rubbed the huge lump and shook his head.

"I'm afraid that headache is just startin'. Best see a doctor," the sheriff warned.

"Wait a minute before you go. I need to complete this account of what you remember and you'll have to sign off on it," the lanky sheriff instructed.

"Like I said, alls I remember was I looked over and saw a buckboard and a black horse a comin' from my right, and that's when I pulled the horses to the left as best I could. It's a miracle we weren't all killed! The girls were thrown clean out the door when the lock broke somehow! Clean out the door! The wagon slammed up against that mountain of a rock on the right there. Ya know the one I'm a talkin' 'bout? I reckon that's what caused it to bust open. I'm not a God-fearing man, but I'll tell ya what, He was looking out today!" The driver was starting to get worked up again.

"In your estimation, was either of you at fault?" the sheriff questioned.

"Naw. To be honest, I figure we both was a goin' at a reasonable clip. Just couldn't see ner hear one 'nother." He stood quietly and waited a few minutes while the sheriff finished writing the information down.

"Well, Ben, sign here unless you have something more to add. You'd best be on your way. Take it easy on yourself and that dandy of a horse."

"Thanks...have a goodin'," Ben returned as he walked toward the door.

51

SOMETHING IS TERRIBLY WRONG

The blacksmith spotted the blonde when she raced into town and forced the horse to slide to a stop. She jumped out of the buckboard, grabbed three bags from the back, and hurried off to the station. He could not believe she had left the horse in the hot sun—overheated and exhausted.

He had seen about everything when it came to the abuse of animals, and it was not in him to ignore one in need of care. He watched the horse until he was certain it had been abandoned and went to notify the new sheriff.

Immediately, the sheriff and the blacksmith could tell the animal was in good health and extremely well cared for, so having been abandoned in such a state did not make sense.

They took a quick look inside the buckboard and noted there were several personal items strewn around and clothing was even hanging out of a trunk, keeping it from closing completely.

A closer examination revealed damage to the left side of the rig, and the blacksmith found a deep, fresh gash on the horse's lower left side. They both recognized the outfit but could not recall the owner.

Concerned for the animal, the sheriff gave the blacksmith permission to take the horse inside for care.

Since the horse was in good condition for its advanced years, the blacksmith did not feel the harsh treatment would cause any permanent health issues. Still, he left his work undone until he was certain the horse was starting to regain strength.

Wanting to be sure nothing had been overlooked, he examined the buckboard once more. But other than a few broken straps, the blacksmith found no significate damage.

Later in the day, the sheriff stopped by to look through the things left in the back of the buckboard. It was obvious the girl had planned to be gone for some time, but the articles scattered around did not match with the neatness of the items packed in the bottom of the trunk.

He found a beautiful shawl with a much used Bible folded inside, but there were no notations or personal information normally found in a Bible.

Bethany could hear women's voices. One was laughing and another sounded angry. Realizing there was something wrong, she tried to lift her head, but the pain was too great and she passed out.

Occasionally, someone offered her sips of water and broth and wiped her brow. Unfortunately, her throbbing head would not allow her to make sense of it all.

Once, she had thought derogatory remarks were being made about her, but it did not matter at the time. She just wanted to go back to sleep so the pain would go away.

Eventually, Bethany opened her eyes slightly and caught a glimpse of a woman standing by a window and another sitting in an unladylike position on a cot. Across the room she could see bars. She raised her head for a better look but had to lie back down to stop the pain. *Something's terribly wrong*! Bethany groaned as the blackness closed in.

52

A BIT OF A MYSTERY

"It never crossed my mind we would meet again—especially after such a brief introduction at the train station," Andrea reminisced.

"I certainly remember being taken with you. I would have tried to strike up a conversation if we hadn't been so concerned about Billy at the time. Although from my perception, you seemed to have volunteered rather quickly when *Stew* asked you to take responsibility for Billy," Matt said to bait her.

"Are you jealous? He *is* considered quite the catch."

"Actually, I'm feeling quite secure in our relationship. After all, you did marry *me*." Matt gave a pleased smile.

"Isn't God amazing?" Andrea said, unintentionally changing the subject. "We've only been husband and wife for two weeks. Yet in a few hours, we'll be a family."

"That little guy certainly made an impression on me. I felt it was so unfair when he lost his mother on the train. Still he continued to trust God. And his *face*...I've spent many sleepless nights thinking about his little, sweet face." Matt gave a slight laugh at the thought.

"As I have," Andrea agreed. "But then again, I've spent a few nights awake thinking of your handsome face too."

Matt lovingly put his hand to her cheek. "I never thought I would want to be a married man...*or* a Christian...but I've certainly been blessed by making those choices. I knew I didn't want to go through life without you when we were reintroduced at church."

"And I felt the same way about you," she agreed. "God had a wonderful plan for our future."

"Conductor! How long is it until the next stop?" Matt asked suddenly.

"About fifteen minutes, sir," the man replied, not slowing down as he passed.

"Fifteen minutes!" Andrea repeated in excitement. "I had no idea we had napped so long!"

"Wow! Calm down! I don't want you climbing out the window." It pleased Matt to see his new wife so anxious.

"I'm sorry, Matthew. I hope I didn't embarrass you. I'm usually more in control of myself." Her face flushed as she noticed a few of the other passengers had heard the outburst.

"You could never embarrass me. Besides, I love it when you're a bit out of control."

Matt Wilson gently touched his bride's waist to guide her through the crowd as they made their way across the platform. He then offered Andrea his arm to lead her to a shaded bench where she would be more comfortable until he collected their luggage and located the horse and buckboard.

To Matt's disappointment, the promised transportation was

not under the tree or anywhere in the vicinity. He sat the luggage down on the platform and walked into the street to scan the downtown area. There was not a rig anywhere fitting the description they had been given.

Matt was irritated since his new wife would need to wait in the scorching heat while he made other arrangements. He knew the horse would have been left alone for an hour or more, so he was concerned something might had prevented the driver from arriving at the station on time. Nonetheless, his first duty was to care for his wife.

"I couldn't find the horse and buckboard...even checked at the ticket office. The man suggested I ask the sheriff since he keeps on top of things. If needed, we should try renting something from the stable. It's not far, so let's find a more comfortable place for you to wait while I see what I can do."

"No, Matthew. It *is* hot, but I'd like to go. We'll be able to leave immediately if I'm with you." Andrea was accustomed to being pampered, but getting to the orphanage was more important than her comfort.

Matt just smiled and held out his arm to guide her.

It did not take long to find the sheriff's office, and Matt was not far into their story before the sheriff asked the couple to follow him to the stable.

"Hey, Sam!" the sheriff yelled to the blacksmith. "Sounds like that buckboard and horse belong to the mission over in Pike City. This couple told me a rig was to be left at the station. They're expected to drive it back to pick up a boy they're adoptin'."

Sam put down the iron in his hand. "That's *right!* It belongs to that group who took over the orphanage. The girl driving the wagon...was she a blonde?" he asked with disgust in his voice.

"We've no idea," Matt was stumped by the man's agitation. "We received a telegram stating a black horse and buckboard would be left under the tree at the station. Someone was leaving on a train not long before we arrived."

"Well, some blonde woman, wearing a blue dress, come ridin' up in the rig, grabbed her bags, and headed off to the station. The horse had been driven too hard in this heat—especially for its age! She just left the animal standin' in the hot sun, all lathered up, and in a bad need of water! I watched him out there 'til I couldn't stand it no more. I finally went and got the sheriff. Nothin' but a self-centered, mean-streaked woman could do a thing like that!" The blacksmith was still spitting mad over the incident.

"There's some damage to one side of the buckboard, and the horse has a big scrape on its left side. May've been in some kind of accident, but that's no excuse for leaving the animal in that shape. She could've *at least* left it at a trough where it could get water. Most anybody around here would've helped her if she was runnin' late," the sheriff added.

"To be honest, I have no idea what to think about it." Matt scratched his head and then pulled some money from his pocket. "Here, let me pay you for your trouble. I hope this will cover the expense." Matt handed the money to the blacksmith.

"Well, I guess that'll more than do, but I don't know if it's a good idea to put the horse back on the road right away. Best give him a night to recover and leave in the mornin'."

"Then do you have anything to rent, so we can get to the mission right away?" Matt questioned. He was feeling somewhat desperate since neither he nor his wife wanted to postpone the trip.

"No, nothin' 'til tomorrow, I'm afraid," the man answered.

"Now Sam, you heard me tell ya this young couple is on their way to adopt a kid. They don't want to wait until mornin'. The horse looks in good shape. Can't they use him if they take it slow and keep an eye out. This young fella looks like he's got some horse sense."

"Well...I reckon'...if they walk him and keep a close watch. I do tend to get a bit overprotective. Come on, I'll get him hitched."

It was not long before Matt and Andrea were on their way after having lost an hour. The ride was slow, hot, and tedious—but one they would always remember. The newlyweds were certain they could not make it back to Tally in time to catch the late night train, but it wasn't important. Being reunited with Billy was all that mattered.

It seemed like an eternity before the couple curved onto the road that would take them to Pike City. Both gave a sigh of relief when the mission finally came into sight. Matt took Rook up to a slight clip, and the horse seemed more than happy to oblige.

When the couple pulled into the mission drive, Sandra was watering flowers and was the first to greet them. She quickly led the two through the corridors and into the pastor's office.

Pastor Goodry, pleased to see they had arrived, shook their hands heartily. "I hope you found everything as instructed."

"As a matter of fact, it's a bit of a mystery," Matt reluctantly replied, not wanting to start out on the wrong foot at such an important time. "The horse and buggy weren't at the station when we arrived. Fortunately, we stopped by the sheriff's office before trying to find other transportation. The sheriff took us to the blacksmith across the street.

"We were told the horse and buckboard we drove here belong to the mission. It appears there might have been some sort of accident, so the horse should be looked after right away."

"You don't say!" The pastor was caught off guard by the news. "Please, let's go take a look. Did they say anything about Bethany?"

"I'm not sure who Bethany is, but from what I understand, the driver was a blonde girl wearing a blue dress. According to the blacksmith, she pulled up, grabbed some bags, and ran to the station. He was upset because the horse had been driven too hard in this heat. I guess she left him exhausted in the hot sun," Matt explained as they walked outside.

"The horse is skinned up on one side and the buckboard has damage that looks fairly new. The smith seemed to think the girl looked unharmed. But, as you can see, she didn't take all of her belongings."

"There's no doubt...that's our buckboard and our horse, Rook."

"Glad to hear it."

"Did the sheriff have any idea what might have happened?" Pastor Goodry asked.

"Nothing more than I've already told you. Andrea and I found some evidence there might've been an accident back at the fork where it curves onto the road to Pike City. The ground was torn up badly in one section."

Sandra opened the trunk and checked the contents. "Her purse and money...best dresses and shoes...and jewelry...are all missin'. But there *are* several things here that Bethany held in high regard." Sandra was bewildered by the sight.

"Why would she leave so many nice things just because of running late? She could have caught another train...unless money was a problem," Andrea mentioned.

"You're right. Our dear Bethany would've waited for the next train rather than leave these things behind. Money wasn't the problem. And she wouldn't have left the trunk—unless something was wrong. I know that for sure. As a matter of fact, the little trunk over there was a Christmas present made by her father," Sandra remarked.

"Bethany would never have abused Rook for any reason. She loved him." the pastor added. "Do you think the blacksmith actually knew what he was talking about?"

"Well, the sheriff seemed to agree with the whole account. I do remember the blacksmith mentioned the girl didn't look like the type who cared about much of anything. I hope you understand I'm not criticizing the young lady...only passing on what I was told," Matt clarified. "I don't mean to insinuate anything, but is there any chance you could have mistaken her character?"

"None," the pastor quickly responded.

"Definitely not!" added Sandra.

Then Sandra took a moment to look at the horse's side. "That *is* a deep cut. Rook, ya've had a hard day, haven't ya, ol' boy? We know it wasn't Miss Bethany who put you at risk, don't we?

"Pastor, I'll take Rook on and have Tom look after him."

"We'll need to give this situation some serious thought before we act. Sandra, would you also send word to the Jacksons asking them to let us know when Bethany arrives? I think that's all we should mention to them for now. Their Remington address is in the black book on my desk."

"I'll do it right away," Sandra said as she hurried off.

"I hope this situation won't dampen this day for either of you," the pastor mentioned with regret.

"I can assure you there is no reason for concern in that regard," Matt replied.

"Well, let's go back to my office to sign the final paperwork. Then I'll take you to the social room where Pete is waiting with our missionary.

"By the way, Pete hasn't been told anything about his adoptive parents. We wanted it to be a surprise."

"Pastor," Matt asked hesitantly, "you've been referring to the boy as "Pete". We *are* talking about the same child, aren't we?"

"Oh, yes," Pastor Goodry gave a little laugh. "You see, when Billy arrived, I evidently didn't recall his name correctly and started calling him Pete. He never corrected us. It was a few days before I went through his papers and discovered his real name was Billy Joe *Peterson*. I guess part of his last name stuck in my mind."

Andrea and Matt smiled in relief.

When the pastor, Matthew, and Andrea entered the social room, they saw a young boy sitting patiently with Miss Jenkins. "Pete!"

Pastor Goodry called, “I want to introduce your adoptive parents.”

Billy looked up and then ran toward them as fast as he could, “Mr. Matthew! I knew it would be you! God told me!” He jumped into Matt’s arms and hugged him with all of his might.

When the hug ended, he opened his eyes and looked at the lady standing beside them. “Miss Andrea?” he asked cautiously, afraid what he saw was not true.

“Yes, sweetheart. Mr. Matthew and I are married, and you’re our son now!” Andrea was overjoyed to tell Billy the news.

“God told me ‘bout Mr. Matthew, but God didn’t say nothin’ ‘bout you!” Billy gushed with excitement. The three of them hugged, and the hugs were emphasized with tears of happiness.

“This is an answer to prayer for Andrea and me. And as soon as we leave here, we’re taking you to our new home in the country,” Matt told him.

Billy grew serious and said, “Can I call you “Mommy” and “Daddy”? I think Mama and Papa would like that, don’t you?”

“I believe they *would*. I know Andrea and I would like it very much.”

53

BETHANY THE LOWLIFE

Bethany was startled by the metal cup being run back and forth on bars by a woman making loud, obnoxious demands. Someone yelled for the woman to be quiet, but it didn't silence her. Then a tall, well-built man took a club and gave the bars a couple of hard slams and told her to sit down and shut up.

The woman gave him a defiant glare but soon recoiled onto a cot.

This time Bethany was awake enough to understand she was in jail and was looking up into the kind eyes of a woman.

"I'm in jail?" she asked, hoping to be mistaken.

"Yes, you are," the lady answered.

"But why? I don't understand." Because of her pounding head, Bethany could barely pull her words together.

"According to Red—that woman over on the cot—you're a saloon girl who joined their gang. The two of you have been convicted of bank robbery. If that's so, then you're going to be in prison for a *very* long time. But you don't strike me as a saloon girl or the bank-robbing type."

"No! There is something *terribly* wrong! I'm Bethany Jackson. I've just finished serving at the mission in Pike City. I was on my way back home." Bethany's protest brought on another series of sharp head pains.

"Honey, that mission has been closed for a while. Besides... Red, over there...she went crazy when you called yourself Bethany while you were out of your head. Ever since then, she's been ranting and raving about you being a liar and a whole lot of other things I won't repeat."

Bethany was in too much pain to defend herself.

A few days later, Bethany's head still ached as she stood to look out the widow of the jail. Sadly, there was nothing to see except miles of brush and land *so flat* that there was not one thing out there to make her wonder what it might be.

Why doesn't anyone believe me? How long will it be before someone finds me? God, You know where I am.

"What's the name of this town?" Bethany asked the lady who had faithfully cared for her.

"Liver," the lady answered.

"Liver?" Bethany started to chuckle, but a sharp pain ran through her head and stopped her. "Why?"

"From what I understand, at one time this place had a real good livery stable and blacksmith. It was the only reason folks came here. So after a while, the town became known as Livery. Eventually, they put up a nice looking sign with the name of the town in carved wooden letters. But over time, the letters weathered...and the 'Y' fell off."

Bethany could not keep from laughing, but she paid for it with head pains so sharp it kept her from speaking for several moments. "So they just started calling the town 'Liver'?"

"It became a big joke among the townsfolk...so no one ever fixed the 'Y'."

"The town seems to be so far away from everything."

"I'm not sure I'd call it a town. There are a few businesses. One's a little general store with a makeshift post office and telegraph—which isn't working. There are a few homes, a tiny little church, a nasty saloon...but the place still has a good blacksmith and livery stable...I guess I should mention the jail.

"It gets pretty monotonous around here. If it wasn't for the church, the town's women would dry up and die. Sometimes it feels like there's no way out. We get a lot of outlaws in this area because the prison is close by. They come through for different reasons. It's usually when someone's being released or when they want to break someone out. The sheriff does a pretty good job of keeping on top of things. He's a good man."

"May I ask why *you* were arrested? You're obviously not a bad person," questioned Bethany.

"I wasn't arrested because I did anything wrong. I was brought in because of debt. Lance, my husband, wanted to try his hand out west, so we sold everything to move here. Then Lance was thrown and killed while breaking a horse. I had no way to pay the bills or the loan on the property. The bank took the land, and the people we owed wanted *me* to pay—one way or another. I don't know what will happen to me. I won't find out until the judge makes his round to this area. No one knows exactly when that will be," she answered.

Even in a plain housedress, the lady was pretty. She had long auburn hair and pretty green eyes. Her speech had a hint of the west, but she had definitely been raised in the east. If she had not been a strong woman before, she was now.

"I'm sorry about the loss of your husband and your property."

"I didn't mean to complain. The people I owe deserve to be paid. I don't even care that I lost the land. I do wish I could've kept a few of my personal things...but, I have my memories." She tucked her head and looked away, not wanting to give in to emotion.

Bethany suddenly felt faint and asked to be helped to her cot.

"The sheriff's mother takes the women prisoners home for a bath and a clean change of clothes ever so often. That is, if the sheriff feels the women can be trusted. It will make a difference in the way you feel. Try to act perky when the doctor comes, so he'll allow you to go. The sheriff will most likely let you. You're too bad off to run. The bath won't be an option for Red," she whispered.

"Before I go to sleep, may I ask *your* name?"

"My name is Sadie Moore, and I already know *both* of yours," she said with a smile.

Bethany felt better the next morning, so she got out of bed early. She and Sadie sat together on the same cot and talked softly since they didn't want Red to wake up.

"So what's your story? How did a seemingly sweet girl like you end up here?" Sadie compassionately asked.

"I don't know," Bethany answered.

Sadie wasn't convinced Bethany was the good person she seemed to be—especially with Red constantly spewing accusations of Bethany being a liar and a fake. Even as mean and crude as Red was, she could be very convincing. "We already discussed this. You were brought in a jail wagon as a partner to that despicable woman over there. How did you pair up with her?"

"I have no idea!" Bethany answered honestly. "As I started to tell you before, I'm not from this area. I was filling in at the Pike City orphanage until the missionary was available. The morning after she arrived, I started for home. I was driving the mission horse and buckboard to catch the train in Tally, and my last clear memory was taking the curve onto the main road. It seems like I recall catching a glimpse of something approaching to my left. That's all I remember. I think we must have collided. I keep worrying about what happened to the mission's horse, Rook."

"That's a real nice story, sweetie, but, as I said, the mission over in Pike City has been closed for a while. It was the only one in these parts. Otherwise, I'd be tempted to believe you," Sadie admitted sorrowfully.

"But it's true! The mission never completely closed. It's been restored and is thriving. The orphanage has been successfully adopting out children for several months."

"Yer nothin' but the liar I told the boys you were! Yer a worthless, bottom of the barrel, saloon gal! Ya may fool 'em for a while, but they'll see through ya! I'll give it to ya though—ya sure can act. She's been playing that routine for years. That scum used to brag about how she used that innocent act to lure men in. She sweet talked the boys into takin' her in and even got me to trustin' her after a while. But she's a lying lowlife from the gutter! Ya turned on me and the boys, trying to save yer own hide! So don't fool yerself, sweetheart...I'll get ya for this!" Red was so worked up and persuasive that the sheriff had to put her in another cell to cool off.

This time Red's ranting wasn't just an act to cover up Melva's escape. Enough time had passed for Red to realize Melva had not gone for the boys. She had taken the money and left her to rot in prison. Bart and Yancy might never figure out where she was, and they might not come even if they did. Bart had roaming eyes and had taken up with more than one woman, and Yancy wasn't the devoted-brother type.

Red was furious for setting herself up by releasing Melva. *Someone* was going to pay for her taking the rap alone, so she had decided to do everything she could to take Bethany to prison with her.

Bethany kept to herself for the rest of the day and throughout the night. During that time, she silently cried out to God for help. Hopefully, her parents and Pastor Goodry were aware she was missing by now. But could anyone find her out here? What would happen to her if she were put in prison?

Still she knew Jesus promised to never leave nor forsake her. He knew where she was.

The next day, the sheriff's mother showed up to take Sadie for a bath. The sheriff walked along with them but returned to the jail to wait. He was having second thoughts on allowing Bethany to leave the jail but concluded it would be fine since she did not look too spry. He would just have to keep a watch on her. Besides, it had been a while since he had sat down for a meal at his mother's home. It would also give him an opportunity to ask the girl a few questions about the accident without Red interfering. Red seemed to have an answer for everything.

Since Sadie had been the sheriff's only prisoner for a long while, his mother, Edna, and she had become very close and often confided in one another. So during their conversation that day, Edna asked about the two new prisoners and why they were in jail. Sadie told Edna what she had overheard but acted hesitant every time she mentioned Bethany's involvement in the gang.

"I can see something doesn't strike you right about this case. What is it?" Edna asked.

"I've been thinking on some of the answers the driver gave the sheriff about the accident."

"So, what are you thinking?" Edna urged.

Sadie then told Bethany's version of the story and of her seemingly Christian character, along with details about Red's accusations. "Red is convincing, but I have a notion the real Melva got the keys and switched places with Bethany while the driver was knocked out. I think the driver brought in the wrong woman."

"Oh, my! I see your point. Have you spoken to Marcus about this?"

"No, I haven't had the opportunity. There's no privacy, and it's not my place. Why should he listen to me?"

"Well, you *must* talk to him. He has a great deal of respect for you."

On the way back to jail, Sadie *did* share Bethany's version of the accident and offered her own opinion on what might have taken place. But, Marcus, having something else on his mind, only nodded. He had a more important topic to discuss with Sadie—and it was *not* the Boyer Gang.

Edna was not one to stay out of a situation she felt needed attention. She and Bethany got along wonderfully, and during lunch they had a long discussion about the Bible and their faith. Edna did not need any further information. She knew the girl was innocent.

While Bethany bathed, Edna shared with Marcus the information she had learned and encouraged him to get involved. He told her his job was to hold the convicts until the prison had room for them, and he had no authority to do otherwise. Only solid proof could change the outcome of the case.

The sheriff, being a sharp witted man, *had* noticed issues with the girl's identity when she first arrived and had immediately concluded the driver possibly had the wrong woman. The girl's shoes were new and fashionable; yet her clothing was old and dirty. Two buttons had been skipped on the dress. An expensive barrette—not typical for a prisoner—held one side of her hairstyle neatly in place while the other side hung in disarray. In addition, unlike Red, the girl was freshly bathed, and her fingernails were manicured.

Marcus did take the opportunity to subtly interview Bethany while they were alone, and he found her consistently well spoken. There was no longer doubt in his mind—the girl *was* Bethany Jackson.

54

GETTING MARRIED

"Bethany didn't get off the train! Did she pass by without us noticing?" Helen was in a panic.

"I don't see how. There were only five or six passengers who got off. I'll see if the conductor will let me look for her. Maybe she fell asleep. Will you check the station...just in case she's there?" Uncertain what to make of the situation, Mel hurried off to find the conductor.

Both parents searched thoroughly but didn't find Bethany. "What do you suppose happened? She may have missed one of the connections." Helen answered her own question as she often did.

"I hope that's what happened. The conductor doesn't recall a young lady of her description getting off at any of the stops. I'm sure there will be a telegram from her when we arrive home."

"Mel, let's go to the telegraph office to notify Pastor Goodry that Bethany didn't get off the train. I thought there was something peculiar when we received a message asking us to let them know when she arrived safely. Wouldn't he have asked Bethany to do it? Something is wrong!"

Pastor Goodry handed Sandra the telegram from Bethany's parents. He was chastising himself for not looking into the unsettling situation when they were first informed.

"She could have missed one of her connections," Sandra tried to reason.

"Sandra, we both know that isn't it. Something has happened to her. If the blacksmith was telling the truth, then it wasn't Bethany he saw getting out of the buckboard. I need to send a return telegram to her parents and tell them what we know. Then I'm going to Tally to speak with the sheriff."

"I'll see if Rook is up to the drive. If not, maybe one of the staff will loan me a rig. Would you like to go to Tally with me?" he asked Sandra.

"Certainly! I'd go plum crazy waitin' for news! I'll let my husband and the staff know we're leavin'."

"I don't understand why the pastor didn't inform us when he first received the information. Our daughter is missing and no one is looking for her!" Helen dabbed her eyes. "Mel, how can we just sit here and wait?"

"We're *not*. We're taking the next train west."

"We've told ya all we know, sir. She weren't exactly the dainty, sweet lookin' type. From the glance I got, she had sort of a hard saloon gal look. Wearin' a blue dress, though," the blacksmith told the pastor.

"Then it wasn't Bethany. No one would mistake her for a saloon girl. I'm certain something happened at the fork. Sheriff, do you know of anyone who might have been passing that way at the time? I don't know where to begin. Any suggestion? Anything at all?" Pastor Goodry pleaded.

"Sorry, Pastor. I haven't heard of anything out that way. There's several roads intersecting with the road to Tally, so if someone was involved in an accident out that way, they may've not even passed through here. Those towns are miles apart, and there's a bunch of 'em. That's all I got for you. I'll get news your way if I hear anything," the sheriff promised.

"Thank you. We appreciate your help." Pastor Goodry was in a solemn mood when he left the stable.

"Sandra, do we have a picture of Bethany?" He was walking so fast that Sandra almost had to run to keep up.

"No, none that I'm aware of, but I do a little drawin'. I'm sure I could do a fair likeness of her. Are you thinkin' of puttin' up a poster or two?"

"I think we should try it—at least it's something. Unfortunately, I've allowed valuable time to pass."

"Bethany, I'm sorry you had to listen to another round of Red's lies and accusation. I must admit she *is* convincing, but I shouldn't have doubted you."

"There's no need to apologize. Red almost had *me* believing it,"

Bethany answered.

"Why aren't you upset? You could end up in prison, and you've done nothing to deserve it. Believe me, that place up on the hill is full of ruthless characters. I'm very worried for you. Red will be the least of your worries there."

"The Lord knows where I am. I have complete peace in my heart about it,"

"It's wonderful you feel that way. I've never felt such assurance from God," Sadie admitted.

"God is a loving Father, and His resources are endless. He'll take care of us."

"I guess I've never felt God was all that loving. I've always been afraid of him."

With that said, the two settled down on a cot and discussed the real truth of God's love late into the night. When they were done, Sadie had given her heart to the Lord.

"Now," said Sadie, "I have a secret to share with you, but you mustn't speak of it for a few days."

"I'll do my best." Bethany was already excited, even though she did not have a clue what the secret was about.

"While Marcus was walking me back to jail...he asked me to marry him." Sadie sat back and waited for Bethany's reaction.

"Seriously! I'm so happy for you! He seems like a wonderful man." Bethany gave her a big hug.

"He *is* a wonderful man! I've known him since we moved out here. He was a good friend to my husband. I thought my life was over, but instead, God has blessed me."

"God's turned your mourning into dancing!" Bethany whispered.

"And there's more! After I accepted Marcus' proposal, he told me he had paid off all my debts. He did it before even knowing if I would accept." Sadie was overwhelmed by the wonder of it all.

55

STEW GOES WEST

Stew was relieved to finally receive a letter from Matt. Although, since Matt had taken so long to respond, he was a little reluctant to open it. He hoped the ordeal with Billy had not caused permanent damage to their friendship.

> *Dear Stewart,*
>
> *I apologize for not answering your letter sooner, but so many changes have taken place in my life that I hardly know where to begin.*
>
> *My job is going well, and it suits me even better than I expected. It's exciting and fast paced, which is something we both appreciate. I've already had one promotion, and I'm looking forward to another in the near future.*
>
> *I'm sure you recall witnessing to me before I left Bay City. At the time, I was extremely bitter toward God because of Billy losing his mother and father. I didn't understand why God would leave a small boy alone in the world to face an uncertain future. I con-*

tinued in that frame of mind until I suffered the loss of my own sweet mother. During that time, I was reminded of the faith Billy clung to, even after he had lost everything dear to him. From then on, your words weighed heavily upon my heart, and Billy's face was constantly in my mind. Finally, I realized how foolish I was to reject Christ and his promised blessings, so I got on my knees and asked Jesus to come into my life. I'm pleased to say the decision has changed everything for me.

I started attending a good church which preaches the gospel and stresses daily Bible reading and prayer. Thank you for sharing the love of Jesus with me. I haven't been the same since, and He has blessed me above and beyond anything I could have imagined for myself.

My most extraordinary blessing happened when my company sent me to New York City on business. I was to be there for an indefinite period of time, so I found a church to attend during my stay. One Sunday after service, I chanced upon your friend, Andrea Landis. She was spending the season with her cousin. We quickly found we shared many of the same interests, which included our love for the Lord and Billy. It wasn't long until we both realized we were in love, and neither of us wanted to carry on a long distance relationship.

Since our relatives live so far apart, Andrea's in the West and mine in the East, we decided to be married in a small ceremony in New York City with only a few relatives present. It was a wonderful day, and I'm a better and happier man for it. I know you must be shocked to read of my marriage, especially after the difficult time I gave you for trying to find me a girl. I look forward to having that crow dinner when we meet again.

There is more to this astounding blessing, but I will make a long story short. I want to thank you for letting me know where Billy was located. Because of that valuable information, Andrea and I decided to adopt Billy, and the three of us will soon be living in our beautiful, country home. He is now being loved by two of the most blessed parents in the world. I'm eternally grateful for the part you played in our lives.

It was almost more than he could comprehend. "Matthew is married to Andrea and they adopted Billy?" Stew didn't know whether to laugh or cry. The truth be told, he did both, and it was witnessed by the butler.

"Andrea and Matt would make the perfect couple now that he's a Christian. They both have tender hearts and are very giving." Stew could see how God's timing had worked to bring the three lives together. The Lord had even used the slipshod way he had tracked Billy. Stew was elated over the wonderful news from Matt and was glad to know his friendship with Matt was still intact.

The butler had no idea what his boss was talking about, so he just smiled pleasantly and nodded in agreement.

Once Stew had absorbed the news, he returned to the letter:

This next bit of information, if true, may be of the utmost importance to you.

When we arrived at the Tally train station, a young lady who was leaving her position at the orphanage was supposed to have left a buckboard and horse for us to use as transportation. The rig wasn't there as promised. However, we later found it at the livery. The sheriff felt there was evidence it might have been in an accident. The blacksmith saw a girl driver take her bags and leave the horse out in the sun in bad shape. He and the sheriff were very upset over the horse's condition.

When we reported the story to the mission's pastor and a volunteer, neither believed the description of their former staff member nor the neglect of the horse was consistent with her character. To add to their suspicion, there were several items left behind which she cherished.

At the time, our concern was to finalize Billy's adoption. However, once we arrived at the hotel this evening, my thoughts returned to the mystery surrounding the girl from the mission. Stew, I distinctly heard the young woman's first and last names mentioned by the pastor. The girl's name is Bethany Jackson, and apparently she is from Remington. I knew the name sounded familiar, but I didn't make the

> *connection at the moment.*
>
> *I have no way of knowing if this is the young lady you were engaged to marry, but I felt you might be interested since you still consider her a friend. This is just a gut feeling on my part, but I couldn't let this pass without bringing it to your attention. I believe the pastor and some of the mission's staff might have felt there was foul play..."*

It couldn't be Bethany. She wouldn't be at a mission in the West. To Stew's knowledge, the Jacksons had never spoken of any connections in the West. He reasoned that Bethany Jackson was a common name. But since Matt had mentioned the girl was from Remington and there might have been foul play, it frightened Stew. He had to know or he would go insane from worry. Stew grabbed his hat to go telegraph his parents. He prayed it was not true.

Later that day, a telegram arrived from his father, confirming Bethany *had* been at a mission out west. Bethany had not returned on the train as expected and was thought to be missing. That's all his father knew at present.

If Bethany is missing, what can I do? I can't just wait around to hear something. I have to go.

Stew paced the floor while he waited to talk to his boss. Even though he loved his work, if need be, he was willing to sacrifice his job to find Bethany. To his relief, the boss encouraged him to take the trip and use as much time as needed.

The train ride west was sweltering. Several of the passengers had become ill from the heat, but Stew was too caught up in the need to find Bethany to care what he suffered. He spent most of his time in prayer, asking God to keep her safe.

Once he reached Tally, Stew went immediately to the sheriff's office to see what information he could gather. The sheriff suggested Stew might begin his search at Liver since it was one of the few settlements in the area that had a sheriff. After renting a horse, he went to buy clothing suitable for the ride. He left his bag in a hotel room and told the manager he did not know when he would return.

Stew stopped at the fork where the accident was thought to have happened, but there was little to go on. Instead of turning to go to the Pike City mission for more details, Stew decided to ride on to Liver since the sheriff there might know something.

It was late evening by the time he reached the town, so the jail was locked up. Stew was hungry and the only place to eat was a saloon and the general store. He found something at the general store to satisfy his hunger and stashed a couple of apples in the saddlebag for later.

He was given directions to the home of an elderly lady who, for a modest fee, offered a bed for the night. Stew found her to be a kind lady who took much pleasure in keeping a tidy home. He was welcome to draw a bath, which he was more than willing to do.

After the bath, Stew took a walk down to the sheriff's office just in case the sheriff might have returned. His hunch was right, the sheriff and his wife were sitting at his desk having a late meal.

"Hello! My name is Stewart Jefferson. I'm sorry to bother you this late, but I've come a long way to get some answers. I'm looking for a girl named Bethany Jackson. She may have been in an accident on the road coming from Tally. Considering the information I've been given about the area, I thought this seemed the most likely place to start." Stew was businesslike, but polite.

"Good evening. I'm Sheriff Newly, and this is my wife, Sadie. We were just completing one of our first meals together as husband and wife. Would you like to join us? My wife is an excellent cook, and there's plenty." The sheriff wore a broad smile as he reached out to shake Stew's hand.

"Thank you, but no. I grabbed something at the store across the street...although it does look tempting." Stew was almost sorry he had interrupted them.

"What a coincidence! We were just speaking of Bethany." The sheriff knew he was going to enjoy sharing the good news with this desperate-looking fellow.

"You know her?" Stew asked, sounding anxious.

"Yes, my wife and she were cellmates for several days. I assume you're here because she was missing, but you can relax. Miss Jackson and her parents have gone back to the mission with the pastor."

"Cellmates! Bethany was in jail! She's safe and well then?" Stew questioned intently.

"Yes, she's fine, but she had a hard go of it for a while. I've heard Bethany speak your name," Sadie said with a hint of a smile.

"How are you acquainted with Miss Jackson?" the sheriff asked very intentionally.

"Well, I'm her...I guess, I'm a friend of sorts. We attended the same church and our families are close friends." Stew felt his answer was deceitful at best.

"Yer not tellin' it all! You were lovers! We all know it! She carried on, a blubberin' and callin' out yer name while she was out of her head!" Red yelled from the cell. Then she gave a big fun-making laugh.

"Red, keep quiet!" the sheriff warned. "By the way, Red, I received word the prison will be sendin' someone for you and Blondie tomorrow. But I'll take you over tonight, if you keep it up!"

Red walked back to her cot, sat down, and remained quiet for the rest of her stay. She knew all hope of the boys coming to break her out was gone.

"She's correct. We were engaged to be married, but it didn't work out," he told the sheriff, ashamed for not admitting it in the beginning.

"As far as the wreck goes, Miss Jackson was turning onto the Tally road and collided with the jail wagon. Miss Jackson and the driver were knocked out. Red was hurt but got the keys and unlocked the cuffs for Blondie to escape. She's the one who impersonated Miss Jackson," the sheriff pointed to Melva.

"But on the train east, she made the mistake of taking a seat by a U.S. Marshall. When she stood to allow him to get out at his stop, the lid on her case flew open and the money dumped on the floor."

"So Bethany could have been put in prison?" Stew had to take a few seconds to adjust to the thought. "You mentioned Bethany was hurt. What happened there?"

"Bethany took a hard hit when she was thrown out of the buckboard. It was a few days before she made any sense at all. It was during that time when she called out for you."

Stew breathed a sigh of relief and relaxed. "But did I understand you to say Bethany and her parents went back to the mission?"

"Yes, when I was sure the driver had brought in the wrong woman, I rode over to the Pike City mission. Her parents had just arrived, so they followed me back here. It just so happened, the judge arrived about the time we pulled in. Since her parents could identify Bethany, the judge released her. *Then* he married me and Sadie, and before they left, Melva was brought in." The sheriff gave a hearty laugh at the thought of everything that had transpired.

"Well, I'd better get a couple hours of sleep. I need to get to the mission." Stew shook the sheriff's hand and thanked them for everything.

As soon as Stew left the sheriff's office, he went to see that the horse was bedded down for a good rest. They would be riding out long before dawn.

56

CLOSE TO BETHANY

It was midmorning when Stew rode up to the mission. The place impressed him as being quite decent, especially compared to most orphanages he had seen. Yet he was disappointed Bethany's parents had allowed her to serve in such a rough section of town.

Stew tied the horse to a hitching post and was just about to knock on the door when Tom showed up. Once Tom realized he was there to check on Bethany, he directed Stew inside and attended to his horse. Annie, another volunteer, greeted Stew and led him directly to the pastor for an introduction. The pastor immediately knew who he was.

Stew found the pastor to be an impressive, young man and immediately wondered how close Bethany and the pastor had become.

Since he was tired and anxious to get to the reason for his visit, Stew spoke hurriedly, "I'm sorry to interrupt your day, but could you tell me if Bethany Jackson and her parents are here?" He knew meeting with Bethany and her parents might be unpleasant, but he needed to be certain she was doing well.

"I'm sorry. Her parents have taken her back to Remington. They wanted her to recover in the comforts of home. She'd been through a lot. I assume you know most of the details."

"Yes, my friend, Matthew Wilson, wrote to me when he realized Bethany was my ex-fiancé. I've already spoken with local authorities." Since Stew was no longer engaged to Bethany, he felt uncomfortable telling the pastor the liberties he had taken.

"I see," the pastor answered.

"By any chance, are you the other man who helped Billy when he lost his mother? If so, this is a very small world indeed."

Stewart nodded and answered, "I *am* the same man."

"Your lawyer told me of the dilemma when he visited the orphanage. It seems to me God has used the entire situation in a most remarkable way. The boy's struggles have brought together a loving family."

"Thank you. I'll try to view it in that light from now on."

"Bethany's doing well physically and mentally. I hope hearing it will relieve any apprehensions you have. I shouldn't have allowed her to take the buckboard to the station...but she can be very insistent," the pastor admitted. "We were blessed the sheriff in Liver was observant and realized the driver had brought in the wrong girl."

"I agree." Stew answered. Then he felt compelled to justify his presence. "I hope you understand why I had to come west. I couldn't just wait to hear something. It's most likely for the best that I missed seeing her. But I wanted to be certain she was safe."

"Bethany and I were very close by the end of her stay, but we didn't get off to a very good start—it was my fault," the pastor shared.

Stew hoped the pastor's statement wasn't the beginning of a confession of love for Bethany.

"She became closer to me than my own sister. I admired her greatly. She stood up to me when I needed it most. I will always feel indebted to her because—"

Just then, there was a tap on the door, and Ella Jenkins walked in. Stew was relieved to see the look of adoration that passed between the pastor and Ella.

Once Ella was introduced, they told Stewart about the accomplishments the Lord had brought to the mission through Bethany's willingness to serve. Then the couple gave him a tour of the mission, which included Bethany's former quarters, and even took him to visit the dress shop to meet Lena and Burt.

After much insistence from the pastor and Ella, Stew accepted an invitation to have lunch at the mission. He enjoyed meeting the children and the staff who had come to know, love, and respect Bethany.

Sadness overtook Stew when it was time to leave. Being at the mission was as close as he had been to Bethany for a very long time.

57

ON TO ANOTHER MISSION

Even though Bethany had felt much better by the time her parents arrived at the jail, they had insisted on taking her home as soon as possible to finish recovering. After the scare of her disappearance, no one blamed them for wanting their daughter in their own safekeeping.

The Jacksons, however, did take time to visit Lena and her husband at the store, and Mrs. Jackson was thrilled to finally see the boutique and her own designs on display. Helen even overheard two ladies discussing how stunning the dresses were. It pleased her to know the mission children were the inspiration behind Lena's venture and *she* was a part of it all. She promised to return to help Lena with the plans to expand the shop. It would be Mrs. Jackson's first business trip.

It was all behind Bethany now. She had been home for a few days and was more than ready for a day of shopping with her mother. They purchased several accessories to bring their wardrobes up to date, had lunch, and spent hours looking at the latest fabric.

Toward the end of the day, Helen needed to run some errands, so she left Bethany to shop on her own for a while.

Bethany was enjoying the stroll through the department stores without having to worry about a budget. She passed the perfume counter and had just turned down an aisle toward the jewelry when she found herself directly in front of Rica Adams.

"Well, Bethany Jackson...so you have returned from living among the misfits. I hope you didn't come home with lice or fleas. That would be most embarrassing." Rica wore her usual gratified sneer.

"Hello, Rica. I see you're well." Bethany had no desire to play games with her.

"I'm much more than well. It appears I'm about to be married...as I'm sure you've heard." Rica wasn't about to pass up another opportunity to humiliate her.

"How nice," Bethany replied, not blinking an eye.

"How insensitive of me! It completely slipped my mind you had hoped to marry Stew. Your engagement party was such a shameful event. People just can't stop talking about it. You must have been mortified!" Rica continued with the digs.

"I'm so sorry I don't have time to stop and chat. I'm to meet with my mother in a few minutes. Have a good day."

Rica was disappointed in the reaction she had received from Bethany but was satisfied with getting in a few hard licks. She assumed Stewart was still unaware of the phony engagement article in *The Remington News*. Until Stew did know, she would use every opportunity to further provoke Bethany.

Bethany's knees had been shaking as she left Rica, and even

though she did not want to admit it, her heart was breaking. She had given up her chance. Stew belonged to Rica.

Stewart found little pleasure in his work after his return from the mission. He felt like a fool for going west to find Bethany, but he would do it again—a thousand times over if need be. Even though he knew she did not love *him*, he would always love *her*. He would never be complete as long as he walked this earth without her.

Stew knew he had no right to chase after Bethany, but he regretted not going home to see for himself that she was doing well. Although, he would not have been so bold as to visit her in person, it would have been comforting to have viewed her from afar.

What happened the night of the breakup was still a mystery to Stew, and even if Bethany gave him another chance, he could not explain what had taken place between him and Rica. He still had no idea how he had allowed the kiss to happen.

Life was pleasant at home, but Bethany missed the fulfilling challenges of the mission. Home was quiet and peaceful, but there was nothing there to give her purpose. She had been to church and attended teas, but the conversation of everyday events was lacking. She had become accustomed to minute-by-minute problem solving—if not with the children then with Lena at the shop or among the poor.

"Bethany," Helen called softly. "Where are you, dear? Sometimes I feel as though we brought home the wrong girl. Do you long for the children?"

"No, my work there is done, but I feel so useless. My days there were full. Now, I have nothing to occupy my time. There must be something meaningful I can do."

"I think I might have a simple solution to your problem," Helen informed her. "Would you consider doing charity work? I know of some children who would benefit from your sewing skills."

"Of course! What was I thinking? You know, I was pleasantly surprised by how much I loved sewing. I believe I share your passion, Mother. So, who *are* these children?"

"Well, Lena and I knew you would soon be bored once you arrived home. So if you are willing, she would like for you to continue as a seamstress for the shop. You can do what you love and help meet the needs of your beloved children at the mission."

Helen pointed to the parcels which had just been delivered. "We have a lot of work to do before the next shipment goes out."

58

DO NOT DISAPPOINT ME

Stew stood on his parents' front veranda feeling relieved the doctor's report had been a good one. His father had fought hard and refused to be taken by the heart attack.

It had been over two weeks since Stew had arrived in Remington, and he had spent almost every moment by his dad's side. Being outside in the fresh air and seeing trees and land all around made him long for freedom, so he went to ask the stable boy to saddle a horse while he changed. A spirited ride through the woods was exactly what he needed.

When Stew returned, he found Storm saddled and pawing. The stable boy was new and somehow had managed to pick Storm from among all the other horses. The horse bobbed his head up and down as Stew approached. Then—to Stew's amazement—Storm walked over and nuzzled his nose into Stew's chest. Thankfully, Storm had not detached from him. He put his arms around the horse's neck and held on tightly to his old friend.

Stew felt renewed as he mounted the magnificent horse and took off in a gallop just like old times. They took their usual route but stopped on top of the rise to look down on the Jacksons' home.

Stew stayed in the saddle surveying the property for a few minutes and then headed back.

Even with his doctor's disapproval, Mr. Jefferson insisted on going to church on Sunday. Stew was neither comfortable with his father's decision, nor was he ready to attend his home church for the first time since his and Bethany's broken engagement.

The Jeffersons made a habit of arriving at church early, so they were already seated when most of the other members entered the sanctuary. Their church family was delighted to see Stewart and his father in attendance, and several of the members took time to lovingly greet them before the service began. The kind reception helped Stew relax among his friends.

The Jacksons were just taking their seats when the pastor asked the congregation to stand for the opening song.

Bethany would not have noticed Stew if she had not overheard someone say they were happy to see the entire Jefferson family at church. Bethany had nonchalantly glanced to see if the Jeffersons were in their usual pew. Stew was standing in the aisle, and even though it hurt to see him, she was pleased he was there.

It was then Mr. Jefferson asked to go home because he was feeling weak. As Stew assisted his father, he was able to catch a glimpse of Bethany. Seeing her made his heart beat faster, but at the same time, he was glad to be leaving since he did not want to cause her any discomfort. Yet he could not stop himself from stealing one more glance. At that same time, Bethany turned her head toward him and their eyes locked as they both felt the intensity of the moment.

Bethany had not told her parents about the confrontation with Rica because she did not want to worry them. However, when she met with Adel and Mandy for Tuesday tea to discuss collecting for the mission, she began sharing the incident with her friends.

"Bethany, we are talking about Rica. Stewart knows what a nasty person Rica is and is well aware of how she operates. *She* was responsible for your breakup. I don't know what happened between the two of them at the engagement party, but I believe Stewart is innocent."

"I agree with Mandy. Rica's not even a Christian. Stew is a good man who loves the Lord, and he could never be interested in Rica for that reason alone. She has conjured up something. Besides, we haven't heard a word about their engagement from anyone else—before or after the newspaper article."

"That's true. And Mrs. Jefferson hasn't even mentioned it to my mother, and we all know how close they are. Rica is just bluffing," Mandy added.

"Mandy, do you suppose anyone has mentioned it to the Jeffersons?"

"Not that I know of, Bethany. My mother doesn't feel it's her place."

"It doesn't matter. It isn't any of my business what Stewart does, but I do want him to be happy. I just can't imagine he could find happiness with Rica...that's all."

Bethany wished she had kept quiet.

A few days later, Rica hurried into Brennon's Fashions. She slammed the door behind her and started ordering Mrs. Brennon around. "You need to help me into that wedding dress you're working on, and we have no time to lose."

"What! I can't do that! This is a very expensive gown, and the bride will be here within the hour for a fitting. I wouldn't consider doing such a thing," Mrs. Brennon protested.

"I think you *will*. If you remember, I caught you with Mr. Sulks. I've never mentioned a word of it to anyone, but I suppose his *wife* might be interested in hearing what I have to say," Rica threatened.

Earlier in the year, Rica had stopped by the shop for fabric samples and had caught Mr. Sulks holding widow Brennon's hand.

"I *tried* to explain the situation was not what it appeared to be, but *you* wouldn't listen!" Mrs. Brennon cried out.

"And I'm *not* going to listen! You *will* help me, or I will go to Mrs. Sulks with *my* version of the story!" Rica warned her. "Now, help me into the dress. And don't say a word unless I need you to back me up." Rica quickly stepped into the oversized dress which easily hid her clothing. Then she shifted her eyes toward the door to indicate someone was about to enter.

"Mrs. Brennon was pinning the back of the dress when Adel, Mandy, and Bethany entered. Rica turned and gave them an analyzing but satisfied stare. "Well Bethany. This is quite shocking, but you didn't need your posse to steal a look at my gown. I would've gladly shown it to you. However, I *am* interested in knowing what pretense of business brought you here," Rica accused.

Mrs. Brennon looked like a whipped pup once she realized she had been forced to participate in such a deception.

"Rica! I'm so sorry. Honestly, I had no idea. This was totally unforeseen—" Bethany was too shocked and humiliated to go on.

Mandy stepped forward, ignoring Rica. "Mrs. Brennon...regardless of *whose* dress you might be working on...you were *expecting us* to pick up your donation for the children's mission."

"Why, yes! It's right there on the counter." Mrs. Brennon quickly responded. "Thank you for the opportunity to participate in such a worthy cause. I'm pleased to hear the mission is operating successfully." She stopped talking when she noticed Rica's glare.

"Thank you very much, Mrs. Brennon. We appreciate your kindness," Mandy answered just before instructing her friends they were leaving. "*Ladies*," she said, then exited the store with Adel and Bethany following closely behind.

Rica gave a hysterical laugh, and then narrowed her eyes on Mrs. Brennon. "Now, get this oversized monstrosity off me!" Mrs. Brennon wasted no time in doing so; she wanted the vicious young woman out of her shop.

"Now, if you want to continue doing business with my family, you will never breathe a word of this to anyone. In return, I will continue to keep your little secret," Rica warned. "Now, hand me my bag and gloves." She gave a hateful smile and walked out.

Bethany walked silently with Adel and Mandy until they came to a secluded area. "Would either of you object if I left collecting for the orphanage to you. I'd like to—"

"Of course not," Adel jumped in. "Mandy and I are perfectly capable of handling it. You go on."

"Thank you. I appreciate it." Bethany hurried off to her buggy.

"Well, I didn't see that coming. It's so disheartening. I thought the entire wedding announcement was a lie made up by Rica." Adel was fuming. "And I couldn't think of a thing to say to the smug, little creature!"

"Adel! Seriously? Didn't you see Mrs. Brennon's face? Rica is up to something."

There were two letters waiting for Bethany when she arrived home.

Ella had written to tell her about her growing relationship with David. She also informed Bethany of Stewart Jefferson's visit and how impressed the entire staff was with him. The second letter was from Sadie, telling her that Stewart had been to Liver trying to locate her.

Bethany was confused by learning of his visit to the mission—especially after seeing Rica in her wedding dress. If he was engaged to Rica, he had absolutely no right to go west to check on her.

A few days later, Bethany took a walk up to the rise. As she reached the top, she was startled to see Stew as he was dismounting Storm.

"Bethany!" Stewart said in shock, having to restrain himself from running to take her into his arms. "It's wonderful to see you. I was glad to hear you made it home safely."

"Stewart!" Bethany returned in excitement...and then sobered. "It's nice to see you too."

"What have you been doing to pass the time now that you're home? I understand you were accustomed to hard work at the mission." Stew had spoken without thinking.

Bethany gave him a defensive look.

"I guess, I should explain. I received a letter you were missing and—"

"Stewart! I know you were at the jail and the mission. You had no right to go looking for me or to present yourself in such a familiar way to my friends—especially under the circumstances." Bethany did not even know if she actually meant to scold him or not. It was terribly awkward.

"I'm sorry, Bethany. I didn't intend to present myself in any certain way. I was concerned for you, and I *had* to go. I would do it again—you *know* I would. I *love* you.

"I was hoping to see you before I went back to Bay City. Although, I *was* expecting a little better reception since so much time has passed. But I'd still like to try to sort things out between us." Stew was hurt and apprehensive since Bethany was still so defensive toward him. But he knew it might be his only chance to talk with her. He *had* to try.

"There's nothing to talk over between us. You belong to someone else. I shouldn't be in your thoughts at all." Bethany had to be firm—even though it took all of her inner strength to do so.

"What do you mean? I've never belonged to anyone except you. I've tried to forget you, but I can't. I will always love you. You know that."

"Stewart! How can you say such things to me? It's so wrong! I know your plans. Please, don't say another word. Don't disappoint me further." Bethany turned and ran.

"Bethany! Please! For once, just listen to me! Let's talk this out!"

59

SHE WANTS TO TALK

Bethany was disappointed that Adel and Mandy had been wrong about Stewart and Rica's approaching marriage. Still, she was ashamed of the way she had treated Stew because of it. And as a matter of fact, if she was to be completely honest with herself, she would need to admit that David was right when he accused her of never seriously praying about the whole affair. She had just reacted at the time of the breakup and had been dishonest to herself and others about her feelings toward Stew. She *loved* him and would *always* love him. He was a good Christian man who made a mistake, and it was her own overactive imagination which made her think otherwise. He had asked more than once to discuss what happened with Rica, but she had been proud and had refused him.

Yet Bethany *did* find him with Rica. She was obviously too great a temptation for him. Rica was extremely beautiful with long, raven hair, and she could be very charming when she chose to be. Bethany felt she could never marry Stewart because of this weakness in his character. And knowing his weakness was *Rica* made the situation even more devastating to her.

Still, it did not excuse her behavior toward him last evening.

She should have spoken to him as a friend. As she sat under the willow, she prayed for forgiveness for her attitude toward Stew and for guidance in becoming his friend—once again.

Stew was hurt to find Bethany was still hostile toward him. It was not like her to be so stubborn and unforgiving. And why did she say he belonged to someone else. Surely she didn't mean Christine? He had never mentioned her to anyone outside of Bay City. His acquaintance with Christine had lasted such a short time that it did not seem relevant. He was intrigued with her but never developed a true affection.

As it was, his father's health was much better, so there was no reason for Stew to remain in Remington. He had tried to speak with Bethany, but she had clearly refused him. It was time to face the truth, Bethany no longer had feelings for him. He would keep his distance. She was convinced she never truly knew him, and Stew had no desire to cause her further torment. He prayed God would watch over her.

Bethany was still sitting beneath the willow when she heard a carriage in the distance. Her heart leaped at the hope Stew might have come back to give her another chance. But when she looked down the lane, she could tell it was Adel.

Adel did not park her carriage to walk to Bethany or even slow down. Instead, she slapped the reins to make the horses gallop across the lawn.

"Bethany!" she yelled and waved her free arm wildly in the air. "You must come quickly! Something horrible has happened!"

"What do you mean?" Bethany questioned, hoping it wasn't Stewart.

"I was on my way to town when I came upon an accident! It's a very bad one! It was Rica Adams! She was riding with Joe Meeker, and he must have been driving recklessly because he missed that turn up on Sawyer Road. Rica was thrown through the railing and onto the rocks below. Joe's doing fine, but she's in terrible shape! Anyway, I waited until they brought her up, and she grabbed my hand as they passed. She begged me to try to get you to come to the hospital. She wants to talk to you. She looked so desperate that I couldn't refuse her. You had better hurry! Jump in, and I'll drive you to the hospital."

"No," Bethany told her, "maybe you should see if anyone has told her parents. I'll ride Shadow."

Adel turned the buggy around and headed back across the grass while Bethany ran for her horse.

Just before Bethany entered the room, the nurse indicated Rica was not doing well. Bethany straightened her shoulders and went in, not knowing what to expect.

There lay beautiful Rica—her body covered in cuts and bruises and her face swollen. It was difficult for Bethany to see her in such condition.

"Bethany!" Rica whispered as though she was shocked to see

her. "Please come in. I need to speak with you."

"No, Rica, I'll sit right here. You need to save your strength. There is nothing you need to say that won't keep." Bethany was in fear for Rica's life.

"You've always been too concerned for others. I've hated you for your Christian goodness...but I want to tell you how sorry I am for the way I've treated you. I was so terribly jealous of you. You were adored by everyone...and I despised you for it. Did you know our birthdays are on the same day?" Rica asked.

Bethany shook her head.

"Most of the children would refuse *my* invitation and go to *your* parties."

"I'm sorry. I didn't—" Bethany started to apologize.

"No...it was easier to blame *you* instead of blaming *my* bad behavior.

"I thought I was in love with Stew. I did everything I could to get his attention...but he chose *you.* I tried *everything* to come between you two, and I succeeded...the night of your engagement party," Rica confessed, looking Bethany straight in the eyes.

"What do you mean?" Bethany asked.

"I contrived the whole scene. It even worked out better than I'd hoped." Rica then briefly explained everything from the incident in the jewelry store up until Bethany had found them together.

"I had planned to *force* a kiss on him. Just before you entered the door, I stepped out in front of him. When Stew realized it wasn't you, he started to back away...and hit his head on a heavy iron piece hanging from a rafter. It must have stunned him momentarily, because he staggered and reached out to grab me...to break the fall. That's when you walked in. It gave the impression we were embracing, but it was all I could do to keep him upright. Bethany...we didn't *kiss*."

"Rica!" was all Bethany could say.

"Your voice caused him to rally, and he looked back...just in time to see you run away. I told him you had just seen us *kissing*. He was disoriented...and he must have believed me.

"I waited until the party was over and followed him into the country. I caught up with him on a side road. He was raging with grief and confusion. I tried to convince him to give me a chance... but he wanted nothing to do with me. After he told me I *disgusted* him...I vowed to get revenge."

"...But you *did* turn his thinking around. You're going to be married."

Rica seemed to be getting weaker, and it frightened Bethany. "You're not in any condition to discuss this now."

"But, Bethany...you don't understand. Stew and I *aren't* engaged. I know you're concerned for me...but I need to explain." Rica's protest gave way to a raspy coughing spell, but she seemed to rally a bit of strength once it was over.

"I'm certain Stewart doesn't know about the news article...or he would have confronted me," Rica admitted, stopping to catch her breath again.

"What?" Bethany was in disbelief.

"I *forced* a reporter to take a picture of Stewart and me the night of the awards. There were flashes going off everywhere. He wasn't even aware the picture was taken."

Bethany didn't respond.

"Bethany...can you forgive me?" Rica's voice was weak and her body was shaking, but she spoke with true sincerity

"I can, Rica," Bethany answered quickly, hoping she would rest.

"Thank you. Maybe God would have loved *me* if I had been more like *you*," Rica said with a slight smile.

"Rica, it's not what *we* do. It's what *Jesus did*...on the cross. It's never too late to give our lives to Jesus. Would you like to do that?" Bethany asked with hopeful tears in her eyes.

"Yes, very much," Rica answered weakly.

Bethany held her hand as Rica prayed and gave her life to the Lord.

"Bethany...I've never...felt a peace like this," Rica said in awe.

"It's because you're a child of God now," Bethany answered as she watched Rica relax and seem to breathe easier.

By then, the nurse had stepped back into the room. "Have her parents arrived?" Bethany whispered very quietly. The nurse shook her head.

But just at that moment, Rica's grip loosened on Bethany's hand. She was smiling when she closed her eyes.

60

I AM NOT GOING TO LIE

Stew was on his way to the train station when he met Adel along the road. "Hello, Adel! It's good to see you. Sorry, I didn't get a chance to visit this trip, but I had to stay close to home with dad being under the weather."

Adel gave him a strange look and asked rather frantically, "Stew, you're not at the hospital? Hasn't anyone contacted you about Rica?"

"No. No one has contacted me about Rica. Is there a reason someone should?" he asked with a confused look.

"You don't know Rica has been in a terrible accident? I thought her parents might have had reason to send word to you," Adel replied.

"How, awful! I'm very sorry to hear it, but why would her parents notify me. Our families have no connections," he answered, still bewildered.

"So, you *aren't* engaged to marry Rica?" she asked, more pointedly than she had intended.

"Engaged? To Rica? Why would you even ask me that, Adel?" He was insulted by the question.

"So you're not?" Adel was astounded by her own stupidity. Mandy had warned her not to fall for Rica's deception.

"Of course not! I can't believe you'd think I'd even consider it!" He had not meant to raise his voice to his friend.

"I should have listened to Mandy. I'm sorry, Stew. But there was a picture in a local newspaper with you and Rica looking into each other's eyes. It was the night you received the awards in Bay City. The article definitely gave the impression you were to be married. Then the other day, Mandy, Bethany, and I went to Brennon's to collect for the mission, and we walked in on Rica being fitted for her wedding dress. She made insinuations to Bethany about the marriage."

"Is that why Bethany was so hostile toward me? How long has she known about it?"

"Her parents wrote to her right after the article was published."

"Do you have any idea where Bethany is? I have to talk to her!" Stew asked desperately.

"The last time I saw her, she was on the way to the hospital to visit Rica. I was at the accident scene, and Rica begged me to ask Bethany to come to the hospital. Rica is very badly injured. It doesn't look good for her."

"I'm sorry to hear it. I was very hard on her," Stew admitted.

"Rica *chooses* to do the mean things she does," Adel said to console him.

Stew nodded in agreement, then turned Storm sharply and galloped off.

Bethany—trying to absorb everything that had transpired with Rica—sat down on the granite rock under the willow. Her mother had heard Stewart was taking the afternoon train back to Bay City. Bethany's opportunity to tell him how wrong she had been was gone. He was innocent. Sorrows of many kinds filled her heart.

"I thought I'd find you here," a familiar voice said.

"Stewart!" Bethany could hardly catch her breath. "I thought you had left for Bay City."

"I was on my way to the station when I met Adel along the road. She told me about Rica. I'm sorry to hear about the accident. I hope she's doing well."

Bethany nodded, "She did accept Jesus."

"Thank God." Stew was relieved to hear it. "You know Rica and I were never engaged."

"Adel told you about the picture?" Bethany asked.

"Yes," he answered.

"Stew, Rica admitted to everything...why she hated me...her feelings for you...and how she schemed to make it look like you were kissing. I was *wrong*.

"Stew, you *weren't* kissing Rica. I'm *so sorry* for the way I've treated you and for *doubting* you." Her apology was honest and sincere with a hopeful heart.

"Bethany...I'm not going to lie. It ripped my heart out each time you refused to listen to me. I was devastated when you just threw our relationship away. My world was shattered in a moment's time. I'd never been so broken and angry.

"But because of it, Bethany, I did find anger deep inside of me—anger I didn't know I possessed. And not too long ago, I learned I *had* made a habit of overlooking Rica and other young ladies' advances. I didn't deal with them as a Christian man should."

"And *I* have been *impulsive* and *stubborn.* It was wrong to believe unjust things of you...and, Stew, I was dishonest when I said I didn't love you...because I *do*...so *very* much." Bethany looked at him with tears of shame in her eyes.

Then he took her hand and got down on one knee. "Bethany, I love you now and forever. Will you, *please*, reconsider my proposal and marry me?"

She looked into his eyes. "Yes...of course I will."

Then Stew took Bethany's hand, pulled her to him...and the kiss they shared began to melt away all the pain they had endured.

61

ALL WHO LOVED THEM

The morning dew had relented to a blue sky with angelic rays of sun filtering through delicate clouds. This was the day God had chosen for Bethany and Stewart to marry.

"*Perfect*," slipped from Bethany's lips as she looked down from her window onto the scene below. It was at least an hour before the wedding, yet several of their dearest friends and family had already arrived.

The lovely, pastel gowns worn by the ladies and the well pressed suits of the gentlemen momentarily caught Bethany's eye, just before she noticed the gazebo ladened with lovely purple and white roses. She quickly tore her eyes away, not wanting to spoil her sister's surprise. Bethany knew Tanna had put much thought into the gazebo's décor. Her sister wanted to erase any unpleasant memories associated with the night of the engagement party. Tanna's thoughtfulness touched Bethany's heart, but nothing, past or present, could in anyway spoil this day.

Then Bethany stepped a little closer to the window to get a better look at some of the guests. *Surely it is my imagination...it can't be!* But it was true. Bethany could clearly recognize several of her dear friends from the West. It was Ella, Lena and Bert, Sandra and Elmer, Sadie and Marcus. And there was little Billy sitting between his parents. Tears filled her eyes at the thought. "Mother...do you know who's here?"

Helen smiled knowingly. "Yes, dear. It was to be a surprise."

Bethany shook her head in disbelief. "*Oh...it is*," she said softly. "I *so* wanted to share this day with them."

As she was closing the curtain, Bethany noticed Rica being carefully escorted to her seat by Joe Meeker. Joe had been Rica's devoted admirer since the day she had apologized for the taunting which had led to their accident and her injuries. On the same day, a letter from Rica admitting to her shameful treatment of others had been read before the congregation of Faith Chapel. Rica also had shared her intention to make amends by living her life in service to her Lord and Savior. The humble confessions had warmed many hearts, and Bethany was pleased to see Rica was well received by those in attendance.

No—not one thing could ruin this day.

It was only a short time before the cheerful voices of Tanna, Mandy, and Adel filled the room as they assisted Bethany into her awaiting bridal gown. Mrs. Jackson added the perfecting touches and then tearfully escorted Bethany to the mirror.

"Thank you, Mother. There is no doubt I *am* wearing the most beautiful wedding gown I have ever seen."

As Stew stood looking out the window of the Jacksons' home, he could visualize his precious Bethany walking down the aisle. Their day had finally arrived. His heart stirred at seeing many of those closest to them had already been seated. His face broke into a smile when he caught sight of Mathew and his family, along with several of the people he had met from the West.

The smile turned to a look of shock when Stew noticed Mr. Derby among the guests. It was all he could do to keep from raising the window and shouting out to him. Derby's appearance meant more than any promotion or pay raise.

Of course, each person in attendance held a special place in his heart, and he thanked God for them all.

It was about then that Stew's parents came to pay a quick visit. His mother hugged him profusely, and his father prayed blessings over his son and Bethany.

Just as the prayer ended, there was a knock on the door and a note was handed to Stew. Unfortunately, his two groomsmen had been detained due to a railway accident and could not make the wedding in time. It was a disappointment, but Stew had to act fast. He quickly wrote two notes which would hopefully settle the matter promptly. There was nothing else to be done.

The eager guests quieted as Stewart, his father, *Matthew*, and *Mr. Derby* appeared at the steps of the gazebo. Stew instinctively gave his father a hug and winked at his mother.

Suddenly, it seemed as if the air itself was holding its breath in anxious excitement.

Bethany smiled at her father. He could not speak—but it did not matter because his eyes said it all. He held out his arm for his little girl.

It was time...

Then with the delicate strum of a harp, lovely Bethany Jackson walked down the aisle toward her *beloved* Stewart.

With the same strum of the harp, Stewart turned to see his beautiful bride coming to meet him. He stood breathless—Bethany was about to become his own.

Once their eyes met, neither could look away. Stew and Bethany allowed the love between them to sift through their hearts. They would soon be one in the eyes of God.

As Pastor David and Pastor Strong performed the ceremony, Bethany fought to keep her mind on the most important words she would ever speak. Thoughts of her building love for Stew through the years proved to be tough competition during those sacred moments.

Stewart's mind was in the present and past as well. He understood the words he repeated and meant every word he spoke. Yet his mind raced between the vows they were taking, their love as it had grown, and the future they were about to enter together. Stew wondered if all brides and grooms struggle in vain to keep their thoughts from wandering.

Soon Pastor Strong proudly informed the couple, "I now pronounce you husband and wife!"

Then Pastor David paused teasingly and, with a sneaky smile, announced, "Mr. Jefferson—you may *now* kiss your bride!"

Stew then quietly spoke to his Bethany, "I have never longed for anything as I have for this moment. I love you, Bethany Jefferson."

At long last—to everyone's delight—Stewart took Bethany into his arms and tenderly kissed his new bride for the first time. They were now Mr. and Mrs. Stewart Jefferson—*one* in the sight of God and all who loved them.

ACKNOWLEDGEMENTS

Over the years, this story has spent more time on the shelf than off, and I had resolved just to copy it and put it in a binder. Because of these people I love, that did not happen:

My sister, Gayle Quinn, and her husband, Gary, who insisted that I publish my story, Under the Willow. I especially want to thank Gayle for her tireless work in helping to refine the manuscript.

My dear friend, Carolyn May, the brave soul who rummaged through the first raw copy and convinced me it still needed a lot of work.

My wonderful husband, Jack, who encouraged me and was supportive—as always.

Kayla Swedberg of The Brand Huntress for her beautiful artwork, her meticulous preparation of my manuscript for printing, and her patience in walking me through the process of self-publishing.

Above all, my Lord and Savior for surprising me with a way to bring it all together.

Thank you.

ABOUT THE AUTHOR

Madge Hurley Jones was just an ordinary grandmother living with her husband, Jack, in the Wilmington, Ohio, countryside when she felt God had put a story in her heart. Although this is only her first romance novel, there is no doubt readers will be anticipating more to come from this talented septuagenarian who writes in the style of the beloved Grace Livingston Hill.

www.ingramcontent.com/pod-product-compliance
Lightning Source LLC
Chambersburg PA
CBHW030603310726
48979CB00003B/552

* 9 7 8 1 7 3 6 5 6 3 0 0 7 *